Chance gave the nod, and the chute gate was opened.

Bellowing loudly, the steer charged into the open arena.

The horse Chance was riding raced off. With the lariat circling his head, Chance bore down on the runaway steer, and cast the rope. Then, giving it a quick tug when it settled over the outstretched horns, he dismounted from his saddle.

The instant Chance came down on his weak knee, he gritted his teeth against the pain, then charged toward the steer to tie up its legs in as few seconds as possible.

Cheers went up around the arena, but Chance's gaze wasn't on the whooping, hollering cowboys. His attention riveted on the beautiful, smiling face of Alexa, who had ambled down to the arena to watch him perform.

The expression on her face, however, indicated she wasn't just being entertained by the performance. It implied she was concerned about the pain in his leg.

Someone who cares...

Chance couldn't remember anyone ever caring if he was safe and sound....

Dear Reader,

Special Edition is pleased to bring you six exciting love stories to help you celebrate spring...and blossoming love.

To start off the month, don't miss *A Father for Her Baby* by Celeste Hamilton—a THAT'S MY BABY! title that features a pregnant amnesiac who is reunited with her long-ago fiancé. Now she must uncover the past in order to have a future with this irresistible hero and her new baby.

April offers Western romances aplenty! In the third installment of her action-packed HEARTS OF WYOMING series, Myrna Temte delivers *Wrangler.* A reticent lady wrangler has a mighty big secret, but sparks fly between her and the sexy lawman she's been trying very hard to avoid; the fourth book in the series will be available in July. Next, Pamela Toth brings us another heartwarming story in her popular BUCKLES & BRONCOS miniseries. In *Buchanan's Pride,* a feisty cowgirl rescues a stranded stranger—only to discover he's the last man on earth she should let into her heart!

There's more love on the range coming your way. *Finally His Bride* by Christine Flynn—part of THE WHITAKER BRIDES series—is an emotional reunion romance between two former sweethearts. Also the MEN OF THE DOUBLE-C RANCH series continues when a brooding Clay brother claims the woman he's never stopped wanting in *A Wedding For Maggie* by Allison Leigh. Finally, debut author Carol Finch shares an engaging story about a fun-loving rodeo cowboy who woos a romance-resistant single mom in *Not Just Another Cowboy.*

I hope you enjoy these stirring tales of passion, and each and every romance to come!

Sincerely,

Karen Taylor Richman
Senior Editor

Please address questions and book requests to:
Silhouette Reader Service
U.S.: 3010 Walden Ave., P.O. Box 1325, Buffalo, NY 14269
Canadian: P.O. Box 609, Fort Erie, Ont. L2A 5X3

CAROL FINCH

NOT JUST
ANOTHER COWBOY

Silhouette®

SPECIAL EDITION®

Published by Silhouette Books

America's Publisher of Contemporary Romance

This book is dedicated to my husband, Ed, and our children: Kurt, Jill, Christie, Jeff and Jon with much love. And to our first granddaughter, Brooklynn Sheree Walls.

 SILHOUETTE BOOKS

ISBN 0-373-24242-5

NOT JUST ANOTHER COWBOY

Copyright © 1999 by Connie Fedderson

Printed in U.S.A.

CAROL FINCH,

who also writes as Gina Robins, Debra Falcon, Connie Drake and Connie Feddersen, has penned fifty-four novels in the historical romance, contemporary romance, mystery and romantic suspense genres. A former tennis pro and high school biology instructor, Ms. Finch devotes herself full-time to writing and working on the family's cattle ranch in Oklahoma.

Ms. Finch is a member of the Oklahoma Professional Writers' Hall of Fame. She has received seventeen nominations and seven career achievement awards from *Romantic Times Magazine* for Historical Love and Laughter, Historical Adventure, Best Contemporary Romance and Storyteller of the Year.

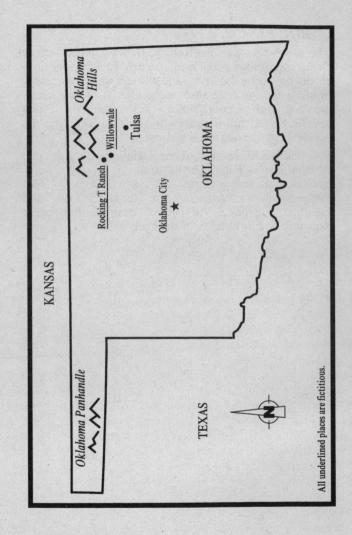

KANSAS

Oklahoma Panhandle

Oklahoma Hills

Rocking T Ranch • • Willowvale

• Tulsa

★ Oklahoma City

OKLAHOMA

TEXAS

N

All underlined places are fictitious.

Chapter One

Just another cowboy, Alexa Tipton mused as she stared out the kitchen window at Rocking T Ranch. When the new arrival slid off the seat of the pickup truck Alexa noticed the brace wrapped around his left leg, and she muttered under her breath. This floundering ranch in the Oklahoma Hills needed a good, dependable hired hand, not another unattached, injured rodeo cowboy who was down on his luck and needed a temporary paycheck to tide him over.

Since her husband, Dan, was killed in a traffic accident on his way to the rodeo in Cheyenne a year earlier, Alexa's father-in-law had turned the ranch into a rehabilitation center for Dan's cronies. Howard's Rodeo Hobos' campsite, she called it.

Alexa knew this was her father-in-law's attempt to keep in touch with his son's life, constantly sharing stories about Dan's rodeo heydays. For Alexa, it was a reminder of the here-today-and-gone-tomorrow kind of man her husband had been.

Grumbling, Alexa turned away from the window as her father-in-law, Howard, led the temporary ranch hand toward the bunkhouse. How long would this rodeo cowboy hang around? Two weeks? A month? She supposed it all depended on the seriousness of his injury.

Same song, second verse, Alexa thought to herself. Every mending cowboy who came and went from Rocking T wanted to draw wages while he recuperated, and he couldn't wait to get back to the rodeo circuit. That come-and-go life-style might be dandy-fine for a man, but Alexa had lived as a rodeo cowboy's wife for nine years, and she didn't recommend it to any woman.

"Mom! Grandpa brought home the new cowboy!" When Zack raced into the house, the door banged against the wall—as usual.

"So I see," Alexa said, smiling affectionately at her rambunctious son. "How bad is this one hurt?"

Zack plunked down at the table and reached for a plate of freshly baked chocolate chip cookies—his favorite. "Banged up his leg real good," Zack reported. "He's a bulldogger and calf roper, just like Dad was."

Alexa made a noncommittal sound. She knew her eight-year-old son, like his grandpa, clung to memories of Dan, but what tore at Alexa's heart was the realization that her life had changed so little since she lost her husband. For years, she had been in charge of running the ranch, tending her ailing father-in-law and raising her son.

All Alexa's expectations of a perfect marriage came crashing down the first time Dan went down the road, chasing his dream of becoming a rodeo superstar.

It was Alexa who had dealt with every crisis life handed her, because Dan had been more of a guest in his own home than a family member. And what hurt Alexa even more than the realization that she wasn't high on Dan's list of priorities was the lack of attention Dan paid to his own son. Alexa had learned to accept the fact that Dan didn't love her to the same extent she'd loved him, but Zack was too young to understand. The poor kid had practically starved for his dad's attention—and found himself brushed aside more times than not.

Each time an injured cowboy took up temporary residence at Rocking T Ranch, young Zack searched for a father figure—and found nothing but the temporary kind of man who spared little boys a few minutes in his self-indulgent life.

Man, you're really turning into a cynic, aren't you? Alexa thought as she watched her son devour his third cookie.

Well, maybe she had, but the tragedies and heartaches she encountered the past thirteen years had turned a fun-loving young woman into a serious-minded older-but-wiser woman. With a younger sister to raise, Alexa had hoped to solve her problems and see her dreams come true when she married Dan. But she had been sorely disillusioned with the institution of marriage.

Dan was always the one who packed his gear and walked away when things got tough, when delinquent bills piled up. Alexa was left behind to solve the problems and raise a child. It made a person take life seriously, Alexa reminded herself.

"Are we going down to the bunkhouse to meet the new cowboy?" Zack asked around a mouthful of cookie.

"I'm sure we'll make his acquaintance at supper. In the meantime, Chester Whitmier and I will be working on the renovations in the barn."

Zack considered that for a minute. "Grandpa says we don't need a bed-and-breakfast in our barn and that we don't need a bunch of citified strangers wandering around Rocking T."

"Grandpa will get used to the idea," Alexa insisted. "When we open for business and begin making money he'll change his tune."

"Grandpa says not," Zack replied. "Grandpa says a

ranch is meant for raising cattle, horses and hay, not entertaining city slickers.''

Alexa didn't argue the point with her son. She refused to place Zack in the middle of the ongoing debate between Howard Tipton and herself. Howard had been trying to brainwash Zack since Alexa presented her idea. But since Alexa had inherited half this ranch, she intended to show profit—somebody around here had to!

The Rocking T was located four miles from the thriving community of Willowvale—just a hop, skip and jump off a state highway. According to Alexa's research, bed-and-breakfasts that offered a retreat from the hectic city life prospered. Most everybody had visions of spending a few days in the great outdoors, enjoying home cooking and taking horseback rides on scenic trails.

And darn it, this endeavor was going to work, Alexa told herself determinedly. She was throwing her heart, soul and energy into this business venture. Her father-in-law could cling to his outdated theories on ranching if he wanted, but Alexa was going to improve this family's finances.

Giving her son a hug, Alexa strode out the door and headed for the stately cedar barn that would soon boast sleeping quarters, a spacious dining area for guests and a kitchen where she could prepare meals. Howard Tipton might be living in the past, clinging desperately to memories of his son, but Alexa knew it was vital to get on with life and plan for the future.

As for the new cowboy with a banged-up leg, Alexa couldn't have cared less. He was just another mouth to feed, another unwanted influence on her son's life, another reminder of the irresponsible man her husband had been.

There had to be a better life ahead, Alexa told herself, and she was going to *make* it better for herself and her family!

''You can stow your gear in the closet.'' Howard Tipton gestured a gnarled hand toward the far end of the bunkhouse.

Nodding gratefully, Chance Butler limped over to stack his luggage in the corner, then sank down on the tattered lounge chair to take a load off his feet. His leg was killing him, though he'd taken a dose of prescribed painkiller before he climbed off the plane that touched down in Willowvale. Even though Chance had to listen to Howard sing praises to his departed son during the ride to Rocking T, Chance was thankful for a place to bed down.

The spill he'd taken at last week's rodeo in Nebraska had forced him to take a leave of absence from the suicide circuit. Climbing in the saddle had become sheer agony on the strained ligaments and tendons that had been reinjured in the recent fall.

Howard Tipton's open invitation to house mending cowboys was a godsend. Chance was able to work with the animals he loved, instead of camping out in a fleabag motel until his injuries healed. If listening to Howard's claims that Dan Tipton was the greatest rodeo cowboy ever to mount a horse was the price Chance had to pay, then so be it. Chance had taken one look at the panoramic hills covered with thigh-high bluestem grass and fallen in love with Rocking T. This was the kind of ranch he'd dreamed of owning. One day he would have a ranch that belonged to him, a home to call his own for the first time in his life, a place where he belonged.

''My daughter-in-law serves supper at seven o'clock sharp,'' Howard announced as he hobbled toward the sofa. ''Her cooking used to be out of this world, until she got this bean-brained idea to refurbish the old barn into a bed-and breakfast.''

Howard pulled off his straw hat and slapped it against his hip. ''Damn fool idea, I told her, but she hired a retired carpenter from Willowvale to help her with the renovations.''

Chance blinked, surprised. "Help her?"

Howard nodded his gray head. "Alexa aims to save money by doing most of the framing and drywall herself. That old coot, Chester Whitmier, does more yammering than actual working. Alexa is the kind of woman who isn't afraid to take on challenges. Claims she likes being a carpenter," Howard said, then snorted.

"My wife, God rest her dear soul, wouldn't have been out in that barn, doing a man's work with a nail gun and Skilsaw, building bedrooms and dining areas. But I guess women have changed with the times. Hell, Alexa even made me an appointment with a *lady* doctor when I had to refill my prescription for these high-dollar arthritis pills."

Clearly, Howard Tipton graduated from the old school that preached a woman's place was in the home. The old man, dressed in pin-striped Oshkosh overalls and faded chambray shirt, was way out of touch, Chance concluded. These days, women were independent, progressive and aggressive. Some of them, like the rodeo groupies who followed him around like puppies, were too aggressive for his tastes. Some men enjoyed being chased and pawed, but Chance Butler wasn't one of them. Furthermore, he had adopted the live-and-let-live philosophy years ago.

He had also made a pact with himself not to take women seriously. Why should he? He wasn't planning to settle down anytime soon. At thirty-three, he still had a few good rodeo years left in him—if his knees held up. He had nothing to offer a woman, and he had just enough brains left, after being bucked off and stepped on—by a wild-eyed horse or cantankerous steer—to know that.

Dan Tipton's fatal accident en route to a rodeo was a grim reminder that life was too short to be spent in turmoil. A man lived the best way he could, spreading his smiles around and hoping he would be remembered for his good disposition.

"One word of warning," Howard said as he stared

Chance squarely in the eye. "My daughter-in-law is off-limits to you and every other cowboy who passes through here. I make sure that's understood from the get-go. My son has only been gone a year and a half. His memory is still very much alive in this household. I expect you to give Alexa your polite respect and do the chores you can handle on your bum leg. If you think she needs a hand with her renovations, then you can offer your help if you want to, but that's not part of your job description. You only answer to me."

Chance nodded mutely as he watched Howard shuffle toward the door. If Chance wasn't mistaken—and he doubted he was—Howard was very protective of his daughter-in-law. Chance wondered how Alexa reacted to the possessiveness telegraphed in Howard's voice.

Well, it wasn't any of his business, Chance reminded himself as he stretched out his stiff leg. He was here to herd cattle, fix a few fences and recuperate. When he mended properly he would be gone. Some other hapless rodeo cowboy would be sitting here listening to Howard's lectures and tolerating words of praise to a man who wasn't exactly the invincible saint his father made him out to be.

Fact of the matter was, Dan Tipton was a hell-raiser who thumbed his nose at the institution of marriage. Dan's heavy drinking had caused the traffic accident that took his life. If Howard knew the truth, he seemed determined to ignore it. In Chance's opinion Dan Tipton took his wife, son and this sprawling ranch for granted. Chance thought Dan was a fool, but he figured things would run smoother if he kept his opinion to himself.

Sighing tiredly, he reached for the confining brace that encased his knee, pulled it off and tossed it aside. Damn, he could use a long, relaxing bath before supper. Then he'd put on his best smile to greet Alexa and her son. He wasn't here to make waves or chase skirts, and he had no intention of letting himself forget that. He didn't plan to be here long enough to get tangled up in the affairs at Rocking T.

Chance stumbled to a halt at the kitchen door. He wasn't sure what he'd expected when he strode into the ranch house, but the impact of the cozy cedar-wall kitchen, country decor and aromatic scents gave him pause. Chance had never been anywhere in his life that shouted ''home'' the way this two-story ranch house did. A reddish-blond-haired boy sat at the table, his head bent over a textbook in profound concentration. The boy's mother worked industriously at the stove.

The scene tugged at Chance's heartstrings, unearthing memories that he thought he had tucked neatly away years ago. When Chance felt the wall that carefully protected his emotions begin to crumble, he stiffened. He remembered sitting at the table doing his homework. Occasionally his mother prepared a meal for her latest boyfriend and Chance was allowed to enjoy the benefits of her labors. Those were the semienjoyable moments, but there had been so much turmoil and uncomfortable moments in his childhood that he...

Chance's troubled thoughts went up in a puff of smoke when Alexa Tipton turned in his direction. The woman staring coolly at him was a knockout in that tank top that matched her cedar-tree-green eyes and trim-fitting faded blue jeans. Auburn hair that burned like a flame in the light streamed over one shoulder in a long ponytail. The visual effect this woman had on Chance stunned him. He stood, tongue-tied. He tried to remember the last time a woman's presence had made such a startling impact on him—and couldn't.

Damn, thought Chance. Dan Tipton was ten-dozen kinds of fool for riding the suicide circuit instead of staying home with his gorgeous wife and young kid. Dan had had heaven at his fingertips and he'd been living in the fast lane, chasing women that didn't compare to the one waiting for him at home.

This was one dynamite woman, Chance mused as his gaze traveled over her in masculine appreciation. Given what Howard had said about Alexa—her independence, her willingness to take on any challenge, her ability to cook food that made a man's taste buds stand up and salute— Chance was immediately impressed.

Zack glanced up from his book and smiled. "You're the new guy. I'm Zack." He hitched his thumb over his narrow shoulders. "That's my mom."

"Glad to meet you, Zack, Mom," Chance replied, flashing a smile. "Howard told me to report for supper at seven o'clock sharp."

The kid thrust out his hand, indicating the chair where Chance was supposed to sit. Mom simply stared at Chance, making him wonder if he'd buttoned his shirt improperly or forgotten to zip his blue jeans.

"Dinner will be a few minutes late," Alex said before pivoting toward the stove. "I was detained in the barn."

"Grandpa says Mom is wasting her time with that old barn," Zack confided. "Mom says—"

"Zack," Alexa cut in, "don't bother our guest with family differences of opinion, please."

Alexa gave herself a mental shake and stared at the pot of spaghetti sauce simmering on the stove. She hadn't expected to feel such a startling reaction to the cowboy who appeared in her kitchen. Even when she turned her back on the man she could still see the image of broad shoulders, raven-black hair and twinkling silver-blue eyes staring back at her. To date, none of the cowboys who had come and gone from Howard's cowboy rehab center had made such a strong first impression on her. She shrugged them all aside, but this masculine hunk of brawn, muscle and good looks made his dynamic presence felt by doing nothing more than favoring her with an engaging grin.

Not that it made a whit of difference, of course. Alexa had absolutely no use for cowboy types, no time or inclination for relationships—casual or otherwise—with men. She was on a crusade to revive this faltering ranch, despite Howard's vocal objections and snide remarks. She would treat this temporary addition to her home with the same courtesy as his predecessors. She certainly wasn't in the market for a husband, because she had been down that road before and discovered that the pathway was filled with potholes. Alexa knew how to take care of herself, and her son. She wasn't looking for security, because husbands didn't come with written guarantees that they could handle responsibility. In her experience, a husband was another responsibility she had to undertake.

No, thought Alexa, although this new cowboy was incredibly easy on the eye, she wasn't interested in getting to know him. Her nine-year marriage to a rodeo cowboy had cured her of that.

Resigned to her life as it was—and as it would stay—Alexa wheeled around to snatch up the pitcher on the counter. "Mango tea or milk?" she asked.

"Mango tea?" Chance repeated.

"It's Mom's special," Zack confided. "It's going to be on her menu at the bed-and-breakfast, along with her Southern fried chicken and spaghetti." Zack grinned, displaying his missing two front teeth. "Spaghetti is my favorite. Grandpa likes the chicken when he can't have steak."

Chance glanced over his shoulder. "Where is Howard?"

"Poker night," Zack reported. "Mom says Grandpa doesn't have money to blow on bad card hands, but he—"

"Zack." Alexa's gaze narrowed on her loquacious son.

"Family matter?" Zack asked.

"You got it, kiddo. Read your book and don't pester our guest."

"No problem, ma'am," Chance felt inclined to say when

the kid's face fell in disappointment. Despite Chance's vow to keep his emotional distance from the Tiptons, he kept seeing a bit of himself in this kid. "What are you reading, Zack?"

The boy's nose wrinkled distastefully. "Science stuff. They make you learn all sorts of dumb junk when you're in the third grade. We even have to learn history."

Chance tried to look properly shocked. "No kidding? I reckon those teachers still want kids to be well-versed in lots of subjects, huh?"

"I guess," Zack mumbled. "Mom says I'm supposed to know more than which end of a horse kicks and which end bites, because most cowboys—"

"Zack, for heaven sake!" Alexa's face blossomed with embarrassment.

Out of the mouth of babes, she thought, exasperated. She swore every reckless remark she'd ever made was stuck in Zack's head and would find its way to his tongue. She should be flattered that her advice didn't go in one ear and fly out the other, but she didn't need Zack spreading the gospel according to Alexa every time some down-on-his-luck cowboy hobbled in here.

When Alexa glanced in Chance's direction to apologize she became the recipient of his good-natured grin—one potent enough to melt her knees.

"Don't worry about it, *Mom*," Chance said with a wink. "I realize most folks think that all a cowboy knows is bulls and broncs and not much else." He turned his attention back to Zack. "But fact is, I studied animal science in college and kinda liked it."

College? Alexa groaned. An educated cowboy. *She* had been deprived of college because of the responsibilities she was obligated to assume. Of course, this cowboy had only himself to consider. Must be nice, she mused resentfully.

"Science?" Zack looked appalled.

Chance nodded. "Yep, a good rancher has to know all

sorts of scientific data if he wants to keep his livestock and land in prime condition. And it doesn't hurt to know the history of the breed of your stock, either. Take the Morgan horse that was developed during American colonial days, for instance...."

Alexa set a glass of tea in front of Chance and watched her son sit up and listen with rapt attention. For the first time since Howard opened his home to mending cowboys Zack wasn't being brushed aside. He was being included in conversation and subtly informed that the "dumb junk" taught in school was important.

But Chance Butler would still be just as gone when his wounds healed, Alexa reminded herself cynically. She couldn't allow Zack to get too attached to this cowboy. Rodeo performers were cut from the same scrap of rope, and Alexa wasn't grooming her son to follow his father's footsteps. No matter what, young Zack wasn't going to be hurt more than he'd already been because his own father hadn't had much time for him.

To Alexa's frustration, she sat through supper watching her son warm to this new arrival by alarming degrees. Chance Butler, damn him, had an appealing way about him. Twice Alexa caught herself smiling at something Chance had said—the man could definitely turn a phrase, making Zack giggle and grin. And when Chance looked to her for acceptance it took all the firm resolve she could muster not to melt beneath his easygoing grin. She wasn't going to get attached to this man—or any man like him. That was that.

When Chance levered to his feet to clear the dishes from the table, Alexa glanced up, surprised.

"It's the least I can do after that sensational meal." He leaned close to add, "Even if Howard has reservations, I think your bed-and-breakfast will prosper. But if you tell him I said so, I'll get fired before I put in my first day of work."

Alex stiffened when the scent of cologne and appealing

masculine presence invaded her private space. Her instinctive reaction to Chance shocked her, unsettled her. She didn't want to feel anything except mild approval of a man who would be no more than a temporary acquaintance.

He's a here-today-and-gone-tomorrow kind of man. Don't you forget it, Alexa told herself as she bounded from her chair to escape the lingering scent of Chance's cologne.

"Zack, put your plate and silverware in the sink."

"I know, Mom," Zack grumbled.

Alexa grimaced when she realized she had offended her son's pride. Zack had taken an instant liking to Chance, and he balked at being treated as though he was eight—which he was. Hurriedly, Alexa tried to compensate.

"After you finish your math assignment, how about if we play catch. I should have the kitchen spiffed up by then."

Alexa could have kicked herself for her suggestion. Zack glanced expectantly at Chance, Clearly, the boy didn't want to play catch with his mom when there was a muscular man around the house.

Trying to spare Zack from disappointment, Alexa shooed him on his way. "Better hit the math book before it gets too dark to see the baseball. I don't want your blazing fast-ball to smack me in the nose."

Chance understood the dynamics of this situation perfectly. He would have had to be blind in both eyes not to realize the kid had taken an instant liking to him. He would also have had to be stone deaf not to catch the tone in Alexa's voice. She intended to let Chance off the hook with the kid, to run cheerful interference. The single supermom was handling her own affairs, expecting nothing from the outsider.

"Thanks for a delicious supper," Chance complimented as he rinsed the dishes in the sink.

"You're welcome. Breakfast is served at six-thirty, so Zack can catch the school bus into town."

Chance recognized a dismissal when he heard one. He limped out the door, reminding himself that he was to keep his distance from Alexa Tipton and that lovable little kid who craved a man's attention.

Not your problem, Butler, he told himself on the way to the bunkhouse. He didn't need emotions crowding in on him, wasn't going to get involved in matters that didn't concern him. Besides, what did Chance know about being a male role model. His own father hadn't set positive examples to live by. Just the opposite, in fact.

Yet an hour later Chance was standing at the window on his aching leg, watching Alexa and Zack play catch. She threw the baseball like a girl—and so did her son. Twice, Chance had to stop himself from hobbling outside to offer unwanted instruction on the fundamentals of throwing and catching. The kid stabbed at the ball with his oversize glove, and he released his pitches so far behind his ear that the ball's trajectory resembled a rainbow's arc. No doubt, this kid would be riding the pine if he tried out for the baseball team—if his mom even allowed him to participate at all.

"Girl, I keep telling you that you can't carpenter unless you have your butt behind you," Chester Whitmier instructed. "Gimme that nail gun and pay close attention."

Alexa wiped the perspiration from her brow, then twisted around to face the fuzzy-gray-haired carpenter. Chester knelt beside the stud wall he had measured and laid out on the floor to be nailed together.

Thump-whack, thump-whack. Nails, driven by the force of the air compressor, thudded into the two-by-fours.

"See, girl, you've got to shoot from the correct angle into these studs or they won't hold when you have the added pressure of ceiling joists and Sheetrock on them. You don't want to have flimsy walls falling down around your guests, now do you?"

Alexa was dry-throated. Hours of hard physical labor made it difficult to speak. She shook her head.

"Now take the nail gun to the far end of this wall and secure the braces. Four nails per stud should do it. And this time, don't overextend yourself on the ladder. You're lucky you didn't hurt yourself the last time you lost your footing and took the plunge."

Alexa lugged the heavy nail gun in one gloved hand and wiped away the stream of perspiration on her neck with the other. Although she knew she was saving money on labor, she was working herself into exhaustion. Between her duties of cooking, cleaning, laundering and renovating there was barely enough time to spend with Zack. But Alexa had made a pact with herself when she began this project that she would give up sleep before she neglected her son. Dan had done too much of that already.

Arm shaking, Alexa hoisted up the nail gun and pulled the trigger. *Thump-thump-whack.*

"Hey, girl, keep a light touch on that trigger!" Chester chided her. "You shot two nails at once. You're damn lucky one of them didn't shoot you in the foot!"

Confound it, Alexa wasn't sure she'd ever get the hang of this power-driven hammer. And Chester, bless his heart, was trying to teach her the tricks of his trade. But he spouted off rapid-fire instructions and Alexa could remember only half of them.

"Okay, now we have the wall nailed together so we can stand it upright and secure it to the floor," Chester said as he positioned himself at the opposite end of the framework. "Grab the level and ladder so you can nail this wall in place."

Obediently, Alexa did as she was told. When she and Chester lifted the wall into place, she balanced one foot on the ladder and grabbed the nail gun.

"Good. Now nail this baby in place."

Alexa pulled the trigger, securing the uprighted wall.

Then she climbed down the ladder to move to another position to nail.

If she'd climbed this ladder once, she'd climbed it a hundred times a day. Her legs felt like cooked noodles, but she refused to complain, refused to give out until the new wall to the first upstairs bedroom was securely in place.

Two quick thumps from the nail gun and the wall stood alone. Alexa climbed down, then stepped back to appraise her handiwork. Pride of accomplishment overshadowed her exhaustion. She was making headway under Chester's constant, critical instruction.

"What time is it?" Alexa questioned as Chester plopped into a folding chair to rest.

"Don't know, girl. Times have been so hard that I had to lay off one of the hands on my watch," Chester said, then grinned. His false teeth flashed in a teasing smile. "My guess is that it's close to four o'clock. The school bus should be here soon, and Zack will be bounding up here to ask another million questions."

"Four o'clock?" Alexa's shoulders slumped. Could it be that late already? She had promised Zack that she would make peanut butter cookies for his after-school snack. She refused to go back on her word.

Don't neglect your son. The rest of your world can go to hell, but never let Zack suffer.

"I'll help Chester lay out the next wall while you see to Zack."

Startled, Alexa whipped around to see Chance Butler leaning negligently against the balustrade that led downstairs. Alexa felt an odd sense of pride spilling through her as Chance's approving gaze drifted over the newly erected wall.

"Nice work," Chance complimented.

Chance had been standing there for several minutes, watching Alexa balance on one leg like a trapeze artist, holding the nail gun in her shaking hand. Chance had held his breath, afraid she was about to take a spill, wondering how he was going to dash across the barn loft on his gimpy leg in time to catch her. The woman was a daredevil, he decided. No woman in his acquaintance would have considered attempting such feats.

Chance had been also been standing there long enough to overhear what Chester said about Alexa taking a previous fall from the ladder. Right there and then, Chance decided to refer to the rickety aluminum ladder as Grace. And as long as Chance was at Rocking T he would find a way to see that Alexa was saved from future falls from Grace.

Chester took a swig from his water jug, then nodded a greeting. "You must be the new cowboy Zack has been carrying on about for the past three days."

"Chance Butler," he said as he limped forward, outstretching his hand.

"Chester Whitmier." He looked Chance up and down. "You know how to carpenter, boy?"

"I've done a little of this and that through the years." He tossed Alexa a wry smile, then added, "I know enough to know that you have to get your butt behind you when handling a nail gun."

Alexa forced herself not to react to his teasing comment and sexy grin. She was the workhorse at Rocking T, and she didn't have time for nonsense. "I'm not sure Howard would approve of your helping me with this project," she murmured as she relinquished the nail gun to Chance.

"And I doubt you want to disappoint Zack after you promised him fresh-baked cookies," he countered.

Alexa was surprised Chance had paid attention to the quiet conversation she'd shared with her son at supper the previous night. As she recalled, Howard had been bending Chance's ear with more stories of Dan's grand accomplishments on the rodeo circuit. For more than a year, Howard had repeated—and embellished—tales of Dan's feats, keeping the memories alive for himself and whomever was polite enough to listen.

"Thanks," Alexa whispered before stepping away. "I'll serve you an extra portion of fried chicken at supper."

When Alexa exited, Chester leaned back in his chair. "She is some kind of woman, isn't she?"

"Yep."

"She's determined to remodel this barn by herself and cut expenses. Even talked me into coming out of retirement to help her, even after I told her no a half dozen times." Chester shook his head in amazement. "Don't know all that many womenfolk who have Alexa's grit. But my money is on the lady and her new bed-and-breakfast."

"Mine, too," Chance agreed.

In between mending fences and moving cattle to greener pastures, Chance had watched Alexa come and go from this grand old barn, carrying lumber, gathering tools, working tirelessly. The woman had impressed the hell out of him, just as she had obviously impressed Chester. Time and time again Chance had asked himself why Dan Tipton had sewn so many wild oats while on the circuit. He'd had every cowboy's dream waiting for him at home and been too dense to realize it.

No job seemed to be too great or small for Alexa to undertake. She astonished him with her organizational abilities, her efficient use of time. He had seen her do two things at once without batting an eyelash or voicing complaints. Weary though Chance knew she was, she made time for her son, had the patience to deal with Howard's constant boasting.

For three days Chance had stood at the bunkhouse window, itching to add his two cents' worth while Alexa and Zack played catch. He was trying very hard not to intrude, to remain outside the circle of this family, to mind his own damn business. But the woman and her kid were getting to him. He wanted to ease Alexa's burden for a few minutes out of each day.

So here he was, offering his skills as a carpenter so she could quit early to keep her promise to Zack.

"All right, Chester, let's build a wall."

And like the shoemaker's elves, he and Chester attacked their tasks, while Alexa baked the cookies she had promised her son.

Chapter Two

Astonished, Alexa stared at the two newly erected walls in the barn loft.

Merciful heavens! Even nursing his bum leg Chance had made more progress in half an afternoon than she had all day.

And why had he even bothered? she wondered. None of the other temporary hired hands had lifted a finger to assist her while she cleaned and swept the old cedar barn. They had spent their spare time sprawled on chairs in front of the TV in the bunkhouse, tossing down the contents of longnecks.

Never once had Alexa asked for Chance's assistance—wouldn't even have considered asking. Never once had she given the slightest indication that she regarded him as anything except Howard's hired hand.

And what did he expect in return for his magnanimous help?

Alexa frowned suspiciously. Was this some new kind of

a come-on? The usual ones she received from cowboys—when Howard wasn't looking—came in the form of come-hither glances and effusive flattery. To date, she had ignored all the come-ons. But maybe the long-legged cowboy who hailed from Montana was trying a different approach, still expecting payment in some intimate form.

That would be the day frogs flew! Alexa had half a mind to march down to the bunkhouse and set Chance Butler straight. Since it was Friday night, she would direct him to the nearest honky-tonk bar in Willowvale. There were plenty of urban cowgirls eager and willing to show a ruggedly handsome man a good time. A subtle hint might assure Chance that he wasn't to expect anything but home-cooked meals and thank-yous from Alexa.

While Howard was showing Zack the scrapbook of Dan's rodeo career—for the umpteenth time—Alexa aimed herself toward the bunkhouse. When she rapped on the door, no one answered. Resolutely, she tried again.

"Hold on a sec!" came that deep baritone voice that had such a pleasing effect on her ears—and certain feminine parts of her body.

Tapping her foot impatiently, Alexa waited for Chance to appear. When he did she stepped back a pace, startled to see his wet hair tumbling down his forehead and water droplets glistening on the dark hair on his bare chest. Apparently, she had caught him fresh from the shower. She found herself staring at a magnificent chest that was nicked by scars—souvenirs of being hooked by horns during steer wrestling events, no doubt. Scarred or not, that was USDA Prime Choice chest—all rippling muscle, vibrant masculinity and bronzed flesh.

Exasperated by her betraying gaze, and the potent effect his brawny male body had on her, Alexa barged into the bunkhouse. When Chance tried to close the door, Alexa whirled to face him.

"Leave it open. I don't want Zack or Howard getting the wrong impression," she said in a rush.

He waggled his thick eyebrows suggestively. "Then I guess you don't mind if I get the wrong impression."

It was the wrong thing to say. The fact that Alexa found his playful smile utterly appealing and disarming only irritated her further. She had tried to be the Queen of Cool in Chance's presence, but there was nothing cool about her response to the man, damn it.

"Put on a shirt, cowboy," she demanded in a no-nonsense tone. "I came here to discuss your chest—I mean the barn project."

When Chance burst out laughing, Alexa's face turned so red that she was afraid it would explode in flames. "I'm trying to be serious here," she snapped, angry, embarrassed. "This is not a social call, Butler."

"Why would I think that?" Chance asked between snickers. "I've nearly suffered frostbite from you since I got here. I've been wondering what I could possibly have done to offend you. Do I talk too much? Not enough? What's the problem here?"

"Are you going to put on a shirt or not?" Alexa muttered, staring everywhere except at his appealing chest.

"Sure, if you think I'm too distracting the way I am."

Now how was she supposed to reply to that? This ornery cowboy had backed her into the proverbial corner. If she kept insisting on the shirt, then she might as well come right out and announce that she found him appealing and distracting. But if he didn't cover his chest, she wasn't sure she could keep her traitorous gaze from wandering all over him while she fumbled to put her thoughts into words.

All right, she did find him exceptionally attractive, she admitted begrudgingly. And she was going to feel considerably more at ease if he covered himself.

While Alexa stood there fighting down her blush and

wrestling with betraying thoughts, Chance let her off the hook. Thank goodness!

"Give me a minute, Al, and I'll get dressed. Does this conversation require boots or is barefoot acceptable?"

Her respect for him elevated a notch when he didn't press his advantage or come on to her. "Barefoot is fine."

"What about a belt? Shirt tucked in?" he teased as he limped toward the closet.

Alexa felt a reluctant smile working its way across her lips. The man was as exasperating as he was amusing and attractive. He had a knack of lightening up her serious moods, of teasing her without offending her. He seemed to be a good and decent man, despite his chosen profession.

Too bad she had a general dislike for men of his chosen profession.

Modestly, Chance kept his back to her while he thrust his arms into his shirt, fastened the buttons hastily, then pivoted around. "If you don't prefer to sit down, I hope you don't mind if I do, Al. The leg is beginning to throb something fierce."

Alexa felt guilty about the extra work he'd done in the barn. He had placed unnecessary strain on his leg—on her behalf. The man had done her a tremendous favor, and the least she could do was thank him properly, though she wanted to make it clear that she didn't repay favors in an intimate fashion.

"First off, thank you for working in the barn. You and Chester made amazing progress while I was baking cookies."

"You're welcome. Any woman who is willing to lug around a nail gun and build her own bed-and-breakfast deserves a helping hand. You're the strongest, most self-reliant woman I've ever met. You impress me, Al. I wanted to show you that I approve of you and admire your work ethic."

Never in all the years of her marriage had Dan bothered

to acknowledge, or even notice, how hard she worked. Alexa was inordinately pleased that Chance admired her, respected her abilities. Hard as she tried to dislike this man, he kept chipping away her barriers of defense. Not to mention the vivid effect his physical appeal and sense of humor had on her, she tacked on silently.

"I'm aware that Howard doesn't approve of my refurbishing project," she said, anxious to put space between herself and her traitorous thoughts of attraction. "But the agricultural industry is still in a state of depression. I'm convinced the B-and-B will be profitable once I open for business."

"With you at the helm I don't doubt it," Chance said with firm conviction. "You've got more energy than a high-strung Thoroughbred, and I've never seen you sit down long enough to gather dust."

"I appreciate your vote of confidence, but that isn't why I stopped by."

Chance grinned. "I didn't think so."

He was curious as hell to know what had prompted Alexa's first official visit to his living quarters. For the most part, she seemed to be annoyed with him for just standing there breathing. She had given him such a wide berth since he arrived that he also wondered if he was contagious—or at the very least, had a serious case of bad breath.

Chance was surprised and delighted by Alexa's reaction to seeing him freshly scrubbed from a shower. It did wonders for his male ego. With his noticeable limp, Chance had been feeling less of a man, more vulnerable. It wasn't a feeling that he was comfortable with.

Yet despite these humbling feelings he was experiencing because of his injury, he wanted to get to know Alexa.

On one hand, he was hesitant to cross the line that Howard and Alexa had established for him. On the other hand, this woman's remarkable strength of character, personality and arresting good looks were hopeless lures. Though she wore no makeup, didn't fuss with that tangled mass of curly auburn hair and dressed down her feminine assets, she still appealed to everything male in him.

Chance wasn't a complete fool, though. He knew he was asking for trouble if he appeared the least bit interested in developing a relationship with Alexa. But hell, what man wouldn't want to try? He'd have to be dead a week not to react to a stunningly lovely woman like Alexa Tipton.

In hopes of reassuring this leery female that he wasn't the slightest threat to her, Chance had quickly nicknamed her Al. He had tried to send a subtle message that he wasn't coming on to her—though the man in him strongly objected to the tactic.

If nothing else, Chance wanted to leave Rocking T with Al's respect and friendship, even if she was the one woman he found himself wishing—in his weaker moments—that he could share a good deal more than conversation with.

When Alexa squirmed awkwardly on the sofa, then stared at the air over his right shoulder, Chance frowned curiously. He reckoned he was about to learn the reason for this unexpected visit.

"Since you are new in the area, I thought I would direct you toward the local watering hole in Willowvale. Bud's Tavern caters to the cowboys who like to kick up their heels and listen to country and western music. Bud hires live entertainment on weekends, and unattached females frequent the place."

Chance's frown deepened. Just what was going on here? Why was Alexa so anxious to send him off to the local honky-tonk?

His gaze drifted to the door that Alexa insisted he leave wide open. Could it be that Alexa had taken an unwanted liking to him?

Well, he'd taken a reluctant liking to her, too, and Chance was as hesitant as she was to complicate the situation. Hesitant but unable to ignore Alexa's magnetic appeal. Hell, every time he made the mistake of staring at those lush lips—like now—he felt the stirring of hungry need.

Yet he kept thinking there had to be some flaw in this all-too-perfect female. Why had Dan Tipton tripped the light fantastic, every chance he got, with the rodeo groupies on the circuit? For sure, Alexa wasn't the type of woman who came on aggressively to other men. Her insistence on an open door, to prevent wrong impressions, signified that she possessed strong Midwestern values.

Didn't sex appeal to her? he wondered. Strong and independent as she was, maybe she didn't like any man, even her husband, being in control of any given situation....

"Well? Are you interested in a night on the town?" Alexa prompted when he dillydallied too long in thought.

"Are you asking me out on a date?" Chance popped off before he could stop himself.

"No! Certainly not!" she denied adamantly.

Fascinated, he watched a blush work its way up her neck to splatter her creamy cheeks. "Fact is that I don't drink," he confided.

His comment caught her by surprise, he noted.

"You don't? I thought all cowboys—"

"My dad is a reformed alcoholic," he cut in. "I lived through hell with that man before he reformed. Believe it or not, you could even call him respectable now, though I have difficulty forgetting what he was like in his wilder days."

For the life of him Chance didn't know why he had imparted that confidential information. He was in the habit of keeping his background to himself, refusing to reveal hellish memories from childhood. But he found himself sharing that part of his unpleasant past with Alexa. Maybe he wanted her to know that he wasn't just another cowboy who'd landed on her doorstep. Maybe he wanted her to realize he *was* different, and that he wanted to earn her respect.

"Now, if you were to accompany me to the honky-tonk for a cola and dancing I wouldn't be opposed to that," he blurted out of the blue.

"Are you asking *me* out on a date?" she croaked, frog-eyed.

Fool that he was, Chance had opened his big mouth and put her on defense with that comment about a date. Geez, sometimes he ought to try engaging his brain before he unleashed his tongue.

"Guess I am," Chance admitted, chuckling. "I like you, admire you. Can't hang a man for that, can you?"

Now she was really starting to squirm. Chance knew he had made a mistake by being too open and straightforward with this overly cautious woman. He could see her retreating behind that wall of cool reserve she'd built around herself.

"I'm sorry, but I can't accept," she insisted. "I have my son to consider. He is my first priority."

"What about your wants and needs, Al?" he couldn't help but ask. "Aren't you supposed to have a life, too?"

Something inside Alexa snapped—emotions half-buried, but still a little raw, grated on her. She knew Dan had been unfaithful to her—or rather she'd suspected it after she found traces of makeup and whiffs of strong perfume on the shirts she laundered after his trips. Dan had led a double life, and she presumed Chance was also accustomed to living in the fast lane. She had a definite aversion to men who slept their way from one rodeo to the next, keeping track of feminine conquests like a gunslinger notching his six-shooter.

Alexa would never allow herself to become any man's casual conquest. She didn't need a man in her life. The one she had married had never been there for her. And sex, as she had learned the hard way, wasn't necessarily fulfilling.

Dan's idea of lovemaking consumed about as much time as his eight-second rides on saddle broncs....

Alexa fought down the blush that accompanied that thought, then focused her attention on Chance's question about having a life of her own. "When you have the responsibility of raising a child, you make a commitment to your child and you put his wants and needs before your own. Children aren't something you take or leave on selfish whims."

"Try telling that to my parents," Chance said, half under his breath.

Although Alexa was curious about his mumbled comment, she was determined to drive home her point. "It is my duty to get this floundering ranch back on its feet. I need to make this bed-and-breakfast prosper. As it is, I have enough trouble finding extra minutes in the day to ensure Zack doesn't feel slighted. My dad never had time for me and my sister, and Zack's dad didn't make time for him. I'll be damned if my son is going to suffer in any way!"

"Mom! Are we going to play catch tonight?"

In Alexa's opinion, Zack's timing couldn't have been better. He had reinforced the point she was trying to make.

"I'm on my way, champ." Her gaze drilled into Chance as she called back to her son. Alexa came to her feet, nodding curtly. "If you'll excuse me, I have to catch the next Greg Maddux, the Cy Young Award-winning pitcher for the Atlanta Braves."

Although Chance was impressed that Alexa appeared well informed on sports celebrities, he couldn't keep his trap shut. "Zack throws like a girl, and you do, too. I'd be happy to give Zack some pointers so he won't end up on the sidelines for the rest of his life."

Her chin came up to a defiant angle. "We'll muddle through the best we can, thank you very much. You won't be here long enough to follow Zack's sports career, after all."

On that parting shot, Alexa strode through the door. Chance sank back in the chair, propped up his lame leg and stared at the blank TV screen.

Such a proud, stubborn, defensive woman, he mused. She wasn't accustomed to accepting help, unless she paid for it. She didn't know how to handle offered assistance gracefully, because she wasn't accustomed to being on the receiving end. From what Chance had seen, Alexa did most of the giving on this ranch and none of the taking.

Wasn't accustomed to accepting help, unless she paid for it...

The thought rolled back to Chance, making him frown ponderously. His feelings of frustration evaporated when he gave the matter further consideration. Paybacks. Was that the hidden agenda in Alexa's visit?

Knowing Alexa as he did—and he had become amazingly perceptive where she was concerned—he was beginning to realize that she didn't want folks doing favors for her unless she could repay them properly. She had a very strong sense of fair play and she didn't expect to get something for nothing.

Chance wondered if Alexa's attempt to steer him to the local tavern and the available females looking for a good time, was her way of assuring him that he wasn't to expect favors of an intimate nature from her, just because he'd framed up a wall in the barn.

A slow, wicked smile worked its way across his lips. He should place a few calls tonight to some friends who owed him favors. This weekend was open—in preparation for the high-dollar rodeo held at the fairgrounds in Tulsa. Alexa would be in a full-fledged tizzy if Chance gathered a workforce to frame her bed-and-breakfast. She'd be so flustered by his generosity, and that of his friends, that she wouldn't know what to do with herself, what to say, how to react.

Well, too bad. She needed to learn how to accept a helping hand graciously, needed to know that she didn't have to depend entirely on herself, one hundred percent of the time.

Out of pure orneriness, and the compelling need to help that strong-willed woman, Chance reached for the phone. He didn't understand his driving need to prove to that wary, defensive woman that he had integrity, that he didn't fit into the mold. But he did. It was high time to redeem the lowly status of rodeo cowboys.

While Chance dialed he silently cursed Dan Tipton. That irresponsible jerk must have really done a job on Alexa. Well, there were a hell of a lot of good and decent cowboys on the circuit. Sure, some of them believed in having a rowdy time, but not necessarily at someone else's expense. Not everyone followed Dan Tipton's philosophy of cheating on his wife.

Alexa was dead on her feet, but determined to put the kitchen in order before she tucked Zack in bed. She had seen Chance drive off in the jalopy truck Howard had offered for use during Chance's employment at Rocking T. No doubt, Chance had taken her suggestion to check out the local bar and its hovering barflies.

So why was she disappointed in him? she asked herself while she practically scraped the Teflon finish off her skillet. Rodeo cowboys were notorious for their raucous nightlife. She knew that, had lived with it during her marriage. Why did she want Chance Butler to be different? Why should she care if he was or wasn't? He was just another walkaway cowboy who came and went from her life.

Alexa stifled the warm, tingling sensation prompted by the lingering memory of seeing Chance half-dressed. She couldn't believe that she was actually pondering the outrageous possibility of accepting a date with him. She knew he would be entertaining company, and she could use a diversion from her daily routine....

But it was never going to happen, she assured herself

sensibly. Aside from the gossip that would fly around Willowvale, Howard would buck and kick to such extremes that he'd throw a shoe. He'd made it clear, on numerous occasions, that he didn't expect her to have a relationship with another man after Dan died. Howard was protective and possessive of his family, and he wanted things left exactly as they were.

Since Alexa's parents had died in a small plane crash when she was in high school, she had no family except a younger sister. Her father's modest savings had been swallowed up by final expenses, leaving two young girls to struggle for survival. When Alexa met and married Dan, this ranch had become Alexa's home. Living life the way Howard expected her to was the price she paid for remaining at Rocking T.

Alexa had learned to accept responsibility and obligation early in life. She had raised her kid sister, Debra, as best she could. That hadn't been easy, because Deb had gone through a traumatic crisis after their parents' deaths.

There had been times when Alexa wondered if she had married Dan just to ensure Deb had the security of a home, until she went to college. Certainly Alexa had loved Dan— or thought she did—in the beginning. She had been swept off her feet by a man six years her senior. But Dan's affection had been distributed nationwide, and Alexa found herself on the heartbreaking end of one-sided marriage vows.

Well, that was all muddy water under the bridge, Alexa reminded herself. She had to make the best of her life, just as she always had. There wasn't time for self-pity and complaint. Besides, what did she have to complain about? She had inherited half this ranch. She had a bright, loving son and a father-in-law who adored Zack. Howard was protective of her, even if he wasn't too thrilled with her construction project, which went against the grain and tradition of a dyed-in-the-wool rancher.

But every once in a while, Alexa found herself wishing for more.

Aren't you entitled to a life, too?

Chance's question returned to torment her. No, she couldn't allow herself such self-indulgent thoughts. She did not need a man, had proved that hundreds of times in the past ten years. She could lead a productive, rewarding life with a successful bed-and-breakfast to manage.

The roar of bad mufflers on the bucket-of-rust truck drew Alexa's attention. She saw the flash of headlights, saw the interior cab lights flick on as she peered out the kitchen window. Her gaze was magnetically drawn to the sinewy silhouette in the front yard.

A moment later there was a firm rap at the door.

Alexa found Chance standing on the porch, his arms laden with plastic bags. He limped inside, uninvited, to deposit the sacks on the kitchen counter.

"I'm having a few friends over for the weekend," he announced matter-of-factly. "Howard said I could have guests if I wanted them. I didn't think you'd mind preparing extra food if I paid for it."

She stared at him as if he had horns sprouting from the sides of his head. "Didn't think I'd mind? I planned to spend Saturday framing the rest of the upstairs bedrooms in the barn. Do you expect me to be two places at once?"

Chance shrugged nonchalantly, infuriating her. "You'll manage, Superwoman. Besides, this is your chance to repay me for the favor of framing the barn this afternoon. And next time you decide to repay me by pointing me toward those glossy honky-tonk angels who hang out at the local bar, don't bother. You probably find this hard to believe, but I can manage to get my own dates when I want them."

Damn, the man was more perceptive than she'd given him credit for being. He seemed to have her figured out, but he was sadly mistaken if he thought she was such a good sport that she intended to spend the weekend chained to the damned stove! Cook for him and his cronies? Like hell!

"You can cook for your own guests, cowboy," she snapped. "I've got more important things to do with my time."

"Consider this practice for cooking at your B-and-B," he suggested, undaunted.

"Consider packing your gear and leaving Rocking T, as of tonight," she hissed, outraged by his presumptuousness, his domineering attitude. "I've got news for you, pal, I'm in control of this ranch. And I don't take orders from temporary hired hands."

"Howard hired me," he reminded her calmly.

"And he can fire you. All I have to do is imply that you tried to get up close and personal and you'll be history."

Chance closed the space between them in deliberate strides. Despite his limp, he could be very intimidating when he wanted to be, she noted. Six feet three inches of brawny, well-muscled cowboy was nothing to sneeze at. Alexa reflexively retreated when Chance loomed over her, sporting that mischievous grin that was as dangerous as it was devastating.

"If and when I come on to you, sweetheart, you'll know it," he said in an ultrasexy voice that sent gooseflesh flying down her arms. "When I pull you good and close like this—"

He hooked his index fingers in the belt loops of her jeans, towing her forward, until her hips collided with his.

Alexa's knees knocked together the instant her body came into contact with muscled, masculine contours. Lord! The man was as radioactive as a neutron bomb.

"When we are well and truly up close and personal, like this—"

His head lowered to hers, his sensuous mouth only a hairbreadth from her trembling lips. Alarm bells clanged in her head, but she found herself rooted to the floor. She couldn't move, couldn't think past that appealing scent of his cologne, the wicked temptation in his eyes, the devilishness in his smile.

If her wobbly legs collapsed like a folding table and dumped her in an unceremonious heap at his feet she was going to die of humiliation. The powerful threat of his male body, the undeniable attraction, were destroying her sense of balance, her sense of well-being. The man rattled her, no question about that!

"That's when you'll know that I'm coming on to you, Green Eyes," he whispered in a voice like liquid velvet.

Alexa knew he was about to kiss her, could see the glint of heightened desire in those entrancing eyes that burned like flaming mercury in the light. The betraying thought that she actually *wanted* to test her reaction to this noaccount cowboy shocked her. Like a fool, she stood there staring up at him, waiting in nervous anticipation of something she wanted—and didn't want.

To her relief, or disappointment—she still wasn't sure which—Chance released her as gently as he had drawn her against him.

"But...I never make unwelcome advances toward women," he murmured, his gaze still fixed on her lips. "I don't believe in using my overpowering strength and size to my advantage, unless I'm bulldogging or lassoing a steer in timed rodeo events."

Chance tipped his hat politely, then limped toward the door. "See ya at breakfast, Al."

When the door creaked shut behind him, Alexa braced her arms on the counter for needed support. Damn, Chance Butler nearly knocked her legs out from under her and he'd barely even touched her! Alexa shuddered to think what would have happened if he had actually kissed her. The man was definitely a threat to her feminine senses, her emotional equilibrium.

Damn it, she had sworn off will-o'-the-wisp cowboys

after her marriage to Dan. How could she be such a hypocrite?

Alexa inhaled a deep, fortifying breath, determined to clear her clogged senses of the scent, feel and sight of Chance—the lady-killer—Butler. Alexa had made one crucial mistake in her life already. She was not about to repeat it. No matter how devastating Chance was, she was going to keep her distance. And he could damned well think again if he thought she was going to cook all the food he toted into her kitchen! She'd let him and his friends starve to death!

Yeah, right, Al. You've spent your adult life placing the wants and needs of others before your own. You think you're going to become self-centered overnight?

Alexa muttered under her breath as she put away the food, then flicked off the light. She was the kind of person who took in stray dogs—like the lame-legged dalmatian puppy someone had dumped out at the ranch, the puppy Zack fell in love with immediately. No way could she dispose of that pup—or let grown men go hungry.

For years she had projected an air of toughness so her husband wouldn't know how much it hurt her to be slighted and betrayed. But on the inside, she was a tenderhearted softy. Somehow she would find time to squeeze in cooking. She had learned to do two things at once during her hectic days. Why not go for three?

Chapter Three

Breakfast was a silent affair. Howard's arthritis was acting up and he had his hands full managing to hold on to his coffee cup. Zack was sleeping late—a habit he developed after rising early to catch the school bus during the week. Chance devoured his eggs, sausage and hash brown potatoes like a man who had been on prison rations for years. Alexa picked at her food and stared everywhere except at Chance, who had seated himself directly across from her.

"I decided to take you up on your offer to invite guests for the weekend," Chance told Howard. "All of my guests are rodeo cowboys who knew Dan. I'm sure you'll recognize the names, since you read *ProRodeo Sports News*."

Howard perked up immediately. Chance figured he would.

"I don't want to impose, but I wondered if you would mind if some of the boys practiced their skills in your arena. You know, sort of casual competition."

Howard sat up a little straighter in his chair. "No, glad

to have the cowboys in for the weekend. It's been a while since Dan and his friends used the arena and chutes for practice. I don't mind a bit.''

Chance spared Alexa a discreet glance. She was silently fuming, he suspected. Her feathers might be ruffled now, but later she would thank him for this weekend—he hoped.

''I know Alexa won't mind feeding a few more mouths,'' Howard said. ''She'll enjoy seeing some of Dan's friends again.''

Alexa would be nothing of the kind, judging by the annoyed glance she shot Chance. If looks could kill, Chance figured he would have been pushing up daisies on the north-forty.

''I suppose the men are passing through on their way to the rodeo at the fairgrounds in Tulsa.'' Howard reached over to refill his coffee cup, and Alexa automatically took the cup from his deformed hand to prevent a spill. ''I've been thinking about taking Zack down to watch the events—''

''No.'' Alexa had kept silent as long as she could stand. Zack was not going to follow in his father's footsteps and become the extension of his grandfather's broken dreams. Her son was going to receive the higher education she'd been deprived of. Zack was going to become a chemical engineer, brain surgeon—whatever he wanted, as long as he wasn't a rodeo cowboy!

When Howard glared at Alexa, Chance felt the tension floating around the kitchen. Clearly, there was a private conflict of opinion at work here. He had unintentionally stirred up a hornets' nest.

''I don't see the harm,'' Howard gritted out.

''Zack is just a little kid,'' Alexa pointed out. ''He needs to be at home, not kicking around bucking chutes like a rodeo rat.''

''It's the only way to learn the profession,'' Howard maintained. ''Rodeo and ranch are in that boy's blood.''

"Then I'll get him a transfusion," Alex shot back.

Chance decided it was time to defuse what was about to become an explosive situation. "Breakfast was terrific." He smiled cheerily. "I haven't eaten this well in years. Since you're anxious to start work in the barn loft, I'll tidy up the kitchen before I feed the cattle."

When Alexa quickly accepted the offer and strode from the house, Howard scowled at her departing back. "I don't know what's gotten into that woman. If she isn't careful she'll mother Zack to death. I won't let that happen."

"Maybe she just doesn't want her son leading the rambling life that rodeo cowboys lead," Chance put in tactfully. "From a woman's standpoint I doubt the prospect has much appeal. Constant travel puts strains on family obligations, I suspect."

Howard considered that for a moment. "Maybe. There was always someplace Dan had to be. Alexa was left on the ranch a lot, but she should have understood the situation."

Chance wondered if the fact had occurred to Howard, who was wrapped up in his son's world and teemed with fatherly pride, that Alexa was the one who suffered most by her husband's lengthy absences.

"I know it's a sore spot among the married cowboys," Chance added. "After a couple of years of constant separation I imagine a woman might start wondering what's the sense of being married. Alexa may have wondered the same thing occasionally."

Howard frowned pensively. Chance suspected the old man was beginning to recall a few tense moments in this household. There were bound to have been some, given Alexa's staunch refusal to lead her son down the trail to rodeos.

"Well, maybe," Howard conceded, "but I don't see why I can't take Zack to a rodeo every now and then. It's not like I plan to load him up every weekend and drag him away from Alexa, you know.''

You're doing it again, Butler. Poking your nose in places it doesn't belong, Chance caught himself thinking.

Despite his better judgment, his personal reservations, he kept getting in deeper with the Tiptons. Who the hell did he think he was? The Tiptons' counselor? He was here to recuperate from an injury that kept him off the circuit. What right did he have to meddle in this family's affairs?

No right at all, just an uncontrollable urge to help a woman who held his admiration, respect…and his growing attraction. Hell, this ticklish situation might blow up in his face, and what was he going to do about it? Walk away, just as Alexa expected *his kind* to do?

Geez, maybe he should have rented a room at Sleep E-Z Motel for a month. Well, it was too late now, he realized. He had gotten attached to that talkative kid who asked more questions than a college entrance exam. And admitting that Alexa had gotten under his skin was a gross understatement. That little scene he'd staged in the kitchen last night had deprived Chance of needed sleep. He kept wondering how that feisty female would have reacted if he *had* kissed her. The mere *prospect* of kissing her had had Chance tossing and turning half the night. Swallowing a pain pill at two in the morning was all that had saved him from total insomnia.

Before Chance got all hot and bothered over a woman who was off-limits to him, he stood to gather the plates from the table. He wondered if thrusting his hands into cold dishwater would be as effective as a cold shower.

A half hour later he was assured that it wasn't.

Chance heard hiccuping sobs coming from behind the barn. It sounded as if Zack was blubbering like an abandoned child. Chance knew how that felt. He'd done some serious crying in private during his troubled childhood.

When Chance limped around the corner of the barn, he found Zack scrunched down in the dewy grass, slamming a baseball into his glove repeatedly.

"Something wrong, kid?" he asked softly.

Zack wiped his tears on the hem of his striped T-shirt, then looked across the rolling pasture. "Don't wanna talk about it," he mumbled.

Chance ambled closer to lean leisurely against the barn. "Sometimes talking things out, man to man, helps. Take me for instance. I've been feeling left out because of this bum leg. I can't do all the things I used to do because of it, either. All my friends are entering rodeos and I've been left behind for a few weeks."

Watery eyes lifted to Chance, causing a constricting sensation in his chest. "We picked teams to play baseball in gym class at school yesterday. I was picked last," Zack confided in a trembly voice. "Nobody wanted me...."

Another sob and hiccup escaped the little squirt. Chance slipped his hand under Zack's arm to hoist him to his feet. "I've been itching to play some catch with you since I got here," he confided. "But I didn't want to crowd in on the time you spend playing with your mom. How about if I give you a few pointers that will make the rest of those third graders sit up and take notice of your baseball skills?"

Zack's face glowed with excitement. "Do you think you could help me get better at baseball?"

Chance nodded. "I'm willing to give it a try if you are. You'd be doing me a favor, too, because I need some exercise to limber up my stiff leg."

Beaming in anticipation Zack tramped off twenty paces, then whipped around. After they had warmed up their throwing arms, Chance limped over to take Zack's arm through the proper pitching motion. For the next half hour he encouraged and instructed Zack.

The boy's eyes were dancing with enthusiasm and a sense of accomplishment when his fastball smacked into

Chance's bare hand. "Wow! I'm gonna tell Mom that I'm getting better and you're helping me!"

Chance held up his hand before Zack dashed off. "Whoa, rookie. Bad idea."

"How come?" Zack wanted to know.

"Well, moms can be kind of touchy about having some cowboy stepping in to replace them for ball practice," Chance explained. "We don't want your mom to feel left out or unwanted, you know."

Zack frowned, pondering the logic.

"We'll practice privately," Chance continued. "That way we can keep doing each other a favor without hurting your mom's feelings. Since you and I know how it feels to be left out, we wouldn't want her feeling that way, too, would we?"

"No way," Zack insisted.

Chance hobbled over to give the kid a quick hug. "Me either. You can play catch with both of us, okay?"

"Okay."

When Zack trotted off to play with his dalmatian puppy, Chance ambled back to the bunkhouse. Alexa would likely raise hell with him if she found out what he was doing, but damn it, he couldn't let that kid go on hiding behind the barn, crying his eyes out because he was a gym-class reject. Zack was putting up a brave front for his mother's benefit, but there was no question that the kid had been hurting in private.

Willfully, Chance turned his thoughts toward preparations for the cowboys-turned-carpenters' impending arrival. He was going to play fairy godfather for every member of the Tipton family this weekend. He just hoped like hell that the majority of them appreciated it.

Alexa worked off her frustration in the barn loft. She had so much energy that lugging around the heavy nail gun didn't faze her. Following the directions Chester had given her during the past few weeks, she set the precut studs on the floor, shoved the two-by-fours in place and nailed the newly constructed wall. She didn't know how she was going to hoist up the wall by herself, but she vowed to figure that out when the time came.

While working, Alexa muttered a few curses to Howard's name. How on earth was she going to convince Howard that Zack didn't need to go chasing around to rodeos without offending the old man who had been generous to her? She should appreciate having a weekend all to herself for the first time since she could remember. But damn it, why couldn't Howard offer to take Zack anywhere except to a rodeo?

There were plenty of activities that an eight-year-old boy would enjoy. Professional baseball games, a Disney movie, a trip to an amusement park. But this wasn't really about what *Zack* liked to do, was it? It was about what Howard wanted, what Howard expected of his grandson.

And Chance, curse him, had fired up Howard when he mentioned inviting a few cronies to play rodeo cowboy for the weekend. Howard ate that stuff up, loved to relive his son's fame and glory with other men in the rodeo circle.

There were times when Alexa wondered how it would feel to pack a suitcase, grab Zack by the hand and shove off, leaving the responsibility of the house and the ranch behind her. Unfortunately, responsibility had become her middle name, her way of life. She never turned her back on obligation, and she didn't have it in her to start now. She was stuck in a rut and couldn't seem to climb out without feeling guilty.

But just once, for one reckless, carefree, selfish moment she would like to live for herself, to follow her own personal whims and thumb her nose at obligation.

Alexa muttered an epithet to Chance's name for putting such irresponsible thoughts in her head. The man was a bad influence on her, was too damn appealing. She didn't want to like him, didn't want to count on him, because he would be gone in a few short weeks. She didn't need another Dan Tipton tormenting her life. One had been plenty.

Alexa's thoughts trailed off when she heard the clatter of footsteps on the staircase Chester had built onto the opening of the barn loft. Twisting around from her squatting position, Alexa gaped at the familiar faces of men she recognized from infrequent ranch visits and action shots taken by rodeo magazines.

"What on earth…?"

To her stunned amazement, six rodeo cowboys, equipped with tool pouches, carrying armloads of two-by-four studs, nodded greetings as they strode toward her. Chance brought up the rear of the procession with his noticeable limp. He, too, was laden down with lumber. The task had to be putting excessive strain on his injured knee.

"The guys and I decided to erect a few walls and save the roping and riding until it cools down this evening," Chance explained with a casual smile. "Al, you remember Skeeter, Jack, Teddy, Lefty, Ray and Sonny, don't you? They all claim to have passed through here a few times in the past."

Dumbfounded, Alexa nodded a silent greeting to the bulky cowboys. Then her astonished gaze fixed on Chance's wry smile. It dawned on her that he had secretly arranged for this barn-raising party and that he was giving her the weekend off from hard labor, if she would agree to cook for the hungry men.

Practice cooking for your bed-and-breakfast, he'd said—or something to that effect. At the time, Alexa had wanted to choke him for what she believed to be presumptuous imposition. Now she wanted to hug the stuffing out of him for accelerating this construction project. Of course, she would never forgive Chance for leaving her beholden to so many men, either, she tacked on silently.

Chance set aside the stack of lumber, then extended a

sinewy arm to her. "Hand over the gun, Al. As sheriff of this here podunk town, we got laws against womenfolk packin' firearms," he said in his best Old-West drawl.

The comment drew chuckles from the cowboys, but Alexa's gaze was locked on Chance's teasing smile. When she handed over the nail gun, Chance lifted it as if it were as light as a pencil.

"Zack is camped out on the couch, watching the Braves take on the Cincinnati Reds on TV. John Smoltz is on the mound. Why don't you go take a look at the man's pitching technique and see if you can't learn to throw with some respectability, Al. Me and the other menfolk got some buildin' to do here."

At that moment, Alexa couldn't find it in her heart to take offense at his playful criticism of her baseball skills. Chance was like a wizard waving his magic wand to fulfill her dream.

Alexa was beginning to understand that Chance was giving her an opportunity, without asking for much in return. He had made it crystal clear the previous night that he wasn't the kind of man who expected sexual favors or made unwanted advances. Any advances, Alexa knew, would have to come from her.

Conflicting emotions assailed Alexa. She wanted Chance to keep his distance before she got too attached to him. She wanted him to leave—she wanted him to stay. She wanted Chance to be Zack's male role model, yet she didn't.

When Alexa continued to stand there staring up at Chance with an indecipherable expression in her cedar-tree-green eyes, he longed to pull her into his arms and assure her whatever emotion was rumbling beneath that carefully controlled surface could be worked out to a satisfactory conclusion. But hell, he wasn't sure things would work out perfectly for her, and he didn't believe in spouting empty promises.

He was going to do this good deed for the year and just

let it go at that, he told himself. Even if by slim chance Alexa yielded to the attraction he sensed she was feeling toward him, there was still Howard Tipton to contend with. That old rooster would be crowing at the top of his lungs if any man dared to intrude on the shrine he had erected to honor his departed son.

No wonder Chance had spent his spare time with uncomplicated women who were interested in one-night rodeos. Complex females like Alexa could put a man's closely guarded emotions in a tailspin.

Before Chance got all mushy and sentimental from staring into that lovely feminine face, he shooed Alexa on her way. "Skedaddle, Al. Us menfolk got lots to do. Your first six guests at the bed-and-breakfast want to get their rooms ready for occupancy."

"Thank you," Alexa whispered soulfully, her eyes misting with tears.

"No thanks needed, Al. A pot of stew simmering over the campfire will be appreciation enough," Chance said in a light tone.

Damn, that watery smile was really hitting him where he lived. Most women bled tears when a man handed over sparkling diamonds, but not Al. She got all sentimental over refurbishing a barn. But then, Chance already understood that Alexa was a unique breed of woman who didn't fit the usual feminine mold.

When Alexa smiled, then walked away, Teddy Cramer lifted a quizzical brow. "Wanna tell us what's going on here, Butler?"

Chance shrugged nonchalantly. "We're renovating a barn."

"No, Teddy is asking what is going on with you and *Al,*" Lefty paraphrased.

"I'm doing my good deed for the year and you're helping me. So clam up and get to work," Chance ordered.

"Go build some walls and make damn sure they're level while you're at it."

"He's sweet on the widow," Jack and Ray chorused.

Chance raised the nail gun threateningly. "I said get to work."

With mocking salutes, the troop of cowboys-turned-carpenters marched off like soldiers on parade.

"Hey, Mom, John Smoltz struck out three batters in a row!" Zack reported when Alexa stepped into the living room. "The Braves are up three to zip in the fourth."

"Has Chipper Jones gotten a hit yet?" Alexa asked.

Thanks to Zack's avid fascination for the Atlanta Braves, she knew the names and positions of the team's starting lineup and the ERA of the bull pen.

"Chipper got a stand-up double," Zack said, in between bites of peanut butter cookies. He tore his gaze away from the TV screen long enough to flick a glance at his mother. "Grandpa says the cowboys are going to practice rodeoing this evening. He said I could take a turn at riding and roping. Do you want to practice, too?"

Alexa inwardly flinched. She hadn't been particularly pleased when her husband planted Zack on horseback and thrust a lariat into his small hand. Dan had shrugged off her concerns, as he did everything else. Now Howard was pulling the same stunt. Alexa didn't believe a young boy had any business playing a man's games, not when high-spirited horses and cantankerous cattle were involved.

"I think we should watch from the fence rail," Alexa insisted.

Zack wrinkled his nose. "I know how to ride already, Mom."

"Famous last words before you fall off a horse and get stamped on."

"Aw, Mom," Zack grumbled. "Grandpa said I could."

"He isn't your mother," Alexa muttered, then whirled away.

She and Howard were destined to lock horns over this, she predicted on her way to the kitchen. She planned to prepare the steaks and fried potatoes Chance had purchased at the supermarket. Howard loved steak—cooked medium rare. When he had his gums wrapped around the juicy meat, she would inform the old man that his grandson would be a bystander, not a participant this evening. Maybe the juicy meat would mellow the old man and make him see reason.

As for Chance, Alexa was still debating between strangling him and hugging him. The surprise he had arranged for the weekend was turning out to be both a blessing and a curse.

Alexa was up to her elbows in peeled potatoes and corn shucks when the phone rang. Zack answered, then came toting the portable phone to her.

"It's Aunt Debs. She wants to talk to you." Zack shook his head in disappointment. "Gee whiz, Mom, she doesn't know who John Smoltz is."

"Just goes to show you what happens when you slack off on your education, doesn't it?" Alexa said, then winked. "I bet she didn't pay attention to her science book when she was in the third grade, either."

"That means I'm supposed to pay attention, right?" Zack asked.

"You got it, champ. Go cheer for Smoltz for me, will you? Let me know if his pitches are clocked over eighty-five miles an hour."

Zack tore off to watch the game. Alexa wedged the phone between her head and shoulder. "Hi, sis, what are you up to?"

"I'm headed to the arts and crafts show this afternoon. I wondered if you wanted me to pick up some knickknacks to decorate your bed-and-breakfast."

Would she ever! Alexa was eager for her sister's expertise. Debra had the amazing knack of selecting inexpensive items and putting them together in a manner that gave a countrified touch to decor. An art major who had opened her own arts and crafts shop in Willowvale, Debra was the perfect candidate to decorate the B-and-B. Alexa was counting on her sister's talents to add just the right touch of antiques and Western paraphernalia to provide a memorable atmosphere in the old barn.

"I'll leave the selection of crafts to your good taste," Alexa said. "Just don't forget that I'm working on a limited budget, sis. The bank loan is increasing so fast that it makes my head spin. The plumbing and lumber bills are staggering."

"Don't worry about bursting your budget," Debra replied. "The knickknacks are on the house. I'll use the crafts and artwork as advertising for my shop. We'll stick a plaque by your cash register—where you'll be raking in the dough right and left—announcing that the decor is furnished by Deb's Craft Mall."

"Are you sure you can afford—?"

"Yep. Thanks to your encouragement, my business is on its feet. It's payback time, sis. I've waited a long time to repay you for raising me and seeing me through my difficult teens. I was too young and immature and bitter at the time to say thank-you. I'm saying thank-you now, and I plan to help you the same way you helped me. Catch ya later, sis."

Alexa set aside the phone and wiped her eyes on her sleeve. It wasn't like her to cry over little or nothing. But Chance's good deed and Deb's words of appreciation had bored through the suit of armor Alexa wore to protect herself from stress and frustration.

She was touched, appreciative and grateful, but she didn't know how to express the sentiment. She was also going to be late putting dinner on the table if she didn't fire up the smoker and get the steaks on the grill.

Grabbing her special blend of seasoning, Alexa coated the steaks, then carried them out to the patio. Zack's dalmatian pup licked his lips and stared beseechingly at her.

"You can chew on the bones after dinner," she said to the spotted dog. "Anything else will earn you a swat on the fanny. So keep your paws and your jaws off these steaks, understood?"

The dalmatian rolled onto its side to sunbathe, but the pup kept a watchful eye on the platter of steaks, just in case one of them plunked on the patio.

While Alexa went in and out the kitchen door, alternately monitoring the cooking temperatures of the meat, potatoes and corn, she heard the rat-tat-tat of hammers, the *whack-thump* of the nail gun and occasional outbursts of laughter.

No doubt Chance was providing entertainment while the men worked. He had a knack for lightening up glum moods. Alexa knew that for a fact, because he had used the technique on her once or twice when he thought she was taking life too seriously.

Damn, why did he have to be a shiftless cowboy? Why not a pharmacist or a shopkeeper, who put down permanent roots? Why did he have to be the symbol representing the kind of men Alexa had made a pact with herself to avoid, hitherto and forevermore?

Sure as the world turned, Chance Butler would saddle up and ride off into the sunset when his injured leg healed. Alexa would still be entrenched at the Rocking T, raising her son, trying to mellow her hidebound father-in-law and managing her bed-and-breakfast.

Chance Butler has been off-limits to you since the moment he showed up, she thought. Don't do anything stupid, like get sentimentally attached to him. He'll be gone and you'll be here wishing you had kept an emotional distance.

Alexa took her own good advice to heart and concentrated on putting a succulent meal on the table for the cowboys, who would show up at high noon hungry for a feast.

While the cowboys were saddling their horses and sorting out steers to rope and bulldog, Alexa ambled into the barn loft. When she reached the landing, she halted in her tracks, her jaw scraping her chest. To her bewildered amazement, the crew of seven men had erected the walls for every upstairs bedroom, placed two-by-ten headers above each door and nailed the heavy ceiling joists into place.

My goodness, how'd they get so much done so quickly? Chester Whitmier wouldn't believe it when he showed up for work Monday morning.

Amazed, Alexa wandered into each room, checking the workmanship. The walls were perfectly level and the doorways were exactly eighty inches high. The framework for the private bathrooms in the suites had been nailed together and set aside to await the arrival of the plumbers. The stack of Sheetrock delivered by the lumber company in Willowvale had been carted upstairs. Six sections of drywall had been nailed up on the ceiling in one of the bedrooms and two walls boasted Sheetrock. The room was beginning to take shape, and Alexa felt a surge of eager anticipation pulsating through her.

This was well and truly the shining example of building a dream. She had walls! She had a partial ceiling. Progress!

Before she got carried away, she pivoted toward the stairs. She had to run interference for her son at the rodeo arena. Howard would have Zack mounted and competing with professional rodeo contestants before she knew it.

Chapter Four

With fiendish haste, Alexa strode to the corrals that Dan had built specifically for practicing his skills. Sure enough, Zack was mounted on his Appy pony, swinging a lariat around his head. Frantic, Alexa stalked past Chance, who was leaning on the fence rail.

Chance snaked out his hand to snag her arm before she barreled into the arena. "Whoa, Al."

Alexa wrenched her arm from his grasp. "I don't want Zack out there. Howard is determined to raise Zack in his father's image but I won't have it!"

"And if you go barging in there, you'll embarrass the kid," Chance predicted.

"Better to be embarrassed than to be flat on his back with a broken neck. He's too young for this!"

Chance wrapped his hand around her rigid arm and directed her attention to Zack. "Check out the look on his face, Al. He's one of the men right now. Part of the cowboy crowd. I've instructed the men not to let him take any unnecessary risks. Every one of us is ready to jump in at the first sign of trouble.''

Alexa stared up at Chance, her eyes wide with apprehension and concern. ''Are you offering me a written guarantee that Zack won't have to be dragged out of there in pieces? Look at you. You have experience galore and you're standing on two bad knees, one of which is wrapped in a support brace.''

''Do you want me to ride behind Zack in the saddle?'' he asked. ''Will that make you feel better?''

''Hell, no. I want Zack planted firmly on the ground!''

''Sh-sh!'' Chance hissed when her voice hit a loud pitch.

''I will not shush,'' Alexa spouted off. ''That is *my* son. He is *my* responsibility.''

''And you are being as dictatorial as Howard,'' Chance dared to point out. ''He says ride and you say dismount. What about what Zack wants?''

''Zack is eight years old. He doesn't know what he wants,'' Alexa contended. ''He doesn't know the risks involved. He just wants to be a hotshot like the rest of you.''

''You think I'm a hotshot?'' Chance asked, offended. ''At no time have I boasted of my skills and abilities. To my recollection I have given no indication that I hold world championship titles in steer wrestling and that I have more award-winning belt buckles than I can wear in a month.''

''You just did,'' she snapped.

''I'm stating my credibility so you'll realize that I can keep a handle on this situation,'' he insisted. ''I'm *not* bragging.''

''I still think you're a hotshot,'' Alexa flung disdainfully. ''Howard constantly boasts of Dan's accomplishments, but Dan was small potatoes compared to you. And if you have a hankering to train a kid to rodeo, then have one of your own!''

''Are you offering your services?'' Chance teased in attempt to cool her simmering temper.

Alexa knew what he was trying to do, should have been grateful, but she was still fretting over the welfare of her son. "No, I'm not and you damn well know it."

"Ready, squirt?" Sonny called out as he positioned himself beside the chute where the restless calf waited to be released.

"No!" Alexa shouted.

All heads turned toward her as she flung herself from Chance's grasp and stalked into the arena. Her footsteps slowed when she saw the look of leery trepidation on Zack's face, saw him glance sideways to gauge the men's reaction to his mother's intrusion.

A riptide of emotion warred inside Alexa. If she humiliated Zack she would never forgive herself. If he was injured, she would never forgive herself. Damn it, why hadn't all these cowboys stayed home? She would have found a way to erect every wall in the barn by herself rather than risk Zack's injury in this arena. This was Chance's fault. She and Zack could be spending a quiet evening playing a harmless game of checkers if Chance hadn't arranged for this surprise building party.

Alexa glanced at Howard, who was puffed up like a toad, ready to croak if she dragged Zack off the saddle. She shot Chance a mutinous look that branded him a traitor. And then she did the unforgivable that went against every fear and concern roiling inside her.

"I just wanted to wish you luck, kiddo," she said, smiling past her apprehension.

Zack beamed in pleasure. "Thanks, Mom."

Spinning on her boot heels, Alexa exited the arena and took her place beside Chance.

"You made the right choice," Chance whispered as he watched Zack back his Appy into position, under Lefty's careful instruction.

"I'm not speaking to you," Alexa muttered resentfully. "I'm going to poison your kibble."

"Fine, but there comes a time in every boy's life when he has to discover that if he does, by chance, take a fall, he can pull himself up to his feet without his overprotective mother rushing in to do it for him."

The comment infuriated Alexa. Macho men were into that taking-it-on-the-chin stuff, in hopes of proving their manliness. In her opinion, it was a waste of time.

"And before you get all huffy," Chance added quietly, "ask yourself who was around to scrape you off the floor when you overextended yourself on the ladder—that I have named Grace—last week while framing the B-and-B."

Alexa whipped her head around, causing her braided hair to ripple over her shoulder.

"Chester told me you were a bit of a daredevil yourself. Let the kid build a little self-esteem and confidence with this baby calf I sorted out for him."

Alexa did not appreciate the fact that Chance pointed out her shortcoming of risking personal injury to get the job done. In her own mind there was no comparison between building in the barn and roping in this arena.

This wasn't a job. This was dangerous entertainment. But despite her serious reservations, she held her ground and sent a prayer winging heavenward. Then she crossed her fingers, her legs and closed her eyes when she heard the chute gate snap open.

Holding her breath, she waited to hear the anguished scream of her son. To her relief, she heard a round of cheers instead.

She opened her eyes to see Zack's oversize loop dangling around the newborn calf that stood in the middle of the arena, bawling for its mama.

"I tried to reduce every anticipated risk," Chance murmured. "Howard is ecstatic, Zack is pleased with his accomplishment, and you lived through another difficult moment."

"You still aren't off the hook, cowboy," she gritted between clenched teeth.

"I thought you said you weren't speaking to me."

"Well, I'm so upset that I forgot. And I hold you responsible for every second of torment I suffered."

"What about Howard? This was his idea, you know," Chance reminded her.

"Him, too." Alexa pivoted toward the house. "Don't let Zack ride again. He had his shining moment at my expense."

"Come on, Al, Zack isn't the first kid to try his hand at steer roping."

"Go to hell, Butler," she threw over her shoulder.

Even at a distance Chance could hear the slamming of the door. Not the one to the kitchen, but rather the emotional one that had crashed closed between him and Alexa.

For the duration of the weekend, while Chance Butler and company completed the ceiling joists and hung Sheetrock, Alexa was conspicuously absent from the barn. She called the cowboy carpenters to meals, then she took Zack to town to visit her sister. When the cowboys saddled up Sunday evening to sharpen their rodeo skills, Alexa found another excuse to drive Zack into town.

Drag the kid into town was more like it, Chance corrected. Clearly, the kid wanted to hang out at the arena and take another turn at roping, but his mother wouldn't let him near the horses and steers.

Howard was none too pleased that his grandson wasn't allowed to participate, but the old man compensated for his disappointment by bragging about his son's moments of greatness in rodeo competition. If Chance heard Dan Tipton's name mentioned once he heard it a couple hundred times. The old man had shoved Dan's name down Chance's throat since he arrived at Rocking T. But what frustrated Chance most was the emotional distance Alexa placed between them after their conflict at the arena. She had begun to warm to him, then wham! She wouldn't even glance in his direction, not if she could help it.

As far as Chance was concerned, he had handled the rodeo incident fairly well. The kid hadn't gotten hurt. His grandfather was exceptionally pleased. Zack had developed needed self-confidence.

Too bad Alexa had paid the price by sweating bullets while Zack rode, then roped the harmless calf. From her standpoint, Chance could understand her objections—partially, at least. Chance's mother had never babied him, overprotected him. He had been left to fend for himself more often than not.

Chance recalled the time that his mother hadn't come home from her Saturday night date. He had awakened early Sunday morning, fixed his bowl of cold cereal, dressed himself and walked through town to attend church. To his dismay, he found the church locked up tight.

At the naive age of six he had assumed the preacher had decided not to hold church services on that particular Sunday morning. Years later, Chance realized he had simply arrived too early for Sunday school and church.

Not the slightest chance that Zack would ever find himself abandoned in favor of a one-night fling, because his devoted, responsible mother would never leave him home alone. But Betty Sue Butler hadn't matured at that stage in her life and was too self-indulgent to worry about her kid.

These days Betty Sue was compensating for the mistakes she'd made early on. She provided model care for the two children from her second marriage. Chance had been the guinea pig that allowed his stepbrother and sister to lead a normal, well-adjusted childhood.

Likewise with Samuel Butler, reformed alcoholic, Chance mused as he bedded down beside the cowboys who shared the bunkhouse. When shuffled off every other weekend to stay with dear old Dad, Chance was usually delegated as the waiter who carted beer and whiskey for the low-life guests who attended Sam's weekly bashes. Drunks camped out on the threadbare carpet, remaining in a near-comatose state throughout the morning. The bed was usually occupied, and it had been years before Chance realized what prompted the moans and groans and squeaking bed frames.

Hell of a way to grow up, he thought to himself. Lucky he grew up at all, in fact. The night Samuel Butler's house went up in smoke—literally—because of a flaming cigarette that fell, forgotten, between the sofa cushions, had nearly done in father and son. Chance had awakened to tow his drunken father outside—and Chance had the scars on his right leg to prove his heroic battle against the flames.

Samuel had climbed on the wagon after his one-week stay in the hospital, and Chance ended up in one foster home after another, because his mother had taken off without leaving her forwarding address.

The Montana ranch where Chance spent his teen years had taught him the meaning of hard work and discipline. He and three orphan boys provided the labor for the slave-driving owner. Chance had learned to ride and rope and wrestle contrary cattle.

From there, he had gone to college on a rodeo scholarship and hadn't looked back. He spent an occasional holiday with his parents and their second families, but it didn't take a genius to realize that he was the family outcast, a reminder of earlier mistakes. Chance had learned to live out of a suitcase and stash his winnings in the bank. It was no big deal to live on the road when a man had never learned the meaning of home and family.

Families hurt each other, he reminded himself. Take the Tiptons, for instance. Howard had his own agenda of erecting monuments to a son who wasn't as honorable and accomplished as Howard let on. Alexa suffered through a marriage with a faithless husband who dumped responsibility in her lap and followed the suicide circuit, seeking personal pleasures and fame. Zack was left without the guidance of a father.

Chance knew that feeling, knew it well enough that he cringed when he saw a part of himself in that reddish-blond-haired kid. If Chance had a lick of sense he would back off. But damn it, every time he looked into Zack's face he wanted to help that little squirt become a man who didn't pitch like a sissy, and didn't shoot hoops that missed the basketball backboard by a country mile!

Atta boy, Butler, set yourself up for the pain you've already lived through as a child. You think you can make a difference in Zack's life? In Alexa's life?

Chance closed his eyes and absently rubbed his aching leg. Whatever his subconscious wanted from Alexa and her son, Chance knew he wasn't going to get, couldn't allow himself to crave. Rocking T wasn't the right place, wasn't *his* place. He should take Alexa's advice and swagger into Bud's Tavern, sidle up to a honky-tonk angel and be content with his lot in life. Maybe feminine distraction would pacify this growing need to hold and touch a woman who was so far out of reach that she might as well have been perched on the planet Pluto.

Debra Parsons opened her apartment door to find her sister and nephew standing on the porch. The petite blonde stepped aside, gesturing Alexa and Zack inside. "My goodness, I've seen more of you the past five days than I've seen in five weeks."

Alexa rolled her eyes at her sister's teasing remark.

"Hiding out again?" Deb questioned confidentially.

Oblivious, Zack tugged on the hem of Deb's blouse. "Can I use your TV, Aunt Debs?"

"Sure thing, kiddo. What are you going to watch?"

Zack shook his head in dismay. "The Braves, of course. Maddux is on the mound tonight."

"Who?"

Zack looked helplessly at his mom. "She sure doesn't know much about baseball, does she?"

"Nope. She's an artist. She's into Rembrandt and Van Gogh."

"Who?" Zack asked.

"Go watch the tube," Alexa encouraged, grinning. "Keep me posted on which pitch is working best for Maddux tonight."

When Zack whizzed off, Deb eyed Alexa curiously. "Are you going to tell me what's up at Rocking T? I thought you had a bed-and-breakfast to build."

Alexa collapsed in the dining room chair. "The renovations are progressing rapidly without me. All the Sheetrock on the barn loft ceilings has been hung, the electrical wiring has been strung and some of the plumbing pipes have been installed."

"So why the glum face? I would have expected you to be elated."

Alexa was—in an exasperated sort of way. The cowboy carpenters had made giant strides, especially after Chester arrived Monday morning to offer his expert guidance. Even the downstairs dining area, kitchen and den had been framed in. But Alexa had to spend every evening on the run, avoiding the rodeo practices at the arena. She had expected the cowboys to pack up and move on, come Monday morning. Turned out that they planned to stay until the day before the rodeo was scheduled to begin in Tulsa.

Alexa had dreamed up excuses to haul Zack to town. They had watched a Disney movie—twice—visited with Deb and made extended trips to the supermarket. Alexa had spent five days looking through Chance as if he were thin air and had conjured up excuses to put off Howard.

"Well?" Deb prompted as she grabbed two glasses from the cabinet. "What's up?"

Alexa cleared her throat, shifted uneasily in her chair,

then dived right into the heart of the problem. "There's a cowboy…"

When her voice trailed off, Debra snickered. "Uh-huh, and there's your solemn vow to avoid, forevermore, that particular breed of men. A real sucker for a pair of boots and a Stetson, aren't you, sis? I don't suppose this cowboy fills out a pair of jeans to such sexy extremes that he should be labeled armed and dangerous, too."

Reluctantly, Alexa nodded.

"Just passing through? Like the rest of Howard's hobos?" Deb questioned as she plunked ice cubes into the glasses.

Alexa nodded again.

"The injured cowboys have been filing in and out of Rocking T for more than a year. What makes this one different?" Deb wanted to know.

There was one person in the world whom Alexa felt comfortable confiding in—her sister. They had been together through thick and thin. Alexa felt the need to air her feelings and frustrations before she burst.

"Chance Butler is the one who rounded up the posse of cowboy carpenters to help with my renovations. He wants to teach Zack to play ball, and he let Zack ride and rope with the visiting cowboys," she said in a rush.

Debra poured diet Coke in the glasses, then shoved one in front of Alexa. Deb's pale green eyes appraised her sister's expression astutely—like a conscientious artist studying a painted portrait. "And what does this Butler character want from you for all his efforts on your behalf?"

"He says nothing."

Deb lounged in her chair, smiling wryly. "And you don't trust him."

Alexa shrugged, then sipped her cola. "He has given me no reason not to trust him. He's proved himself to be a hard worker and a gentleman, even though we have differences of opinion on whether Zack should be allowed to hang out with the cowboys while they practice in the arena.''

"How does Zack feel? Does he like Butler?''

Alexa rolled her eyes and smirked. "Not much, just worships the ground Chance floats over, just follows at his heels like a devoted puppy. I caught the two of them playing catch behind the barn after Zack came home from school yesterday, and again today. I told Chance not to bother, but he defied my request.''

Deb frowned, bemused. "What's the big deal? It's not as if you're a qualified baseball coach, you know. You never played the game. If Butler can give Zack a few pointers that improve his skills, what's the harm in that?''

Alexa straightened in her chair and stared at her dense sister. "This isn't about baseball.''

"No? Sounds like it to me.''

"The harm is that Chance will be going down the road as soon as his injury heals and he won't be back. Zack is entirely too attached already, though I've tried to keep them apart. Dan was always leaving Zack behind. I don't want my kid growing up thinking that's a man's way.''

"I think you're being paranoid and overprotective,'' Debra declared bluntly.

"That's what Chance says.'' Alexa glared at her sister. "I never thought you'd take sides with a man you never even met.''

Debra grinned, undaunted. "Hey, sis, I know what you're like. You are overprotective. You nearly smothered me after our parents died.''

Frustrated, Alexa scowled at her sister. "Talk about ungrateful!''

"Not!'' Debra chuckled, then sipped her drink. "I told you how much I appreciate everything you've done for me, the sacrifices you made. You kept me from going down the wrong path when I was a troubled kid. But admit it, sis, your noteworthy strength is also your weakness. You like to be in control.''

Alexa slouched in her chair, pondering Deb's insights. Was she a control freak? Had she been put in charge and left to handle so many diverse situations since she was seventeen that she was trying to run other people's lives in accordance to her own expectations?

''Hey, Mom!'' Zack called out excitedly. ''Lopez just knocked one out of the park. Braves take the lead!''

''Way to go, Braves!'' Deb cheered enthusiastically, then glanced quickly at her sister. ''What was that pitcher's name again? Murdock?''

''Maddux.''

''Let me know how Maddux does when he comes to the base—''

''The plate,'' Alexa corrected hastily.

''The plate,'' Deb called to her nephew.

''Sure thing, Aunt Debs.''

Deb focused her full attention on Alexa. ''I think you should let the cowboy get close to Zack, even if only for a few weeks. Zack needs another man besides Howard to emulate. Howard has gone overboard trying to keep Dan's memory alive, but Zack needs more than that. If Butler is a decent guy then let him play substitute father for a while. It might do Zack a world of good.''

Alexa found it difficult to accept Deb's advice. Letting go of her son, after she had been in complete charge for so many years, felt unnatural. But maybe she would try being less protective. Placing faith in a man wasn't going to be easy, though, not after Dan had disappointed her ten dozen different ways.

Or maybe the truth was that Alexa sensed that Chance wouldn't disappoint her, that she—like Zack—would become overly attached and left aching when the cowboy rode away. When Chance left, Alexa didn't want to be wishing for something that would never be, didn't want to be hurt again.

"Come on," Deb said as she shot out of her chair abruptly. "Let's go out to Rocking T. I want to get a look at the stud muffin cowboy who has turned my solid-as-a-rock sister into mush."

Deb whizzed off to grab her car keys and round up Zack, who objected to missing an inning of play. Deb cajoled her nephew into leaving the house by promising to buy him an ice-cream cone.

Alexa smiled fondly as she watched Deb scoop Zack off the floor and haul him out the door. Deb had always been the spirited, uninhibited sister—the one with the bubbly personality, the zest for life.

And Alexa had always been the plodding workhorse who took the world seriously. Ah, wouldn't it be nice to shed her obligations for a few hours and let loose. Alexa couldn't remember when she'd done anything so frivolous and reckless as trotting off to show herself a good time.

"Zack is riding with me," Deb said on her way out the door. "We'll meet you at Rocking T."

During the drive home Alexa tried to make an attitude adjustment. She was going to stop taking life so seriously—on a trial basis, at least. She was going to stop being so leery of a friendship between Chance and Zack. And she was going to follow the feelings in her heart instead of relying solely on her head. She might wind up getting hurt if this fond attachment she had developed for Chance intensified. But she had been hurt before, she reminded herself. Dan had taken her for granted and turned his affection elsewhere. Alexa had survived it, would survive again.

"Okay, Butler," she mused aloud. "You want me to lighten up. Fine, I'll give it my best shot."

Chance glanced sideways when he heard the crunch of gravel in the driveway. From his position on horseback he had a clear view of the miniconvoy—consisting of a flashy red sports car and the Tiptons' no-nonsense, no-frills farm pickup truck—that pulled up at the house.

Alexa was back, he noted.

Chance frowned curiously when a petite blonde, wearing a colorful T-shirt and formfitting jeans, appeared beside Zack. Curious about the new arrival though he was, his gaze settled on the crop of curly auburn hair that blazed like wildfire in the sunlight.

Silent yearning plowed through Chance. With each passing day the need to touch Alexa, to tear down the Queen of Cool's defenses, gnawed at him.

Oh hell, this wishful thinking was nothing but an exercise in torment, Chance lectured himself. He would do himself a tremendous favor if he polished his roping skills and focused on recovering from injury. Maybe when he left Rocking T he could put Alexa out of his mind.

"Yo, Butler!" Jack Pearson hollered from the chute. "Are you going to try your hand at roping this steer or just sit there on horseback gawking?"

Chance swiveled around in the saddle to see the congregation of cowboys grinning wryly at him. They knew what—or rather who—had captured his attention.

"Do you have that bad knee braced up good and tight?" Sonny questioned, biting back a snicker. "This here steer ain't no mama's baby, I can tell you for sure. He's half-grown and anxious as hell to take a flying leap from this chute. You're going to have to pay more attention to your business here. Watch yourself, pal. This steer has horns as big as antlers, and you aren't operating at one-hundred percent efficiency yet. Some parts of you aren't, that is."

"Thanks, Mommy," Chance flung at the ornery cowboy.

When Sonny thumbed his nose playfully, the other cowboys guffawed. Howard Tipton grinned, clearly enjoying the mischievous camaraderie, even if the subtleties of the conversation had escaped him.

The old man was in the height of glory, Chance noted. Howard thrived on these nightly practices that put him back in touch with his son's life.

Chance checked his lariat, tied one end of the thirty-foot rope to the saddle horn, then twirled the loop over his head to loosen it up. He clamped the pigging string between his teeth and positioned his bum leg so that it wouldn't take excessive pressure when his mount lunged off in a gallop.

When Chance gave the nod, Sonny opened the chute gate. Bellowing loudly, the steer charged into the open arena, headed for the distant corner.

The horse Chance was riding gathered itself behind and raced off. Chance felt a twinge of pain shoot up his leg when he instinctively clamped his knees against the mount's ribs. With the lariat circling his head, Chance bore down on the runaway steer. When the horse was a body length behind the steer Chance cast his lariat, then gave it a quick tug when it settled over the outstretched horns.

The well-trained roping horse kept tension on the lariat while Chance dismounted. Chance was out of the saddle by the time the steer reached the end of the rope and struggled for freedom.

The instant Chance came down on his weak knee, he gritted his teeth against the pain, then charged toward the steer. He was determined to toss the animal to the ground and tie up its legs in as few seconds as possible.

When Chance hooked his arms around the steer's neck, the 250-pound animal braced its legs to avoid being levered to the ground. Chance stifled a groan as he used his knees to upend the struggling steer. Growling in pain and determination, Chance flanked the steer, leaving it lying on its side in the dirt. Racing against time, he, wrapped the pigging string around the steer's forelegs and hind legs, securing the piece of rope with the customary half hitch.

"Eight point four seconds!" Jack Pearson called out as he clicked the stopwatch. "Not bad for a lame old man."

Cheers went up around the arena, but Chance's gaze wasn't on the whooping, hollering cowboys. His attention was riveted to the smiling face of the young boy, and his mother, who had ambled down to the arena to watch him perform.

The expression on Alexa's face indicated that she wasn't just being entertained by his performance. Her expression implied that she was concerned about the excessive pressure he put on his leg.

Someone who cares... The thought kept hovering in his mind as he retrieved his pigging string and released the downed calf. Chance couldn't remember anyone caring if he was safe and sound.

Oh certainly, rodeo cowboys watched out for one another, tended to one another after a bad fall in the dirt. But Alexa's expression was different somehow. Reluctant to care perhaps, but her concern showed in those expressive cedar-tree-green eyes that were surrounded by a fan of thick black lashes.

"Way to go, Chance!" Zack yelled, then waved his arms so enthusiastically that he lost his balance on the railing and fell into his mother's waiting arms.

Alexa was the kind of woman who would always be there to pick up the pieces, Chance realized suddenly. Ms. Responsible and Dependable was the *rock* in Rocking T. Dan Tipton had married a rare jewel, but self-indulgence blinded him from seeing Alexa for the sparkling diamond she was. Damn fool, Chance thought as he limped toward his mount.

"Chance, this is my aunt Debs," Zack introduced from a distance.

Chance pasted on a greeting smile, though his leg hurt like a son of a bitch. "Nice to meet you, ma'am."

The other cowboys tipped their hats politely to Deb. After a round of how-do-you-dos, the next contestant mounted the sorrel gelding to rope and wrestle another calf.

''Your leg must be better,'' Zack presumed.

''Some,'' Chance lied. Truth was, he had jumped the gun. His attempt to get his mind back on rodeo—and off his futile fascination for Alexa—had probably caused a setback. He would spend the night packed in ice, in hopes of reducing the swelling.

''Are you sure you're all right?'' Alexa questioned as she watched Chance attempt to conceal his limp. She knew he was hurting. His compressed lips—ones that looked as if they had been hermetically sealed—indicated he was biting back pain. Riding, roping and hog-tying that steer had to be a strain on his injured knee. ''I don't think you're ready to—''

Deb elbowed her in the ribs—a sharp, immediate reprisal that warned her to mind her own business instead of trying to control the world around her.

''So…'' Deb cut in, smiling breezily. ''This is the cowboy Zack was jabbering about during the ride home.'' She stuck out a hand, which boasted cherry-red fingernails. ''I'm Deb Parsons. I'm Alexa's kid sister.''

Chance appraised both pretty women, noting the family resemblance in the similar expressions around their heart-shaped mouths and luminous eyes. His gaze darted back to Zack's smiling face. And without thinking, he reached out to ruffle the thick mop of reddish-blond hair.

Instantly, he withdrew his hand, remembering that Alexa insisted on a physical and emotional distance between him and her son. Unfortunately, Chance made a habit of ruffling the kid's hair after they played catch behind the barn. It had become reflexive habit.

When Alexa simply stared at him without getting all huffy and defensive, Chance breathed an inward sigh of relief. He enjoyed the time spent with this adorable kid. It made him wish for a child of his own—during his weaker, more sentimental moments. But Chance was also reluctant to put any child through the anguish he had suffered when his parents remarried and he was left out in the cold, left feeling like an extra person in the world.

There was no guarantee that marriages would last, that kids didn't suffer emotional scars when they were caught in the war zone of feuding adults. No way in hell would Chance want to see Zack suffer as he had.

Chance would have to be absolutely, positively certain that his relationship with a woman was the death-do-us-part kind. No sir, no kid of his would endure the hell he'd been through. And for that reason, Chance had never even considered marriage, hadn't happened onto a woman he believed could stand beside him long past eternity.

"When you finish practicing, why don't y'all come up to the house for refreshments," Alexa invited the cowboys. "I've got ice cream, two freshly baked pies and pineapple upside-down cake."

The cowboys grinned and gave Alexa thumbs-up. Chance did a double take. She was inviting the cowboys into the house after she had given them a wide berth the past few days? What happened to her never-trust-or-associate-with-a-cowboy policy?

When Chance peered quizzically at Alexa, she smiled. It was a devastating kind of smile, which nearly knocked Chance's bad leg out from under him.

Good thing he already planned to pack himself in ice tonight, he decided.

"Give us thirty more minutes to finish up and tend the horses," Chance told Alexa. "We'll be up at the house with mouths watering."

As Alexa turned away, Chance watched the graceful sway of her hips, the confident carriage of a woman who drew his thoughts and his gaze more than he preferred. Although Deb was a real looker, with a cheerful disposition and easy smile, Chance didn't have much interest in blondes these days.

He wondered when he had developed such an avid interest in spellbinding green eyes, curly auburn hair...and lost causes.

Chapter Five

"Damn, sis," Deb murmured as she and Alexa hiked up the hill to the house. "You neglected to mention that Butler is a lot more than good-looking. He's an absolute hunk and he's good at what he does. Maybe you're leery of cowboys, but I'm not."

Yes, Alexa was definitely leery of cowboys, but after watching Chance perform, she felt that funny twitter in her heart. That old cliché about poetry in motion applied to Chance. He seemed so at ease in the saddle, with a lariat in his gloved hand. His riding and roping techniques were so fluid and efficient that watching him in action left Alexa staring at him in rapt fascination. No wonder Chance was such a strong contender for another world title. The man was thrilling to watch!

And yet, Alexa refused to let herself get caught up in that world of rodeo again. Just because she found herself fascinated by Chance Butler didn't mean it was sensible.

"Looks aren't everything," Alexa told her sister. "At

twenty-six, you're supposed to be mature enough to figure that out.''

''I am, but there's nothing wrong with appreciating an exceptionally handsome man when I see one,'' Deb parried. ''Now that is exactly what I was trying to tell you earlier, sis. Try a different perspective for a change. Quit being so cautious. Flirt a little, live a little.

''Jeepers, it's not like I'm advocating that you marry the guy on the spot,'' Deb clarified. ''But a little excitement in your life certainly wouldn't hurt. Lord knows there wasn't much excitement with Dan.''

When Alexa frowned warningly, Deb shrugged. ''I wasn't blind, you know. It was you who tried to make that marriage work. You gave your all and received very little in return. You may decide you do want to marry again someday and—''

''No, I don't think so,'' Alexa put in quickly.

Deb threw up her hands in exasperation. ''Fine, be a thirty-year-old fuddy-duddy. I'll flirt with Butler. I'm single and unattached. I believe in enjoying the moment, putting a few interesting sparks in my life.''

''Sometimes I wish I could be as carefree as you are,'' Alexa admitted on her way through the kitchen door.

''You can be, need to be,'' Deb insisted. ''You missed out on early adulthood, married young so you could provide security for me.'' When Alexa's mouth dropped open, Deb patted her shoulder. ''It took me a while but I figured that out, sis. Believe it or not, I'm not as dumb as I look. Furthermore, I think you should start grabbing for the gusto in life.''

''I don't know any Gustos to make a grab for,'' Alexa said flippantly.

''Very funny.'' Deb snorted. ''The point is that a woman has her own needs and they shouldn't be ignored. You really need to loosen up, sis.''

Alexa stared at her sister in a new light. Suddenly, Deb

was telling *her* what to do. "You did grow up, didn't you? When did that happen?"

Deb grinned. "While you were holding the fort and tending to your baby, I was working my way through college—at your unwavering insistence, as I recall," Deb replied. "Now I'm a mature, responsible career woman, not the clueless teenager you raised. I can take care of myself now. And if a stud of a cowboy could brighten up my life, then I'd give him a whirl."

"Then go for it," Alexa said.

Deb shook her head ruefully. "You did it again, Alexa. Even though I know you're interested in Butler—and I can tell by the way you look at him, and he looks back—you would stand aside if you had the slightest inkling that I might be interested in him. When are you going to stop placing the needs of everyone else before your own? Don't you realize you're entitled to a few rays of sunshine in your life?"

Alexa drew herself up to determined stature and wheeled around to gather paper plates and glasses for refreshments. Live for yourself a little, she repeated silently. Put some spark in your life. The thought was so foreign that Alexa figured it was going to take some time to adjust to the idea.

Chance limped outside the bunkhouse, then paused to massage his aching leg. The other cowboys were gathering their gear in preparation for an early departure the following morning. Chance had been bumped into twice in the cramped spaces of the bunkhouse, and he felt the need for fresh air and the privacy to curse his throbbing knee without being overheard.

The high humidity was playing hell with bones and joints that had suffered years of strain and fierce impacts. Chance wasn't about to whine and complain to the other men, but he was feeling as old as Methuselah…and incredibly lonely in that crowded bunkhouse.

The ultimate irony, he thought as he limped down to the stream that glistened like mercury in the moonlight. Anybody who felt lonely in a crowd was in big trouble. Chance had never felt like this before, even after years of crowded confines behind the scenes of rodeos or during the nightlife that accompanied them. But suddenly, something was missing.

This is as good as it gets for you, pal, came that independent inner voice.

Chance stared across the rolling terrain, soaking up the peaceful tranquillity that was Rocking T. Damn, what a panoramic place this was. He would have to set aside time to bring Zack down to the stream to fish. The kid would like that, and so would Chance.

Stiff-legged, Chance maneuvered himself onto the carpet of grass to give his knee a rest. He sighed appreciatively at the moon-dappled trees that surrounded the creek. He hadn't realized how much he had needed this dose of peace and quiet until he got here.

"Did your friends kick you out of the bunkhouse?"

Chance jerked upright when Alexa's unexpected voice came from nowhere. He half twisted to see her ambling down the slope, her auburn hair fanning around her shoulders like a fiery cape. God, she looked good, would feel even better, he speculated. Too bad he had vowed to keep his hands to himself and not push Alexa in the direction this leery woman was reluctant to go.

"What's up, Al?" he asked as nonchalantly as he knew how.

Alexa sank down cross-legged beside him. "Nothing much. I was standing on the porch when I saw you walk out of the bunkhouse. I saw you rubbing your leg and presumed you were hurting worse than you let on."

"Yeah," he admitted, then chuckled. "I suppose my machismo got the better of me after watching the other cowboys practice. Pride can do as much harm as good, I guess.''

He slanted her a quizzical glance. ''Did you come down here to say you told me so?''

''Nope.''

To his shock—and pleasure—Alexa leaned over to kiss him right smack-dab on the mouth. It was the briefest touch of lips, but the impact of the gesture sent desire flooding through him. For a moment Chance forgot his leg was killing him.

He stared curiously at Alexa as she retreated into her own space. ''What just happened here?'' he had to ask.

Alexa chuckled. ''And here I thought you were a worldly, experienced cowboy. Come to find out you don't know a kiss when it lands on your lips.''

The previously concealed side of Alexa's personality intrigued Chance. There was a playful tone in her voice, a teasing smile on her lips. Chance decided to go for it, even if he got his face slapped. He had been as gentlemanly around Alexa for as long as he could stand.

''Ma'am, where I come from that ain't no kiss,'' he drawled. ''That's a peck. Now this is what we call a kiss up yonder in Montana—''

With a flair, Chance twisted her sideways, draping her across his lap, then lowered his head, inch by inch, so as not to overwhelm her. He gave her time to protest if she had a mind to. To his everlasting relief she simply stared up at him, waiting.

As tenderly as he knew how, as gently as a woman like Alexa deserved, Chance slanted his lips over hers. The urge to crush her against him and plunder her mouth was nearly overwhelming, but Chance proceeded with care and restraint. He had waited for more than two weeks to hold her in his arms, to sip the sweet nectar of her lips. He wasn't going to blow it by letting animalistic desire run rampant.

In all his born days, he couldn't remember being so attuned to a woman's reaction to him, so thrilled by the shivers he felt sweeping through her body. Oh man, if ever there was a woman he wanted to savor, to prolong every delicious sensation she aroused in him, it was this woman. He felt as if he had been starving to death for a taste of her, had bent over backward—and that wasn't easy to do on a bum leg—to please her, help her, reassure her.

When he heard Alexa moan softly, felt her hand glide up his arm to anchor on his shoulder, Chance deepened the kiss. And suddenly, his breathing altered. So did hers. His arm contracted around her, pressing her breasts to his chest, her hips against his arousal. The fire blazing in his knee spread through every inch of him.

The cool evening air was suddenly stifling. He couldn't breathe without inhaling the alluring scent of her. She was consuming his senses, and need pounded through him with such shocking intensity that it caught Chance completely off guard. Talk about an instantaneous, radioactive reaction!

Instinctively, Chance rolled sideways, bringing Alexa down beside him so he could graze his hand over the pebbled peaks of her breasts. When she arched into his hand, silently encouraging him, he slid his fingertips beneath the hem of her shirt to explore the flat plane of her belly, the undersides of her breasts.

Somewhere within the mind-clouding fog of desire that condensed around him he heard Alexa whisper his name. And then he lost touch with reality. He drew her T-shirt out of his way to suckle her, caress her. He wanted to excite her to the same heightened frenzy. He wanted to skim his hands over her flesh, learning her by touch, by shivering response.

And respond she did, like a woman brimming with so much suppressed passion that nothing could restrain her reaction. She was a sensual wild woman beneath that veneer of cool reserve. Again, Chance felt himself wondering why Dan Tipton had been unfaithful when he had a woman who could more than match him in the heat of passion.

No matter which fence in eternity—heaven's or hell's—that Dan was sitting on, he had to know he was a fool to betray a woman like Alexa.

When Chance felt Alex's hand glide along the band of his jeans, then dip lower, his lungs nearly collapsed. He held what little breath he had left, wanting her to touch him intimately—afraid she *would* and he'd lose all vestige of self-control.

Yet something about the tentative way she smoothed her hand over the bulge in his jeans stated that she was exploring uncharted territory. Chance had the feeling Alexa needed to know that her touch pleased him, that he wanted it as badly as he wanted to touch her. He hoped his perceptions weren't off base or he'd come off sounding like a fool.

"You're driving me crazy," he rasped. "You know that, don't you?"

The comment pleased her, he could tell by the expression on her face. "Am I?"

He moaned when her hand swept down with more confidence. "Mmm," he wheezed.

"Was that a yes?"

The languid stroke of her hand over the fly of his jeans made him want to throw back his head and howl at the moon. Instead, he caressed her in the same gentle fashion, wishing there weren't so many layers of cotton and denim between them. But yet, he was thankful there was, thankful he had enough sense left not to rush through to completion. This wasn't a woman accustomed to one-night stands. She was too responsible, too much in control of her life. She would be plagued with regrets. Chance would bet his rodeo winnings on that.

The fact that she permitted things to go as far as they

had amazed him. He knew her reservations, understood her fears, respected them.

Although it took the sum total of the self-discipline he possessed, he withdrew his hand from her hip to cup her chin, then bent to press a whisper of a kiss to her lips. When he raised his head, Alexa stared unblinkingly at him. Somehow he knew he had made the right decision to call a halt before things got completely out of hand—or in hand as the case might have turned out to be.

Chance grinned playfully at her. "Darlin', I guess you know I'll have to crawl back to the bunkhouse now. You have a fierce and powerful effect on me."

Alexa felt a sense of pleasure streaming through her. She was astounded by Chance's gentleness, his sensuousness, his patience. He left her wanting so much more, left her aching with unappeased desire. Her respect for him rose a dozen increments while he smiled that sexy smile.

"Try crawling all the way to the house and up the stairs, cowboy."

"Is that an invitation?" he questioned, grinning roguishly.

"I was referring to myself."

He nodded in understanding, then grinned again. "It's nice to know I'm not the only one feeling the dizzying aftereffects of that kiss."

He implied that she devastated him as thoroughly as he devastated her. Alexa was immensely pleased with the knowledge. Though she didn't want to make comparisons, she was discovering that passion didn't necessarily have to be as rushed and unfulfilling as she had previously thought. Chance knew how to make a woman want him.

The sad, undeniable truth was that Dan Tipton did not.

When Chance rolled away, trying to gain his feet, Alexa vaulted up, then extended a helping hand. He didn't push her away, but rather accepted her assistance. He was man enough to admit his physical limitations. Some men weren't.

"Kick me," Chance requested out of the blue.

Alexa blinked. "What?"

"I had no business getting on that horse and bounding off to hog-tie that calf this evening," he grumbled as he hobbled up the hill, his arm draped around her shoulder for support. "At this rate, I'll be laid up here longer than originally planned."

Alexa wrestled with the words stuck to the tip of her tongue, then she reminded herself what Deb said about enjoying every pleasurable moment for as long as it lasted. "That's okay by me, cowboy. I kinda like having you around."

Chance stopped short, then peered down at her. "Alexa?"

"And furthermore, you don't have to sneak off behind the barn to play catch with Zack. Any pointers you can offer are welcome. Can't have the kid throwing like a sissy, after all. Bad for his image and all that. One thing, though, you need to teach me the fundamentals so I can continue with them after you're—"

Silence filled the space between them. Alexa knew Chance realized what she intended to say.

"Tell the rookie that we'll play catch after he has his after-school snack tomorrow. If you want to take notes, we'll be in the front yard. Bring along a bat," he requested. "Zack's swing has a hitch in it."

"Yes, sir, anything else?" she said saucily.

"Yeah." He brushed his lips over hers. "I'm not going to sleep worth a damn tonight. Not because of the leg. Because of you. I'll need coffee as strong as motor oil for breakfast to jump-start me in the morning."

When Chance hobbled toward the bunkhouse, Alexa watched him go with a smile playing on her lips. She liked that about Chance—the way he made her grin, made her anticipate their next encounter. She intended to spend the following day hanging Sheetrock, but she would be ready and waiting in the front yard when it came time for ball practice.

Alexa strode toward the house, very much afraid she would end up getting her heart broken when that cowboy rode away. Then she decided to follow Scarlett O'Hara's advice and not worry about that today. She would worry about that tomorrow.

"Okay, rookie, now remember what I told you," Chance prompted. "Make a level swing toward the ball. Don't come out of your shoes, swinging like a wild man. We aren't looking for home runs here, just solid base hits. Watch the ball meet the bat, kid."

Chance limped a short distance away from the piece of scrap carpet that served as home plate. He was vividly aware that Alexa was sitting on the front steps, scribbling notes. She was taking this coaching session seriously—as she did everything else, until last night....

Stifling the distracting thought, Chance concentrated on Zack's shoulder-width stance, the position of his arms. "Look for the laces on the ball while it's coming at you. If you can see them you're watching closely. Ready, rookie?"

The reddish-blond head nodded vigorously. The boy's gaze bore down on the ball. He was the picture of intense concentration.

Chance tossed the ball underhanded—right down the middle. Zack swung, and the ball blazed back at Chance. His lack of agility made it difficult to move aside, so he stuck out his glove to snag the hit.

"Perfect. Now, here comes a low ball. Stay down with it, kid. Drive it back to me."

Again the red-blond head nodded—as mighty young Casey stood at bat. A funny little tug contracted around

Chance's heart as he stared at the kid. Zack wanted so much to succeed, to imagine himself in the Atlanta Braves' lineup. With sound fundamentals and encouragement Zack could begin his sports career. Every bit of confidence he could develop would mold him into a strong, self-reliant individual. Chance wished he could be around to see how this rookie turned out.

Don't get ahead of yourself, Butler. The kid is years away from his high school sports career, and Howard Tipton has no intention of any man becoming Zack's substitute father, and Alexa refuses to let another man into her life who lives on the road....

The crack of the bat connecting with the ball jerked Chance to attention—a second too late. The ball thumped him on the shoulder.

"Wow!" Zack said excitedly.

"Are you all right?" Alexa called out to Chance.

Chance rubbed his shoulder. "The rookie packs a wallop. We've got a player on our hands, Al. Are you getting all these tips down on paper? Feet shoulder-width apart, short stride, level swing?"

"Got it," Alexa declared.

For the next few minutes Chance tossed balls to Zack and the kid smacked them back. When Zack sent a line shot soaring over Chance's head, he called a halt to batting practice. Chance intended to leave the kid with a vision of a perfect hit to motivate him until tomorrow's practice.

"Always quit on a winner," Chance told Alexa.

After Chance sent Zack off with instructions to toss the ball onto the roof of the barn, then catch it properly in his glove, Alexa strode forward. It touched her deeply to observe the way Chance paid attention to Zack, the way he playfully ruffled the boy's hair. Those small gestures of affection and acknowledgment pleased Zack immensely. The boy hadn't received those positive responses from his father.

"You're putting me to shame, you know. Where did you learn all this stuff?"

"From my junior high and high school coaches. Big and strong as I was, they decided it was a waste of athletic ability not to know sports skills. They taught and I listened," Chance explained.

"I don't suppose you played basketball, too," she asked hopefully. "Zack idolizes Michael Jordan."

Chance eyed the rickety basketball goal attached to the barn. The ten-foot pole was entirely too high for an eight-year-old kid. The boy needed a goal that adjusted to fit his height and a ball to fit his small hands.

And Zack would have them, Chance decided. The spare pipe from the corral fence, and left-over plywood from Alexa's building project, would serve the purpose. The future Michael Jordan would have a new goal and backboard as soon as Chance completed the list of chores Howard scheduled for him the following day.

"Thank you," Alexa murmured. "I hope you realize how much your help means to Zack…and to me."

Chance wanted to pull Alexa into his arms and assure her that a kiss was payment aplenty, but he'd established the fact that sexual gratitude wasn't expected for his assistance.

"My pleasure, Al. Any kid who lives and breathes sports the way Zack does deserves a chance to improve his skills. He has the desire to succeed. You've done well by him. He's a good kid."

"Howard still insists on taking Zack to the rodeo in Tulsa this weekend," she said as she watched her son position himself under the ball and make a clean catch.

"And?" Chance prompted.

"And I said okay…reluctantly."

"Afraid the kid will join the rodeo circus and run off?" he asked teasingly.

She met his gaze head-on. "Afraid he'll think that putting down roots is a woman's work, not a man's," she confided softly.

"A lot of professions demand travel," Chance reminded her.

"Not the kind rodeo requires, not the kind that comes with a built-in nightlife. Dan spent more than two hundred days a year on the road. He barely knew his son, never took time with his son."

So that was the crux of Alexa's inner fears, Chance mused. "Didn't he have time for you, either?"

Chance could have cheerfully kicked himself for posing that question. It was out of his mouth before he could bite it back. The pinched expression on Alexa's face spoke volumes. The high and mighty Dan Tipton was so wrapped up in his own potential stardom that he neglected his wife and son. And if Chance were a betting man—which he was on occasion—he'd bet that Dan's lack of time and consideration also reached the bedroom. In some ways, Alexa seemed an inhibited novice at intimacy.

"Hey, Chance, my arm is all warmed up now. Can I pitch?"

"Sure thing, rookie," Chance called back. "Grab a bucket for me to sit on while I catch you. My lame leg forgot how to squat."

Leaving Chance and Zack to the pitching lesson, Alexa turned toward the house. "I'll start supper," she offered. "What are you craving, cowboy?"

"You," he said, and grinned wickedly.

To Chance's amazement, Alexa didn't frown in disapproval. She tossed him a sassy smile. "Served on a bed of rice or a medley of mixed veggies on the side?"

"Surprise me," he murmured before he pivoted on his good leg and limped off to play catch.

While Howard was attending his weekly poker game in Shorty McClain's basement, Alexa and Zack were glued to the tube. The Atlanta Braves were in a hitting slump and Zack was beside himself. When Alexa announced that it was bedtime, Zack grumbled about missing the end of the close game. Promising to catch the score and report it to him at breakfast, Alexa coaxed Zack to bed.

She leaned against the door that led into a room filled with posters of Zack's sports heroes and memorabilia Howard had added to remind Zack of his father. It was a boy's room, and Zack was all boy. He was anxious to grow up, to become the next Cy Young Award winner. Alexa couldn't imagine life without him. He was her center focus, her motivation.

"Mom?"

"This isn't going to be another one of those long conversations aimed at postponing lights-out, is it?" she asked suspiciously.

"Nope. I was just going to say that I sure like Chance."

Alexa felt a constriction in the vicinity of her heart. "Me, too, kiddo."

"Dad never played with me like Chance does."

The constriction became worse. "I know, son."

"How come Dad didn't? Didn't he like me very much?"

Alexa couldn't help herself. She crossed the room in a rush to plant herself on the edge of Zack's bed. "Your dad loved you. Don't doubt that. He was involved with his career and he couldn't spend much time at home."

"You're busy and you find time for me. Chance finds time," Zack pointed out.

Yes, Chance did, and Alexa was grateful for it, though she still had concerns about how Zack would deal with Chance's inevitable departure.

Zack linked his fingers behind his head and stared quizzically at his mother. "I sure hope Chance comes back again. He's teaching me all sorts of things about baseball. He even said we were going fishing next week, after he buys the poles and bait."

Alexa knew this bond between man and boy was getting complicated. Zack had gotten too attached, thrived on Chance's attention. "If Chance comes back here it will mean that he is injured and needs time to heal. We wouldn't want to wish him bad luck on the rodeo circuit, would we?"

"No, I s'pose not," Zack mumbled.

Alexa kissed his forehead, then graced him with a cheery smile. "You better get to sleep. Grandpa has big plans for you this weekend. You'll need to rest up if you're going to Tulsa for the rodeo."

When Zack rolled to his side and snuggled beneath the cover, Alexa headed toward the door. "Love you, champ."

"Me, too, Mom."

Alexa went downstairs and saw Howard staggering in the door. He reeked of cigar smoke and whiskey. She wished Howard and the other old coots would find a more constructive form of entertainment, but there appeared to be no end to these weekly gatherings in Shorty McClain's basement.

"I won enough money to pay for the trip to Tulsa," Howard slurred. "Lady Luck was sitting on my shoulder tonight."

Alexa mumbled a reply that Howard couldn't decipher and didn't ask her to repeat.

"How's your building project coming along?" he asked.

"With Chester's help, and that of the cowboys, I'm making rapid progress. I plan to help Chester bed and tape the walls tomorrow."

"Still think it's a waste of good money," Howard grunted. "This is a working ranch, not an entertainment center for city slickers. Dan wouldn't have approved, either."

"Dan isn't here, never was around all that much," Alexa said before she could stop herself.

Howard's bloodshot eyes narrowed and his graying

brows swooped down in a sharp V. "That was the nature of his business. Rodeo superstars have to travel the circuit to keep up their standings so they can compete at National Finals Rodeo in Las Vegas. Injury is all that keeps a cowboy off the road."

When Howard ambled toward his ground-floor bedroom, Alexa stood in the kitchen, her hands clamped on the edge of the counter. As if Howard's constant reminders weren't enough, memories of Dan and his gypsy life-style cluttered this house. The family room was overflowing with plaques, photographs and belt buckles. Howard's room was practically wallpapered with pictures of his son!

Alexa was beginning to resent those constant reminders—and she knew they grated on her more than ever before. She wanted to be free of those bitter memories…because Chance Butler was beginning to matter to her.

Frustrated, Alexa paced the room. These days, she was feeling as if her skin no longer fit properly, as if she were outgrowing previous wants and needs. The woman who had a down-to-earth mind and feet firmly planted on the ground was growling increasingly restless.

A steady thump wafted through the open window. Alexa wheeled around to stare out the door.

Thump, creak, thump.

Frowning, she exited the house to investigate the peculiar sounds.

Chapter Six

Alexa was stunned to see Chance's silhouette in the security light that glowed in the darkness. The man was digging a post hole at eleven o'clock at night? Had he lost his mind?

"What the blazes are you doing?" Alexa questioned as she strode toward Chance.

"Digging a hole."

"I can see that. What for?"

"I'm putting up a new basketball goal for Zack."

Alexa stared at him as if he'd lost his mind.

"I heard the weather forecast. There's a seventy-percent chance of rain tomorrow afternoon. I told Zack I'd have this goal up by tomorrow night."

A man so true to his word that he constructed a goal for a kid, after a long day of ranching chores on a gimpy leg? Alexa admired his dedication. If Chance was willing to make the effort on Zack's behalf, then so was she.

"I'll help. What do you want me to do?"

Chance gestured toward the tin can that glittered in the light. "The nuts, washers and bolts are in the can. The goal needs to be bolted onto the backboard. I've already secured the plywood to the pole."

Alexa scooped up the wrenches, nuts and bolts and set to work.

Chance grabbed the post hole diggers and braced his legs under him. "I designed the goal so it can be adjusted easily as Zack grows. All you need is Grace—"

Alexa smiled, amused that Chance constantly referred to the ladder she'd fallen off of as Grace.

"—and a couple of wrenches. You can elevate the backboard. But it's going to be a two-man job, so don't go thinking you can do it by yourself. This backboard is heavy, and I don't want you to end up on the ground with plywood on your chest and a goal around your neck."

Together, they mixed concrete to secure the pole in the ground, then pushed the goal into position. Alexa stood back to appraise the goal, then peered curiously at Chance.

"Why are you doing this?"

"Because my dad never bothered to do it for me, and my mother wasn't as mechanically inclined, or as interested in my wants and needs, as you are," he answered. "By the time I was eight, my mom was heavily involved in the dating game and my dad was at the bottom of a liquor bottle. Seems to me that every kid should have his own basketball goal. I'm giving Zack what I never had."

Alexa was saddened to think of Chance being shuffled back and forth between two irresponsible parents. From the sound of things, he had been left to grow up on his own. Her heart went out to him, realizing he'd endured a miserable childhood. He had himself to thank for his admirable code of honor, his strong moral fiber and strength of character.

Impulsively, Alexa towed Chance away from the beaming security light, then reached up on tiptoe to kiss him.

"Hey, lady," Chance said in mock affront. "I told you that I don't take intimate favors in exchange for completing jobs."

Yes, he had, and he was true to his word, Alexa mused. "Come on, cowboy," she said, giving her best Mae West impression. "Good-lookin' as you are, honey, you must have women all over you like a rash. Why would you think I'd be able to resist the urge to kiss you?"

Chance arched a thick brow. "Is this the same Queen of Cool I met when I got here?"

Feeling deliciously wicked, Alexa slid her hands up his chest and sidled closer. Flirting had never been her forte, but Chance made her feel safe and unthreatened. She enjoyed full body contact with this particular cowboy. He made her feel relaxed, allowed her to toss aside inhibitions and be herself.

"The Queen of Cool has the hots for you," she admitted openly.

Deb would be so proud, Alexa thought to herself.

Chance's brows rose like exclamation marks. "Correct me if I'm wrong. This *is* another come-on, isn't it?"

"Feels like one to me. How am I doing so far?" She grabbed his shirt collar and pulled him closer.

"You're doing exceptionally well," he murmured.

The invitation was offered and readily accepted. Chance's arms closed around her and he cherished the feel of her body pressed familiarly to his. He wasn't sure how long he could be satisfied with stolen kisses and tempting caresses in the darkness. He didn't know how long he could keep up the pretense with Howard hovering around. But this was sure as hell more than polite interest in Alexa. She made him hunger for the fire and flames of passion.

He wanted her, and he thought she wanted him too, despite the complications swirling around them, despite everything.

His hands wandered possessively over her, reacquainting

himself with each luscious curve and swell that lay hidden beneath cotton and denim. Arms shaking with need, he pulled her ever closer, letting her feel his desire for her, and she ground her hips into his, driving him insane—her, too, if her muffled groan was anything to go by.

Tonight she would have to be the one to call a halt. Chance was too lost in intense sensations and forbidden pleasure to withdraw. He wanted to bury himself so deeply inside her that he became a part of her, that she became a living, breathing part of him....

"Alexa? Are you out there? I spilled ice water on my bed. Will you change my sheets?"

The sound of Howard's voice jerked Alexa back to reality. She was shaking, aching, barely capable of drawing enough breath to reply. "On my way, Howard," she bleated.

"What the devil are you doing out there?"

Doing? Frantic, Alexa mentally scrambled for a logical excuse, but her brain had short-circuited.

"You're checking to make sure there's fresh water in the tank for the cattle and horses," Chance whispered in her ear. "You noticed the tank was low earlier this evening."

Alexa repeated the supplied excuse. Satisfied, Howard disappeared from sight. Alexa sagged in relief.

"Thanks, Chance. You kissed me blind and speechless. I didn't have the foggiest idea what I was going to tell him."

Chance curled his hand beneath her chin and smiled down at her. "If we keep meeting like this, I'm liable to forget Howard exists. Now get out of here. I'm too old to be making out beside the barn like a sneaky teenager."

When Chance turned her around, swatted her playfully on the fanny and urged her on her way Alexa wobbled off on weak knees. She vaguely remembered changing Howard's sheets and climbing the stairs. Her mind, and body, were swirling with the tantalizing thoughts and riveting sensations Chance had aroused in her.

While she lay there alone in bed, begging for sleep that was slow in coming, Alexa felt herself inching ever closer to the dangerous prospect of following a whim. She knew there was nothing casual about her attraction to Chance Butler. The man set her on fire! And when he left Rocking T—as she knew he would eventually—she was very much afraid that he would be packing her heart with him.

Alexa knew she was taking a risk in letting this relationship intensify, but she couldn't seem to stop herself. Despite all her solemn vows to avoid rambling cowboys, Chance Butler was the one man who had earned her respect and left her hungering for the tempting pleasure she sensed awaiting her in his arms.

Damn it, she muttered as she flounced in bed. Why did he have to be a cowboy? Wasn't that just her luck?

"Damn!" Howard spouted as he came through the door, dripping puddles on the tiled floor. Chance was one step behind him. "We still have a pasture of hay waiting to be baled. The rain couldn't have come at a worse time."

Alexa was quick to note that Chance took time to wipe his feet on the mat before entering the kitchen. Howard, on the other hand, never gave a thought to the mess Alexa had to clean up.

"Did you get the motel reservations for Zack and me?" Howard asked as he shrugged off his jacket.

"All taken care of."

"Gas up the truck?"

"Done," she confirmed.

Chance frowned, annoyed. Cinderella was certainly expected to handle every errand around here. Chance was tempted to tell Howard that he could have seen to the matters himself. Apparently Howard, like Dan, continually took Alexa for granted.

Chance wished he could whisk Alexa away from all her expected responsibilities, but knew that was impossible. All he could do was offer a few stolen moments of enjoyment in a secret rendezvous that probably weighed heavily on her conscience.

Damn it, when had he gotten in so deep? Where had he left his good sense? In his effort to help, he was probably doing more harm than good. He'd never felt so helplessly restrained in his life. Feelings of protectiveness swamped him, yet he was forced to hold his tongue and pretend Alexa was none of his concern.

Although Chance praised Alexa's cooking, and Zack seconded the compliment, Howard didn't catch the hint. The old man had his jaws wrapped around another tale of Dan's impressive feats at Calgary Rodeo. Near as Chance could recall, Dan hadn't won half the events Howard claimed. Chance ought to know since he'd been there and had won the bulldogging event himself!

As had become his daily habit, Chance cleared the table and loaded the dishwasher. While Howard and Zack headed for the family room, Alexa lingered behind Chance, watching him work. He pivoted to flash her a smile and felt a tingle of pleasure ricochet through him when she grinned in return.

"I'm asking you out on a date for tomorrow night," he said quietly. "Dinner and dancing, or a movie, whichever you prefer."

Alexa cast a cautious glance toward the doorway. "All right."

"Good, now that that's settled and out of the way, what do you want me to do with the leftovers from supper?"

Alexa scooped up the lasagna and grabbed the aluminum foil. "Your lunch tomorrow," she announced.

"Alexa! Bring me some more of that mango tea, will you?" Howard called from the other room.

Chance muttered under his breath when Alexa automatically answered the summons. Her slave status around here was really starting to irritate him. How had she tolerated this nonsense for so many years?

He posed the question to her the moment she reentered the kitchen.

Alexa shrugged. "I put up with what I had to so my sister could come to live with me until she graduated from high school."

When she explained about her parents' death Chance got a clearer picture of the life of responsibility Alexa led. She was the prime example of a woman trapped, making decisions and sacrifices for the benefit of her family. She was loyal and steadfast and reliable, and Chance admired her for it, even though he wished a far more rewarding life for her.

The urge to hold, comfort and reassure her nearly got the better of him. But Chance knew this wasn't the place or time—years too late, in fact. Alexa had learned to accept, to adjust, to expect very little. As for Chance, he had the chivalrous urge to lay the world at her feet, to recognize her for her unsung accomplishments.

"Prepare to enter the shrine," Alexa murmured as she led the way into the family room.

Shrine was right! Chance squirmed uneasily at the invisible presence that filled the room. Pictures of Dan Tipton were everywhere. What could have been a cozy room, paneled with cedar, was indeed a monument.

When Zack invited Chance to play checkers, Chance eagerly accepted. He would have played with Barbie dolls—anything to avoid staring at the lighted trophy case and enlarged photographs.

Come this weekend, while Howard and Zack were in Tulsa, Chance vowed to introduce Alexa Tipton to a different way of life. She'd have flowers, a gift, the whole nine yards. He'd treat her like a queen.

And then what? Would he cast her back into her role of

Cinderella? Leave her wishing she had never known that some men treated women with the respect, attention and courtesy they deserved?

Okay, so maybe that wasn't such a swell idea. Or perhaps that was exactly what Alexa needed to make her demand a few rights and some well-earned notice from Howard!

Alexa toted Zack's suitcase downstairs to find Howard pacing impatiently.

"'Bout time," he grumbled, checking his watch. "We'll miss the first go-round if we don't hit the road."

Alexa ignored her father-in-law and squatted to stare at Zack face-to-face. "Behave yourself, champ," she murmured affectionately. "I'll call you in the morning to see how the events went."

Zack gave her a hug, then picked up his suitcase. "Oh, wait, Grandpa. There's something I need to do!" He dashed out the door before Howard could stop him.

"Now what?" Howard muttered impatiently. "He already fed that puppy. What else does he possibly need to do before we leave?"

Alexa shrugged, then rose to her feet to confront Howard. "You know I'm not thrilled with this excursion, but I know it means a great deal to you."

"Damn right it does. The boy needs to see what his dad did for a living. I don't want Zack to forget. If you had your way, you'd have me packing away all the photographs and mementos and putting Dan's memory to rest."

Alexa braced herself for the reaction she knew would follow the comment she felt compelled to make. "I don't think living in the past is the answer, Howard. I know you miss Dan terribly, but—"

"But nothing," Howard interrupted. "I don't want to talk about this now. Don't bring it up again, either. My son died in the prime of his life. He deserves to be remembered, deserves to have his story told so that his son will never forget.''

Alexa turned away to retrieve the homemade cookies she'd prepared for the trip. "Have a good time, Howard. And drive carefully.''

Howard nodded curtly before heading to the door. Alexa noted that he didn't bother wishing her well for the weekend. Howard was so wrapped up in his plans, in his son's memory, that she wasn't his slightest consideration.

Like father, like son, she mused as she watched Howard turn and walk away.

Chance glanced up to see Zack burst through the bunkhouse door. To his surprise, the boy rushed over to hug him around the waist.

"I wanted to tell you goodbye. Grandpa is ready to leave.''

"Have a good time, rookie," Chance said, ruffling the boy's hair. "Don't forget to get the names of the cowboys who win the bulldogging and calf roping events. I want to know who my toughest competition will be when I return to the circuit.''

"Sure thing." Zack tipped his head back. "And Chance?''

"Yeah, kid?''

"Love you…''

Zack wheeled around and raced off, leaving Chance staggering from the emotional blow. Damn it, why did the kid have to go and wrap himself around Chance's heart? Leaving Rocking T was going to be hell enough. That hasty, self-conscious confession Zack delivered was making it worse.

Chance stood at the window, watching Howard splatter through the water holes as he drove away. The temptation to stride up to the house to see Alexa was strong, but Chance defied it. He had work to do. Howard had left a list of chores to be done on the ranch and errands to run in town. Chance intended to knock out the tasks this morning, so he could move the recently delivered kitchen cabinets into the bed-and-breakfast for Alexa.

Bright and early Monday morning, the plumbers would arrive to install the fixtures. Alexa's construction project was near completion. Chance wished he could be around for the grand opening, but he was scheduled to ride at Forth Worth.

He knew it was time to move on, before he got so damned attached to Alexa and that kid that he would leave too much of himself behind.

Now there was a laugh, Chance thought as he plucked up the list of errands. He'd done that already. He'd lowered the drawbridge to carefully guarded emotion and got himself hooked on a woman who was out of his reach. And the kid, Chance thought, sighing morosely. That little boy's memory was going to follow him around for a long time to come. It would be right alongside Alexa's.

When Chance took the spill that injured his leg, he had never dreamed there would be more to heal than just tendons and ligaments around his knee. Turned out he was going to leave nursing a wounded heart.

"Help!" Alexa exclaimed the instant she walked into her sister's arts and crafts shop.

Deb appeared from beneath the front counter, frowning in concern. "What's wrong?"

Alexa blushed when she realized there were two older women browsing at the back of the shop. The women were staring curiously at her. Alexa pasted on a nonchalant smile and waved in greeting. "Hi, Freda, Evelyn. Lovely afternoon, isn't it?"

"Yes, dear, it certainly is. How are things at Rocking T?" Freda questioned.

"Is the bed-and-breakfast ready to open for business?" Evelyn wanted to know.

"Things at the ranch are dandy fine. I'll be open for business next month," Alexa called out, then turned as casually as she knew how to face her sister. "I need your help, Deb. On a whim I accepted a date with Chance. I have no makeup or suitable dress, nor do I have money to spare to make frivolous purchases. Do you have anything I can borrow for tonight?"

Alexa must have looked harried and desperate, because Deb patted her shoulder consolingly. "Leave it to me, sis. I'll turn you into Cinderella for your first official date with that Prince Charming cowboy."

Deb waved her arm in expansive gestures to draw the older women's attention. "Yo, Freda, could I impose on you and Evelyn to mind the shop for a half hour. I have an errand to run with my sister."

"You girls go right ahead. Not to worry, we'll take care of things here."

"Are you sure you want to leave the shop in their hands?" Alexa asked worriedly as Deb ushered her out the door. "You might find a few crafts missing when you return."

Deck clucked her tongue. "Oh ye of little trust. Freda Mayse was my sixth-grade teacher. You think she would rip me off?"

"Stranger things have happened," Alexa reminded her as she made a beeline toward her pickup. "I really appreciate this, sis. I haven't dated in eleven years."

"And you're as nervous as a caged coyote," Deb teased. "Not that it shows or anything."

Alexa put the truck in gear and sped toward Deb's apartment. "Why did I agree to this? My head tells me this is a mistake."

"What does your heart tell you?" Deb questioned.

"My heart shouldn't have a say in the matter. I'm simply

following your advice and putting a little diversion in my life. I'm not planning to date every eligible man in town, as you've done.''

"Thanks a lot," Deb said, then giggled. "You make me sound like a third-rate floozy."

"I'm sorry." Alexa's shoulders slumped and she tried to relax. "Men have been attracted to you since you were fourteen. I should know, because I had to beat them off the front porch with a broom. You've got that natural inner sparkle that men find irresistible. I never drew that kind of attention."

Deb shook her head. "Give yourself some credit, sis. You're an attractive woman with a great body and paralyzing green eyes. Problem is that you've downplayed your femininity and do so much physical work that your supply of makeup has long since dried up and been discarded. If you ask me, Chance Butler is the first good thing that has happened to you in a long time. This date is your opportunity to remind yourself that you are a woman with your own needs."

"A woman with a son to raise, a father-in-law in the same house, a ranch to run and a bed-and-breakfast to complete," Alexa added, then threw up one hand—the other one was clamped around the steering wheel. "I must have lost the good sense I've spent years cultivating. What have I done? I have no business going out on a date."

"You're getting a life. You need this date," Deb tried to convince her. "You *deserve* this date."

Boosted by Deb's enthusiasm and encouragement, Alexa parked in the driveway, then followed her sister into the apartment. Deb headed for her closet, and Alexa marveled at the rack of fashionable clothes at Deb's disposal. The woman had always had a knack for bargain hunting. She selected flashy, eye-catching garments that accentuated her feminine assets.

Alexa, on the other hand, had three mix-and-match ensembles she wore to church. The rest of her wardrobe consisted of faded blue jeans and T-shirts, which suited her life-style of working on the ranch.

Deb thumbed through the garments, then pulled out a sleeveless silk dress.

Alexa gave her head a firm shake. "No way. I don't even have a bra that I could conceal under that plunging neckline. I absolutely refuse to go without one."

"I have a Wonderbra you can borrow," Deb said helpfully. "Come on, sis, let loose a little. You'll look fantastic in this dress."

When Alexa hesitated, Deb thrust the dress at her, then grabbed the Wonderbra from the dresser drawer. "Put these on so I can do your hair and makeup. I only have thirty minutes, you know. Don't want the gun-toting Freda and thieving Evelyn to make off like bandits at my shop."

Reluctantly, Alexa peeled off her blue jeans that had seen better days. She fastened herself into the dress, which fit like a glove. More cleavage than she'd displayed in her life reflected in the mirror. Self-consciously, she tugged at the neckline—to no avail.

When Deb returned two minutes later, Alexa crossed her arms over her exposed chest—it only made things worse. "This isn't me," she grumbled.

"Oh, it's definitely you and you'll definitely have to borrow my trench coat for the drive home," Deb said, eyes gleaming with sisterly pride and satisfaction. "You'll have men chasing after you. Good thing you'll have that hunk of cowboy to protect you this evening. Wouldn't think of sending you out alone in that dress. You'd start a riot."

Alexa stared seriously at her grinning sister. "Do you really think I look okay?"

"Okay?" Deb hooted. "You're dynamite." She motioned Alexa toward the chair that sat in front of the makeup table. "Sit, Cinderella. Your fairy godsister is working on a short clock."

Alexa sat, then grimaced when Deb grabbed her hair and brushed it vigorously. In record time, Deb twisted the mass of curly auburn hair into an elegant twist and pinned it atop Alexa's head. Then Deb tugged a few wispy curls loose around Alexa's temples. With dedicated concentration Deb applied base, powder, eyeliner and mascara. With a flair she brushed on blush, then stood back to appraise her handiwork.

"You're going to knock that cowboy dead," she announced.

Alexa wrinkled her nose. "Gee, that should be a fun date."

"Do that again."

"Do what?"

"Use that playful, teasing tone and rely on the dry wit you've stifled since you turned into Ms. Serious and Responsible."

Deb squatted down in front of her sister. "Let the real you shine through tonight, okay? Even if Butler turns out to be a cowboy who walks away without looking back, dance with him, talk to him, laugh with him. You've spent most of your time simplifying the world for young Zack and catering to an old man who lives in the eternal past. You need to share adult companionship. You really need this, Alexa."

One night, Alexa promised herself. She would honestly try to put all thoughts of her complicated life aside for a few hours of carefree enjoyment.

Deb patted Alexa's nylon-clad knee. "Now get me back to the shop, pronto. I have to close up, then run back here to shower and change for my own date."

"With whom?" Alexa asked as she followed Deb through the bedroom door.

Deb paused to grab the trench coat, then draped it over Alexa's shoulders. "I'm going out with a groping drug pusher," she said saucily.

"Deb!" Alexa squawked, appalled.

"He's the new physician in town." Deb snickered mischievously. "We bumped into each other at the grocery store—literally. I pulled out in the aisle and slammed into his basket. We had lunch together yesterday."

"Divorced?" Alexa quizzed.

"Nope, never married. He's a city slicker from back East, but I promised to teach him to fit into rural America."

"Such a dedicated humanitarian," Alexa said, then grinned.

"Keep that up, sis," Deb encouraged. "Saucy and spirited become you."

Alexa repeated the compliment during the drive home. She felt like a cross between Cinderella and My Fair Lady. Gosh, she hoped this wasn't a mistake. She knew she needed a diversion, but she would probably be better off going out with a man she didn't care all that much about. If she had a grand time with Chance, it would only make it more difficult to bid him goodbye.

But truth was, she wanted to dress up to please him. She shouldn't feel guilty or irresponsible because she was going out on the town for one night. It wasn't as if she was going to make a habit of this, after all. This was one night, a space out of time, and she was going to let herself enjoy it!

Chapter Seven

Chance sat on the broken-down sofa, wrestling with his blue jeans. Trying to tug his breeches over the brace strapped to his leg was like pulling teeth—and it hurt like hell. But he refused to strap the damn brace on the outside of his pants, not when he was going out on an official date with Alexa.

Muttering, Chance wiggled and tugged. Finally, the denim slid over the straps. Awkwardly, Chance came to his feet to zip his fly. That done, he limped over to grab his best blue Western shirt.

After fighting the battle of pulling on his boots with a lame leg, Chance set his Resistol hat on his head and stared at his reflection in the mirror. He was scrubbed clean and didn't look too bad for a beat-up cowboy, even if he did say so himself.

On his way to the door, Chance realized he was more nervous than he'd ever been when he rode into a rodeo arena that was teeming with spectators. Roping and throwing a calf didn't faze him. Flinging himself off a galloping quarter horse to bulldog a steer didn't bother him. But walking up to the ranch house to pick up Alexa had his belly twisting like a pretzel. He realized that it was important for him to make a good impression, to show her a good time. Lord knew she deserved it, knew she rarely allowed herself personal pleasure.

Damn, talk about operating under pressure! Chance tugged at his starched collar, startled by the constricting feeling in his throat. You'd think this was the first time he'd gone out with a woman. That was a laugh. Up to this point in his life he had picked up—and been picked up by—dozens of women. The only difference was that Alexa Tipton was unlike the feminine masses who'd come and gone from his life.

Chance halted on the porch, composed himself, then held behind his back the bouquet of flowers he'd purchased while running errands in town. The small velvet box was tucked in his shirt pocket. He was raring to go and had come bearing the niceties that dating a true lady required.

When the door swung open, every cheerful pleasantry he'd rehearsed flew out of his head. The woman standing in the doorway, wearing a sleek red dress that showcased the full swells of her breasts and accentuated the trim curves of her hips, was strikingly beautiful. It was the first time Chance had seen Alexa with makeup and a dress. The effect left him speechless...aroused.

Holy mackerel! This diamond in the rough was a sparkling jewel, whose radiant—yet tentative—smile blinded and beguiled. Chance felt himself stagger back, felt his mouth drop open.

"Alexa..." he bleated like a stunned lamb. "You're absolutely gorgeous."

She looked enormously pleased with the compliment. "Think so?"

His gaze ran the full length of her once, twice, three

times. Sure enough, the effect she had on him intensified with each sweeping appraisal. He could feel himself growing hard, felt hungry need thrumming through him with each accelerated heartbeat.

Before the temptation of casting the bouquet aside and pouncing on her overtook him, Chance gave himself a mental slap. "You take my breath away," he wheezed as he pulled his hand from behind his back to present her with the flowers.

Alexa's jaw sagged, her eyes rounded. She stared, bewildered, at the red roses, then at him. A mist glistened in her eyes, and Chance had the feeling Alexa had never been courted properly, at least not in a decade or so.

She touched the velvet petals appreciatively, then bent to inhale the delicate fragrance of the roses. "I don't know what to say. I didn't expect this."

Chance fished out the jewel box from his pocket. "Then I suppose you weren't expecting this, either." He opened the box, displaying the delicate gold chain and heart-shaped pendant.

Alexa's jaw scraped her chest as she reached out a trembling hand to uplift the necklace. "Oh, my…"

"It's a rhinestone, not a diamond," he told her. "It caught my eye while I was in town this morning. Just as you caught my eye the moment I saw you."

The look she gave him was priceless—a real Kodak moment that Chance wished he could have captured for all times. She seemed honestly shocked by his consideration and generosity. It was as if he had made her day, maybe even her decade.

Alexa Tipton, Chance decided, had never been truly appreciated or recognized for the incredible woman she was. It made him feel small and insignificant to realize that while he had been surrounded by fame and recognition—a well-known name in the rodeo world—Alexa worked tirelessly, unselfishly, expecting and receiving no gratification.

God, he wanted to hug her to him and tell her that she was special, unique, appreciated. But if he did, he'd never set off on this official date. The hug would become a kiss, a caress, and he'd be lost to these tormenting needs he'd been trying to hold in check.

"Here, let me fasten the necklace in place," he offered as he lifted it from her fingertips.

He moved behind her, trapped in the essence of this lovely woman and feeling a little light-headed. His hands were shaking slightly as he grazed her bare skin and fumbled with the clasp.

"I don't know how to repay you," Alexa murmured.

Chance felt her shiver delicately as his hand skimmed the back of her neck. He couldn't help himself, he pressed his lips to her scented skin and felt the jolt of heightened awareness sizzle through him.

"Bake me a cake," he suggested in a strangled voice. "A chocolate layer cake." His mouth glided to the auburn ringlet that dangled by her left ear. "With lots of thick chocolate icing."

He heard her breath catch, felt his heart race. Clutching desperately at his failing self-control, Chance took her hand and towed her toward the door. "Come on, darlin', if we don't get out of here now, I'm going to run out of reasons to leave."

Practicing every gallant manner he'd ever learned, Chance opened the door of the pickup truck and assisted Alexa into the cab. As she eased onto the high seat, Chance was granted an enticing view of hose-clad legs. Gorgeous legs, he noted appreciatively.

Get in the danged truck, cowboy, Chance snapped silently. Don't stand there gawking. Show her the best time she's ever had and don't let her think for even one minute that you're expecting anything except an enjoyable evening in the company of a beautiful woman.

Chance took his good advice and clambered into the

truck. He kept thinking of the movie, *Pretty Woman,* marveling at the transformation in Alexa's appearance. Though he considered Alexa devastatingly attractive even when she dressed *down,* she was every man's fantasy when she dressed *up.*

An hour later, while they sat in Willowvale's most exclusive restaurant—the only one that had a name that didn't end with Bar and Grill—Chance realized that Alexa was unaware of the attention she was attracting. The woman honestly didn't know how stunning she was, how male gazes kept drifting magnetically, repeatedly, in her direction. Chance felt like Ms. America's escort for the evening.

"I was so moved by the flowers and gift that I forgot to tell you how handsome you look," Alexa said as she leaned forward. When she realized she was providing him with an unhindered view of cleavage, she straightened in her chair. But it was too late. Chance had to pry his gaze off her chest. Damn, she was easy on the eye, and hard on a man's blood pressure.

"I really like your blue shirt, Chance," she murmured.

He grabbed his cup of coffee to occupy hands that itched to caress. "Thanks, ma'am. I save it for special occasions," he drawled.

Her thick, mascara-lined lashes swept down, then up. A saucy smile pursed her lips, and Chance inwardly groaned at the devastating effect she was having on him.

"You are a special occasion," she confided. "I haven't been out for dinner, except to pick up burgers and fries with Zack, in years."

All the more reason to treat Alexa like a queen, Chance thought as the satisfaction of her compliment flooded through him.

"Well, look who's here!"

Chance twisted in his chair to see Debra Parsons and the distinguished-looking Suit at her heels. Deb cleaned up as spectacularly as her sister did, Chance noted. The plum-colored dress Deb wore suited her fair complexion and blond hair. The Suit seemed out of place in the surroundings that bobbed with cowboy hats.

"Hi, Chance," Deb said, eyes twinkling. She reached out her hand to draw the Suit to the table. "Chance Butler, this is Kurt Stevenson, M.D. And this is my sister, Alexa."

Chance thought the preppy doctor spent entirely too much time giving Alexa a visual examination before he extended his hand to her in greeting.

"Good looks obviously run in the family," Kurt observed.

"Mind if we join you?" Deb didn't await a reply. She parked herself at the table.

Chance scowled to himself. He had been perfectly satisfied having Alexa all to himself. He didn't need the good doctor and Miss Cheerful crowding his space and cramping his style.

He did note, however, that Alexa relaxed. She and Deb chitchatted while Chance was left to gab with the physician. As it turned out, Kurt Stevenson made interesting company. He was intensely curious about Chance's profession and offered to examine his knee during an office visit, if Chance was so inclined.

Throughout the meal, which didn't begin to compare to Alexa's exceptional cuisine, Chance made small talk and sat there, amazed, as Alexa came to life. Her dry, quick wit prevailed as she bantered playfully with her sister.

"So, where's your next stop?" Deb asked curiously. "Movie or dancing?"

"A movie, I guess," Alexa replied. "No need to put undue stress on Chance's knee."

"The knee is fine," Chance lied. He would have run a marathon if Alexa wanted to. Tonight was all hers, he promised himself.

"Good, then we can hit the honky-tonk," Deb insisted. "I promised to teach Kurt some country-western dancing."

Alexa glanced questioningly at Chance, leaving him with the choice of accepting or rejecting the invitation. "Sounds good, Deb. We'll meet you at the dance hall."

When Kurt and Deb exited, Alexa dug into her purse to pay half the ticket for dinner. Chance raised his hand to forestall her. "Dinner is on me," he insisted.

"Interesting concept," she countered, grinning. "But you've spent entirely too much on me this evening. The least I can do—"

"The least you can do," he interrupted, "is salvage my male pride here. This was never intended to be a Dutch date."

"Well, if you're sure."

"Very sure," he insisted.

Chance levered off his chair, then drew Alexa to her feet. Male gazes lingered on Alexa as Chance escorted her to the door. Impulsively, he took her arm, as if to stake his claim on a woman who was drawing more attention than hundred-dollar bills cast from an upstairs window.

He hadn't realized how possessive he'd become of her, wasn't comfortable with the feeling that sneaked up on his blind side. This nonsense had to stop, Chance lectured himself during the drive through town. He wasn't a complete fool, after all. He knew the complications of Alexa's situation. She was entrenched at Rocking T, determined to make a go of the B-and-B and focus her life on raising her son. She was guarded by a father-in-law who was obsessed with keeping his departed son's memory alive.

Chance would forever be the outsider. As it was, he was pushing his luck by taking Alexa out on the town, living for the moment. Even if he wanted to accept the responsibility of providing a permanent distraction for Alexa and allowing himself to become a father image for Zack, he couldn't. Alexa had no faith in rambling cowboys. Her long-term relationship with Dan had evolved into life-altering cynicism. Furthermore, Howard had posted No

Trespassing signs all over his daughter-in-law. Chance knew better than to expect more than just one night.

This was a place out of time, he reminded himself. This was Cinderella's chance to paint the town red. Come Sunday evening, her life would return to normal, and Chance would be plodding through ranch chores, same as he'd done for more than two weeks.

Be satisfied with one evening, Butler, he told himself as he drove to the honky-tonk on the outskirts of town.

Alexa was thoroughly enjoying herself, despite the smoke that made her eyes water in the dance hall. Chance had been charming company. Deb's arrival had made Alexa's first date in a decade less awkward. Alexa had tried out a few sassy remarks, flirted occasionally and tossed around dozens of smiles. All that disturbed her was the fact that men kept staring at her, both in the restaurant and at the dance hall. It made her self-conscious, wondering if she had a giant runner in her panty hose. She was probably making a conspicuous fool of herself and Chance was too polite to tell her.

Finally, she leaned over to ask him, speaking loudly to be heard over the music of the band. "Do I have something pinned to the back of my dress, a sign maybe? One that says Kick Me?"

Chance frowned. "No. Why do you ask?"

Alexa glanced toward the bar where several urban cowboys were waggling their eyebrows and staring at her. "Then why the silly grins that I keep intercepting?"

Chance eased his arm around her and chuckled. "Stunning women always draw that reaction from men. Watching the rear view of a sexy walk has drawn male attention since time immemorial."

Genuinely surprised, Alexa stared at him. "Me? You've got to be kidding."

"Nope. You've got a to-die-for walk, darlin'. Believe

me," he assured her with a wink. "I shamefully admit that I've had an ulterior motive for walking behind you tonight."

Alexa grinned at his infectious smile. "You're doing wonders for my self-confidence."

"Always glad to help a lady, ma'am," he drawled. "Care to dance?"

Alexa stared longingly at the dance floor where Deb was quietly counting the rhythm in Kurt's ear so he could match the beat of the two-step. "Are you sure your leg can stand it?"

He flashed her a devilish smile. "It's not the leg that's going to suffer from being so close to you, it's the male equipment. If I don't keep a respectable distance from you, just elbow me."

Chance came to his feet, then held out his hand gallantly. "Shall we?"

Alexa found herself guided expertly across the dance floor, moving to the tempo of one of Garth Brooks's popular songs. Despite his gimpy leg Chance moved gracefully as he spun her away, then drew her back into his arms. Alexa responded instinctively to him, matching him step for step, though she knew she was out of practice.

She caught herself wondering how many woman had danced in these brawny arms, then told herself it didn't matter. She had no claim on Chance, had no right to feel possessive. To him, she was just another of the many dates he'd had.

When the band struck up a slow ballad, Alexa hesitated, but Chance drew her close. She maintained a respectable distance between them for a few moments, then eased closer. She felt Chance's arms tighten around her, then relax, as if he, too, were fighting the arousing feelings of sharing the same electrically charged space.

With each frayed breath, each gliding motion, Alexa felt the tug of emotion pulling her ever nearer the powerful contours of Chance's body. When her arm curled over his shoulder, his hand folded tightly around hers, pressing it against his chest. She stared up at him, seeing the flicker in his silver-blue eyes. His head was so temptingly close as they moved as one to the music.

Alexa licked her dried-out lips, and Chance moaned softly in her ear. "What you do to me, woman, should be a criminal offense."

She hesitated, then gave way to the need to lay her head against his shoulder—and felt tingling pleasure for the first time in years. Although Alexa could see Deb grinning at her in the distance, nodding in approval, Alexa was a captive of her own secret longings. She wanted this man the way she'd never wanted anyone else, ached to enjoy the tenderness that she knew awaited her.

Alexa sensed this cowboy, despite his rough-and-tumble profession, would be a gentle, patient lover, unlike the one whose name Alexa vowed not to speak in comparison.

For the space of that slow dance, and the one that followed, Alexa let herself revel in the undercurrent of sensations swirling through her. She savored the feel of Chance's masculine body pressed familiarly to hers. This was her bright, glittering, selfish moment, before stepping back into her no-nonsense world.

"I'm aching," Chance murmured against her neck.

"The leg?"

"Not even close," he whispered, then skimmed his lips over her sensitized skin. "Guess again, darlin'...."

Alexa felt as if she had stuck her finger in an electrical outlet. Chance's warm breath sent paralyzing tingles through every fiber of her being, then left her to burn in unfulfilled desire.

"I can't take much more of this, Alexa," Chance groaned. "Your call, princess. Either we sit down so I can cool off or we go somewhere private. Hanging onto a bucking bronc is easier than what I'm doing now. A rodeo ride only lasts eight seconds, but there seems no end to the torture I'm enduring now.''

Alexa lifted her head to see the grimace that bracketed Chance's mouth. He was giving her a choice? A *choice?* Someone cared what *she* thought, what *she* wanted? How utterly novel.

''I'll get my purse.''

Chance stopped dancing and stared intently at her. ''You're sure? You know what's going to happen, don't you? If you view this as a possible mistake, tell me here and now. I want no misunderstanding, no belated regret. I don't want to kiss you good-night at the door and wake up alone in the morning. You understand what I'm asking, don't you?''

Suddenly, the world shrank to a space no larger than the area this ruggedly handsome cowboy occupied. Alexa met his intense, probing gaze. The tension between them vibrated as he held his breath, awaiting her reply.

Tell him no. You'll only get hurt. You'll probably discover what it's like to be loved properly and then spend years wishing you didn't know what you've been missing. You'll never be the most important priority in this man's life. He'll leave you and you'll be picking up the pieces of a forbidden dream. Just say no!

''I don't want to wake up alone, either.'' Alexa heard the words trip off her tongue, as if someone else—with considerably less sense—were speaking.

Chapter Eight

Chance pressed on the brake and stopped in front of the two-story ranch house. "I'll be back in a minute," he said before climbing down from the clunker truck.

In purposeful strides, he entered the house to retrieve the roses. He wanted candlelight and flowers, and he wanted them in the bunkhouse—away from the shrine of memories that loomed in this house.

Alexa cocked a quizzical brow when he handed the roses to her. "I want them with me in the bunkhouse to remind me of tonight," he explained as he drove downhill.

Chance winced as he stepped down with more haste than caution on his bad leg. Trying to conceal his limp, he circled to Alexa's side of the truck. He wanted to scoop her up and carry her across the threshold in a spectacularly romantic gesture, but he wasn't sure his knee would hold up. Lacing her fingers in his, he led the way into the bunkhouse.

When Alexa stood awkwardly in the middle of the room,

Chance smiled to himself. She didn't know what to do, how to begin. In some ways she seemed so sweetly innocent that it touched his heart, made him feel as if he had taken on the colossal responsibility of initiating a virgin. In some ways, he supposed she was. She didn't seem familiar with the preliminaries of passion, only the end result.

Well, she would discover how it felt to be cherished and enjoyed, Chance promised himself. If it took all night, he would assure Alexa that she had been loved and loved well.

As a symbol of this night together, Chance strode over to light the candle that sat on the table, bathing the room in tones of muted gold and drifting shadows. When he turned around, Alexa reached for the back zipper of her dress. She hesitated, then looked at him uncertainly.

Chance grinned devilishly. "I'd like to do that, if you don't mind. I realize you're accustomed to doing everything by yourself, but…"

His voice trailed off as his hand glided around her waist and she flinched. "Easy, honey. I won't hurt you or rush you. I thought I'd made that clear already."

She looked trustingly at him, then nodded. Chance felt as if he'd been crowned king for the night. Gaining Alexa's trust was a monumental milestone. She was silently assuring him that he wasn't just another irresponsible cowboy, that she had placed faith in him. That meaningful glance was like an arrow through his heart—and his conscience. He didn't want to complicate Alexa's life—or his—but he ached to forget everything that was remotely close to reality for this one night. He wanted to let each moment converge into the next, to discover, explore and enjoy.

The hiss of the zipper was all that broke the sizzling silence. As Chance eased the dress from her shoulders, exposing the bra that called attention to the rounded swells of her breasts, he dipped his head to brush his lips over her satiny flesh. He felt her heartbeat racing, heard her breath catch. While he devoted attention to tasting her scented skin, he drew the dress to her hips, then let the garment drift into a pool around her feet.

She was still holding the roses in a death grip, and Chance smiled to himself. He pulled one rose free, then let the velvet petals glide over her breasts in the same lingering fashion as his kiss. Fascinated, he watched her eyes drift shut, her head tilt back. He traced the scented rose down her belly, across the apex of her nylon-clad thighs. Alexa trembled, wobbled and moaned aloud.

Chance led her toward his narrow bed, wishing for a king-size mattress he didn't have at his disposal. As he feathered a kiss over her shoulder, he hooked his thumbs in the band of her panty hose and eased them out of his way. With the practiced efficiency of a man who handled a lariat, he tossed the garment over the back of the sofa, then focused absolute attention on her luscious feminine curves.

She was as perfect as he had imagined, and he wanted to dedicate the night to memorizing the feel of her silky skin, to pleasuring her—and himself.

After Chance eased her onto the bed and stretched out beside her, he brushed the thornless rose over her lips, her throat, her breasts, her belly. She arched like a stroked kitten, then reached for him, but Chance was in no particular hurry. He was fascinated, intrigued that he could arouse her without laying a hand on her. The rose was his caress, their shared secret of intimacy.

He trailed lazy patterns over the skimpy fabric of her panties, then followed the curve of her inner thighs to her knees. He heard her gasp, her muffled sigh, watched her melt and surrender to the sensations he'd aroused. He longed to let his lips follow the path of the rose, his hands join in the gentle explorations, but Alexa writhed sideways and tugged at his shirt, making pearl snaps pop like popcorn.

He grabbed her wandering hand and smiled at her.

"You'll get your turn later if that's what you want. I'm being purely selfish right now."

"You're being purely tormenting," Alexa wheezed. "You like driving me crazy, don't you?"

"Love it," he said as he flicked his tongue at her nipple. "Love the taste. Love the touch and feel of you...."

Chance stopped talking when he became engrossed in the need to pleasure her to the extreme, to satisfy her to the living end. He stripped her down to her bare skin and made a banquet of her. His name became a litany on her lips as she gave herself up to his intimate touch.

When he glided his lips over her nipple, and plucked gently at the other, she breathed a ragged sigh. When he suckled each rigid bud, her hand clenched around his forearms, as if to steady herself against the tide of sensations flooding through her.

With tender care he coasted his hand over her belly to skim the satiny flesh of her inner thighs. Chance bit back a groan when he felt her feminine heat so close to his fingertips. He cupped her in his hand, delicately tracing her secret heat, feeling the honeyed fire of her desire summoning him closer.

When he glided his finger inside her Alexa gasped for breath. Her nails dug a little deeper into his arm as he caressed her, excited her until she was pleading for him to end the sweet torment. But this odd sense of power he held over her was heady stuff. Chance was mesmerized by her potent reaction to his lovemaking. He brought her to the brink of oblivion, marveling at the pleasure he derived when she shimmered around his fingertips, burning him with the heat of her passion.

Gasping for breath, Alexa arched toward him. She fumbled with his belt buckle. Her fingers seemed to have turned to thumbs, and Chance chuckled inwardly as she tried to draw him closer. She was wild with need—and he was still fully dressed.

His smile evaporated when he remembered he'd had one hell of a time pulling his jeans over that bulky brace. But damned if he would make love to Alexa with his clothes on. He wanted to be chest to bare chest, hip to bare hip with Alexa—nothing between them but this blazing passion that threatened to bring down the night.

When Chance rolled away, he heard Alexa curse. He was cursing, too, when he pulled his jeans down to his knees—and could get them to go no further.

"Damn, cowboy," she muttered as she slid to the floor to tug impatiently at his boots. "You ought to be horse-whipped for starting something you can't finish."

"Hey," he said in mock offense. "I can finish what I start— Ouch! Go easy on that leg, darlin'. The denim is tangled up with my brace."

After several impatient moments Alexa wriggled his jeans down his legs, then glanced at his brace. "Off or on?"

"Oh, I'm most definitely turned on," he assured her huskily, eyes twinkling.

She pulled a face at his corny joke. "I meant the brace."

"Off, baby. I want to be wearing nothing but you," he said in a low, seductive drawl.

Her playful smile vanished as she unfastened the brace and noticed the scar on the inside of his calf. "What happened?"

"My dad accidentally burned down the house during one of his drunken binges, but I managed to get him, and myself, out, with only a few narrow brushes with the flames."

"I'm so sorry," she whispered as she pressed her lips to the scar.

"Don't be," he wheezed, touched by her loving gesture. "It was a lifetime ago, and I try to avoid those long trips down bad-memory lane. Makes me too travel weary. At the moment, the only pain I'm suffering is from aching with the want of you...."

When she reached up to tug at the band of his briefs, Chance forgot to breathe. Couldn't remember why he needed to. Her fingertips grazed his fierce arousal and fire sizzled through every part of his being. He was instantly at her mercy. Whatever she wanted, however she wanted it, her wish was his command, his greatest desire.

"Later, I'm going to figure out how to torment you to the same degree you tortured me," she whispered as she pressed her palms to his chest and pushed him back to the bed. "But not now, Butler. You are definitely going to put out the fire you left burning...."

Her lips came down on his so hotly, so sweetly that Chance nearly lost the ability to think. Dazed and frantic, he groped for his discarded jeans, reminding himself that he'd better grab the foil packet in his pocket before he forgot everything except the hungry need to fulfill his long-awaited fantasy.

Impatient, Chance fumbled for protection and cursed every delay that prevented him from satisfying the ache of being so incredibly close to her, and yet so maddeningly far away.

Finally! When he had dealt with the protective preliminaries, he turned Alexa in his arms, and moved above her. He couldn't remember if his knee ached or not. All he knew was that he'd spent sleepless nights dreaming about the possibility of this moment, wondering if he would ever know what it was like to share Alexa's passion.

When he came to her, trying to restrain the hungry need that simmered inside him, she welcomed him into her silky heat, held him suspended in her arms. Chance discovered the true meaning of rapture. Sweeping, consuming, soul-splitting sensations assailed him. For the first time in his life he discovered how it felt to leap freely into oblivion.

There was no yesterday, today or tomorrow. He gave all that he was, the best of what he was, to Alexa. She accepted him, matched his ardent passion, as they tumbled through time and space—two souls merging as one. Ecstasy cascaded over him as shudder after helpless shudder seized him. Chance held on for dear life, clutching Alexa as tightly as she clung to him.

Later, when Chance could manage thought, he lifted his tousled head, refusing to move away, refusing to lose this marvelous sense of belonging, this sense of indescribable contentment. When Alexa pursed her kiss-swollen lips and her green eyes twinkled in the candlelight, satisfaction spilled through him. Chance knew right there and then that this night was far from over. Once hadn't been nearly enough to appease him—or her, apparently. Once had fed the fire raging between them—a fire that demanded so much more.

And there was definitely more. Alexa had her turn with him—sitting up on the couch. She held a rose in each hand, drove him insane with her playful kisses and caresses, and he loved every minute of her titillating seduction. He repaid her for her teasing mischief on the carpeted floor, then on the dining table, just to see if he could.

He could.

They created memories of their wild, sweet passion in every available space in the bunkhouse.

And sometime before dawn they ended up back in his bed, reveling in slow, sensuous lovemaking that left them drifting off into exhausted sleep, cradled contentedly in each other's arms.

Alexa awoke to see the sun glaring through the window. She glanced at the digital clock. Ten-thirty? Criminy, she hadn't slept this late since she couldn't remember when.

She stirred sluggishly, feeling a presence beside her. Alexa pried open one eye to see Chance propped on his elbow, his hand supporting his head. He was watching her intently, and she blushed at the thought of him studying her while she was asleep.

''Morning,'' he murmured huskily.

''Morning.''

''Short night,'' he said, and grinned rakishly.

Alexa turned a ferocious shade of pink. ''Sure was.''

''I'm starved,'' he whispered as he reached out to trace her lips.

''I'll go up to the house and fix breakfast.''

He shook his head. ''In the shower.''

She blinked, puzzled. ''What?''

''I want breakfast in the shower. You and me. Then I'll fix brunch at the house.''

''Demanding, aren't you? I don't deal well with dominating men these days. You realize that, don't you, Butler?''

He nodded, his seductive smile still intact. ''*Please* join me in the shower. I've had this water-world fantasy about you for days on end.''

Alexa let her gaze stray down his magnificent body, noting that his fantasy was beginning to affect his gender-specific equipment. She delighted in knowing she had the power to excite him without actually touching him, delighted in knowing how much it aroused him when she did touch him.

The way she was feeling this morning, she would have given him the moon if he'd asked for it. A shared shower sounded fascinating.

''Lead the way, cowboy,'' she offered generously.

''No,'' he contradicted. ''We'll go together. That's the way I want it to be with us, Alexa. No one leads or follows. Equal footing.'' He grinned. ''Or as close to equal as I can get on this gimpy knee.''

When he drew her to her feet, she curled her arm around his bare waist, and he curled his around hers. Together they made another secret memory to cherish in private moments, when no one else was around....

Chance glanced out the window, realizing that he'd been hearing a bawling cow for the past hour and hadn't gone to investigate. He'd been so content sitting in front of the television, with Alexa dozing on his lap, that he hadn't paid the slightest attention. Easing away, he limped to the window to see a Limousin cow lying on her side in the corral.

"Alexa," he called out.

She roused slightly, then came fully awake when Chance called her name urgently. "What's wrong?"

Chance scooped up the work boots he'd left by the door. "Difficult delivery is my diagnosis. Do you know where the obstetrical chain and ratchet-style calf puller are, just in case we have to pull the newborn?"

Alexa was on her feet in a flash. She dashed out the door, headed for the tack room in Howard's modern, metal barn.

Chance limped along at a slower pace, cursing the throb in his leg, wishing he could keep up—physically—with Alexa, and trying to tell himself it didn't matter if he could, because she had accepted him, limitations and all.

Alexa reappeared with the silver chain and ratchet tool in hand. "Miz Elsie always has trouble with deliveries," she said as she led the way to the corral. "She's one of Howard's oldest cows. I've tried to persuade him to sell her, but he insists that Miz Elsie always drops good calves."

It had been years since Chance had pulled a calf during a difficult delivery, but he speculated that it hadn't been too long for Alexa. Knowing Howard, he had his daughter-in-law providing the muscle for him. And why not? Howard expected Alexa to do everything else around here.

Calling softly to Miz Elsie, so as not to alarm her, Alexa approached. The cow bellowed and strained, but didn't attempt to gain its feet.

"Damn, the calf is coming backward and upside down," Alexa muttered. "I'm not sure it's still alive."

Taking the surgical gloves from her pocket, Alexa

handed a pair to Chance, then slipped a pair on her hands.
"Don't risk hurting your leg," she insisted. "This looks to
be one hard pull."

Together, they knelt down to loop the chain around the
calf's hooves. Slowly, steadily, they pulled the calf. Chance
felt the strain on his knee the instant he dug in his heels
and applied muscle. This unnatural birth was as hard on
him as it was on the calf and mother cow. All of them
would walk away gingerly from the experience, he predicted.

Several tedious minutes later, the newborn calf lay
slumped in the grass—unbreathing.

Chance grabbed the calf by its legs, lifting it, then drop-
ping it, forcing it to breathe. "Come on, fella, do us both
a favor and suck some air," he demanded.

Eventually, the calf's ribs rose and fell. A feeble bawl
broke the tense silence. Grinning triumphantly, Alexa gave
Chance the high five.

"Nice work, cowboy. Howard needs every calf he can
get to keep his half of this ranch afloat."

A strange sensation pooled in Chance's belly as he stood
aside to watch the Limousin cow struggle to her feet to
cleanse her newborn. Working side by side with Alexa to
bring new life into the world had the power to touch even
the toughest cowboy.

Somewhere along the way, he and Alexa had become
more than co-workers. They'd become friends and lovers.
Chance wasn't sure that was a good thing—given the complicated situation. He didn't need to get tangled up in an
emotional bond that might eventually pull his heart out by
the taproot. He didn't want to hurt Alexa, either. She was
beginning to mean too much to him. Neither did he want
to upset Howard, who had opened his ranch to injured cowboys.

Damn, as much as Howard annoyed him for taking Alexa
for granted and singing high praises to an unworthy son,

Chance was still grateful for a place to recuperate. Talk about mixed emotions!

And how the hell would Chance cope when he returned to the circuit and felt loneliness creeping up on him? He'd never dealt with a situation remotely close to what he was experiencing with Alexa and her son. Did he dare hope for more? How was he to handle this relationship?

Certainly not the way Dan Tipton had, Chance mused. He couldn't bear the thought of putting Alexa through the same unhappiness she had discovered with Dan and his rambling way of life. Dan had cut and run when things got tough on the ranch. To Chance's way of thinking that was a coward's way out.

Maybe it was better to run first, to maintain a safe emotional distance. Any ties formed at Rocking T were dangerous to Chance's peace of mind, and everyone else concerned.

Chance was still wrestling with those disturbing thoughts when he heard the truck pull into the driveway. He hadn't realized he was standing so close to Alexa until she glided away, putting a respectable distance between them. What they had shared ended abruptly, and Chance was forced to retreat behind the wall of pretense…and he told himself it was for the best.

"Mom! We're home!" Zack hollered as he bounded from the truck.

Alexa waved her arms to gain Howard and Zack's attention. "Down here!"

The old man hobbled downhill, while Zack sprinted to the corral.

"You should have gone to the rodeo with us," Zack said excitedly. "It was really fun. Me and Grandpa—"

"Grandpa and I," Alexa correctly gently.

"Yeah, we got to see the saddle bronc riding, the bull riding and some bullfights!"

Howard leaned his forearms on the fence rail and smiled

in satisfaction. "I see Miz Elsie came through like the trouper she is."

"She had considerably more trouble than usual," Alexa informed him. "Chance and I had to pull the calf. She can't handle another difficult delivery like this one. This should be her last calf."

Howard waved off her concern, as if her opinion was of no consequence to him. Chance gnashed his teeth. The old man needed a serious attitude adjustment.

"You just stick to your bed-and-breakfast and let me handle the cattle operation."

Chance had to turn away to prevent from rushing to Alexa's defense. He told himself he was a fool to become more involved than he already was.

Damn it, who did Howard think was doing most of the work around here? Alexa had proved to him that she could handle cattle, had done it many times before. She knew about livestock, but as usual Howard gave her little credit.

While Zack yammered about the rodeo contestants he'd met, Howard motioned his family toward the house. Chance was left standing outside the circle—where he belonged. That was where he had always been, stuck outside, he reminded himself. He knew the role, knew his place at Rocking T. Too bad he had such a hard time playing the role established for him.

Chapter Nine

For two days, Alexa worked feverishly on renovations. The kitchen appliances were to be delivered at the end of the week, and she was down on hands and knees laying tile, while Chester provided instruction and assistance in his limited physical capacity.

"Chance stopped in yesterday to help me hang the ceiling fan in the dining room," Chester said conversationally. "Nice man, that cowboy. Noticed the two of you were at the restaurant together Saturday night."

Alexa's hand stalled over the tile. If Howard got wind of her date, he would come unglued. Suddenly, Alexa was filled with wary trepidation. She had been so wrapped up in her struggle of conflicting emotion that she forgot to consider the possibility of being seen and having to explain her date to Howard.

Although she kept telling herself she was entitled to her own life, could do as she pleased, she knew she was kidding herself. Her life hadn't been her own since she married Dan and moved to the ranch with her younger sister in tow.

"Howard wouldn't like it if he knew," Alexa murmured.

"Probably not." Chester handed her another ceramic tile. "He's got a regrettable fixation on his son. No offense intended, girl, but Dan wasn't the saint Howard makes him out to be."

"No offense taken. I've tried to convince Howard to get on with his life, but he is determined that Zack believes his father is here in spirit."

"That leaves you in a bit of a fix, I'd say."

Alexa glanced up at the spry old man. "A bit. But I'll have the B-and-B to occupy me soon. Everything will work out."

"Maybe, but a pretty gal like you shouldn't settle for less. Won't be as much fun around here without Chance cracking corny jokes, referring to that stepladder as Grace and lending a helping hand when we need it."

"Chester?"

"Yeah?"

"Hand me another tile."

"And keep my nose out of your business?"

"You've got it."

Chester chuckled. "Sorry. Living with my wife for forty years must have caught up with me. Mildred thinks nosing into somebody else's business in a natural-born right."

"How is Mildred doing these days?" Alexa asked, anxious to switch topics of conversation.

"She's fine. Says they couldn't get along without her at the hospital, so she refuses to retire. I keep waiting for her to give up her position as chief nurse so we can do some traveling. If she stays on the job much longer, I'll be too old and feebleminded to remember where I'm going and my eyesight will be useless for sight-seeing."

Alexa sniffed at that. "Old, my foot. You can still climb

around on rafters with the best of them. I've seen you do it—"

"Hey, watch what you're doing, girl," Chester erupted. "That last tile you laid isn't square. I don't want to look down the seams of grout and see a flaw on this dining room floor. Pull up that tile and scrape off part of the mud beneath it."

Things were back to normal, Alexa mused, sighing thankfully. Chester was in his usual form of supervising the construction project, without touching upon sensitive subjects.

Alexa had seen very little of Chance the past few days. Howard had him riding fences and repairing sections where the cattle had reached through barbed wire to chomp on the johnsongrass that filled the ditches. The restlessness plaguing Alexa prompted her to pack up Zack for a drive into town. She didn't want to be alone with memories and futile longing.

What she was afraid might happen had happened. Her growing affection for Chance occupied her thoughts and she wrestled with her emotions more often than she preferred...

"Hey, Mom, where are we going?"

Alexa jerked her thoughts back to the present—and her attention to the road. Daydreaming while driving was dangerous business.

"I thought you said we were going to pick up Aunt Debs, then swing by the park. This isn't the way to Aunt Debs', is it?" Zack asked as he surveyed their surroundings.

"Sorry, that's what happens when you don't pay attention to your driving," she murmured. "When you lollygag you miss your turn. Don't forget that when you're old enough to drive."

"Are you okay, Mom?" Zack asked. "You sure haven't

talked much since me and—'' He halted abruptly. ''Since Grandpa and I came back from the rodeo. Chance hasn't said much, either. I asked him ten questions this afternoon before he finally answered one.''

Alexa wondered what occupied Chance's mind. Was he becoming restless, anxious to go down the road?

Howard had mentioned that Chance planned to ride at Fort Worth Rodeo the upcoming weekend. Howard had also mentioned that Chance's name had come up dozens of times during the trip to Tulsa. Although Howard hadn't come right out and said so, she knew the old man was concerned that Zack was getting too attached to Chance. In Howard's book, anyone who overshadowed Dan's shining memory was a threat.

For everyone concerned it was best that Chance gathered his gear and left Rocking T. That was what was best, but Alexa's heart twisted in her chest at the prospect of telling Chance goodbye forever.

Time was running out for her. Blessing though it probably was, Alexa knew she was going to miss Chance terribly. He'd taught her to smile again, taught her not to take every facet of her life so seriously. He'd brought joy back into her life and had made a place for himself in Zack's heart.

The anticipation of opening the bed-and-breakfast wasn't as intense as it had been. Far as Alexa could tell, her work was going to be a miserable substitute for the sensations that channeled through her when she became the recipient of one of Chance's roguish smiles.

Damn that cowboy! She had accepted the limitations of her life—until he came along.

Alexa pulled into the apartment parking lot to see Deb waiting. Deb was dressed in blue jeans and a ragged T-shirt that had various colors of paint splattered on it.

''Howdy, kiddo,'' Deb said as she climbed into the truck.

''What happened to you, Aunt Debs?''

"I spilled a little paint," she informed her nephew. "There's more on me than on the canvas." She cut Alexa a quick glance. "Yoo-hoo, anybody there?"

Alexa forced a smile as she drove off to pick up one of Zack's schoolmates for a romp through the park. "I'm here, just thinking."

"Must be deep thoughts."

The instant Zack and his friend, Sid, raced off to the merry-go-round, Deb wheeled on Alexa. "Okay, the boys are out of earshot. So what's going on, sis?"

"The only thing going on is that I'm tiling the dining room floor at the B-and-B," Alexa said evasively.

Deb pinned her sister with a dubious stare. "You've been distracted since you picked me up. I assume this has more to do with your weekend date than laying tile."

"The date was fine," Alexa insisted.

"Fine?" Deb echoed sarcastically. "Considering the way you and Butler were making sheep eyes at each other while you were dancing, immediately before you ducked out of the honky-tonk, I'd say the electromagnetic field surrounding you was sizzling with sparks."

"Drop it, nosy."

Deb eyed her sister for a long, ponderous moment. "So you slept with him," she concluded.

Alexa's temper flared like a blow torch. "Did you sleep with the doctor?" she flung back.

"Certainly not. It was our first official date," she replied. "He did make a house call Sunday night, but we only rented a movie for the VCR."

Alexa stared into the distance, watching Zack and Sid barrel toward the trio of slipper slides. "I should have stayed home from that date," she admitted miserably. "It was a mistake to think I could have a life outside the confines of the ranch. Chance will be leaving at the end of the week, and I don't want him to go."

"Uh-oh." Deb sighed audibly. "You did it, didn't you?

You fell for that handsome cowboy. I convinced you to take a walk on the wild side and I dressed you up like a Barbie doll. You were supposed to kick up your heels and live a little.

"Oh, Alexa, I feel awful about this. I just wanted you to get away from all your responsibilities and enjoy yourself for the first time in years. I didn't want to see you hurt and suffering!"

It was only natural for Alexa to wrap her arm compassionately around her sister. Alexa had done it for thirteen years. She had become the shoulder Deb cried on when life dealt staggering blows. Even now, aching though Alexa's heart was, she set aside her own feelings to console Deb.

"It's okay, sis. It's not like this is the first disappointment I've had to overcome. I can handle it. Don't worry about it."

"I'm responsible," Deb muttered as she hugged Alexa close. "I opened my big mouth, tried to dole out advice and you took the fall. I should have known this was serious or you wouldn't have contemplated accepting the date. You never accept dates. Criminy, what have I done to you!"

"You wanted me to have a good time. I had a grand time, in fact. It's my fault that I take things more seriously than you do. When you make up your mind that you're dating for the simple pleasure of a man's companionship you keep the situation light and carefree. But not me, I'm too much out of practice to keep my feelings casual."

Deb stared at her intently. "Does Chance know how you feel about him?"

Alexa plunked down on the park bench. "I'm not certain how I feel," she hedged.

"Yeah, right," Deb sniffed. "Are you in a state of denial here?"

Yes, maybe she was. Alexa was too humiliated to come right out and tell her sister that she'd fallen in love with a rambler. But what did it matter if she had fallen in love?

It changed nothing. Chance would still be just as gone this weekend.

"You didn't tell him," Deb guessed accurately. "Does Howard suspect anything?"

"No, thank goodness. If he knew, I expect he would have exploded long before now. Things seem to be progressing as usual with Howard, except that he mentioned Zack's growing attachment to Chance, and is concerned about it."

"It seems to me I should introduce you to this friend of mine. I'll make arrangements so the two of you can go out."

Alexa stared incredulously at Deb. "Are you out of your mind? That isn't a solution to my problem."

"Sure it is," Deb said enthusiastically. "First of all, it will take your mind off that cowboy. Secondly, it will allow Howard to adjust to the idea that you need a social life."

"No, it wouldn't," Alexa contradicted. "In Howard's eyes, one date constitutes an unforgivable betrayal of Dan's memory. Two dates would suggest I'm running fast and loose."

Deb waved away Alexa's concern with the flick of her paint-splattered wrist. "This whole strategy is designed to give Howard the reality check he needs and to take your mind off Butler. Once Howard grows accustomed to the idea of your dating, he'll simmer down, especially when he realizes you're not serious about any of the men I set you up with."

"There are too many flaws in your scheme," Alexa insisted. "No matter how casual the dates, Howard will think I'm fooling around, tarnishing the memory of my marriage. Howard never saw another woman after his wife died. He expects no less of me."

"You're thirty years old and Howard is more than sixty, for crying out loud!"

"That makes no difference to Howard. He believes in eternal loyalty, and I'm the one who has to live with him."

Deb slumped onto the park bench. "I totally disapprove of the hold Howard has over you. He should get down on his arthritic knees and thank his lucky stars that he has you. Instead, he makes you fetch and heel, has you afraid to enjoy male companionship, even on a casual basis.

"And as for Butler, I'd like to kick his butt all the way back to Texas."

"Montana is his home state," Alexa informed her.

"Montana then," Deb fumed. "If he isn't as crazy over you as you are over him then he's the world's biggest fool!"

"Just drop it, sis," Alexa requested. "I'm going to be fine. Life will be back to normal by next week."

To Alexa's relief, Deb backed off. She chatted about the cute odds and ends she had selected to decorate the bed-and-breakfast, then described her latest landscape painting. For the next hour, Alexa sat back and watched Zack enjoy himself. Not so long ago, that had been Alexa's only form of entertainment.

Her commitment was—first and foremost—to her son, Alexa reminded herself. That's the way it was. That's the way it would stay, no matter what the personal sacrifice.

Chance tapped lightly at the kitchen door, prompting Alexa to glance up from the financial ledgers scattered on the table. "I came to get Zack. I promised to take him fishing when he finished his homework."

The words were no sooner out of his mouth than Zack appeared in the doorway. Sheer excitement glowed on his face.

"Wanna come with us, Mom?"

"I'd love to, but you men better go without me. I have bills to pay and a budget to balance."

Chance's gaze remained fixed on Alexa while he held

open the door for Zack. The distance growing between them bothered him. Not that he could do a damn thing about it. But that sadness he detected in Alexa's luminous green eyes, even when she smiled, tore his heart out. He caught himself thinking that she was missing him, just as he was missing her. But then he reminded himself that if she fell in love with him, he wasn't sure what he could do about it. The responsibility of being loved held too many pitfalls, especially around here.

Chance knew Alexa well enough to realize that she wasn't into reckless flings. He also knew her distaste for men of his profession. But something had sparked between them, something hot and wild and volatile. Hell, he still woke up in cold sweats, wanting her until he ached with it, telling himself he'd had all of Alexa that he was ever going to get.

"Aren't you coming, Chance?" Zack prompted.

Chance mustered a carefree grin and turned away from his troubled thoughts, away from the woman who provoked them. "Sure thing, rookie. Let's go bait some hooks."

Twenty minutes later, Chance and Zack were sitting on a blanket, watching their colorful corks drift across the surface of the stream.

"How long do we have to wait for the fish?" Zack asked impatiently.

"Until the fish get hungry."

Zack frowned pensively. "*We* ate two hours ago. What time do fish have supper?"

Just then Chance's cork bobbled. "Better come help me, kid," he requested. "I can't stand up very fast on this gimpy leg. You need to be ready to take over for me if we get a bite."

Chance tugged on the line, ensuring the fish was snagged before he handed the fishing rod to Zack. "Reel it in and let's see if we caught something."

Zack yanked back, just as Chance had instructed. When

he reeled in again, he stumbled backward, plopping down on his rear. "Whoa! This must be a big sucker."

The fish ran away with the line, forcing Chance to lift Zack onto his lap so he could help reel in their catch.

"Pull…reel," Chance instructed.

Zack did as he was told, his eyes glued to the stream, anxious to catch sight of the fish.

"Again, kid. Don't let the big sucker get away."

By the time they reeled in their catch, Zack was hopping up and down in excitement and yammering ninety miles an hour. "We did it. We really caught a fish!"

Chance braced his weak leg to pull the channel cat ashore. "We won't have to wonder what to have for supper tomorrow night, will we—?"

When Chance tried to step sideways to steady himself, he realized Zack was underfoot, hoping for an up-close view of unhooking the fish. Chance shifted awkwardly on his unstable leg, then tripped over Zack.

"Argh!" he yelped when his legs got tangled up with Zack's. Thrown off balance, they both landed with a splash.

Chance swallowed a mouthful of water before he could come up for air.

Zack clambered to his feet in waist-deep water and stared apprehensively at Chance. "Are you gonna yell at me for tripping you up?"

The kid looked so uneasy and miserable while he stood there with moss clinging to his shirt that Chance threw back his head and laughed. "No, rookie, I'm not going to yell at you," he said between snickers. "I needed a bath after the hard day's labor I put in."

The kid relaxed noticeably. "Sorry 'bout that, Chance."

"No problem," Chance said as he floundered to his feet, still holding the wriggling catfish.

"Hand me the knife from the tackle box," he requested. "We'll clean this sucker, right on the spot."

While Chance dressed the oversize channel cat Zack studied him intently. "Are you married?"

"Nope."

"Neither is my mom. Not anymore."

"I know," Chance murmured, wondering where this conversation was headed.

Zack peered up at him very seriously and Chance felt that now-familiar tug on his heartstrings. "If you want to marry my mom, I can ask her if it would be okay with her."

Chance nearly sliced off his forefinger. "Um…well, kid, that's not exactly how it works."

While Chance went about the task of skinning the fish, Zack peered questioningly at him. "How does it work?"

Chance squirmed in his skin. Never had he imagined himself having this kind of conversation with a child. He felt inadequate, awkward. "Well, the first thing you're supposed to do is fall in love, then you make a commitment—"

"What's that?"

"That's when you promise to care for someone, to look out for them, make them happy."

"Care for somebody, like when they're sick?" Zack asked.

"Not just when they're sick, but all the time, even if you'd rather do something for yourself. But you don't want to see that very special person in your life unhappy so you put their feelings and needs first."

Zack nodded thoughtfully as he watched Chance clean the fish. "You mean like when I want your leg to get better so it won't hurt you anymore, but I don't want it to get better because I know you'll go away and never come back."

Chance swallowed the lump that suddenly clogged his throat. "Yeah, like that, kid. You want what's best for someone you love, even if you have to sacrifice something you want to see them get it.''

Wide, innocent eyes lifted to Chance. ''That's the way I love you,'' he said honestly, openly. ''I said my prayers and asked for you to be my dad.''

''Ouch!'' Chance shook off the burning sensation. Zack's comment had caught him off guard, causing him to cut a chunk out of his finger.

''You okay, Chance?''

''I'm okay,'' Chance mumbled.

But he wasn't the slightest bit okay. This kid was killing him by inches, making him want things he wasn't sure he deserved, things he wasn't sure he could handle, especially since his father had proved such a lousy role model for him.

Chance had no positive experience to draw upon when it came to raising children. He wasn't sure how to offer guidance to this young boy. Damn, how'd he get into this mess in the first place?

''I never had anyone to teach me to play baseball and basketball, except Mom. She's not too good at it, but I didn't tell her that,'' the boy confided. ''I never had anyone to take me fishing before, either. The other kids at school do this kind of stuff all the time with their dads.''

The kid was breaking Chance's heart. He felt himself getting so choked up that he couldn't breathe. And damn it, he was a grown man, callused with years of hard lessons and unpleasant experience.

No one had been around to do those things with Chance, either. He'd grown up thinking it was his fault his parents divorced, his fault that neither parent wanted anything to do with him. Since his arrival at Rocking T, Chance had found himself offering Zack uncounted hours of fatherly companionship, hoping he could make a small difference in the boy's life, hoping it would be enough.

But would it ever be enough? There was an empty space

in Zack's life and he was reaching out, looking for someone to fill it. Zack was a bright kid. He knew his friends shared a closeness with their fathers, a closeness that he was missing. Zack needed a man in his life, but Howard forbade it. Howard, good as he was to the boy, couldn't supply all the things Zack needed.

Chance felt the impulsive urge to haul this adorable kid off with him, to become the father Chance had never had himself. But, of course, that was an impossibility. Zack's place was with his mother and grandfather, not some rambling cowboy who had nowhere to call home.

Damn, Chance thought to himself as he gave way to the urge to hug Zack. He had warned himself not to get too attached to the kid, knowing they would both be hurt. Chance had known better, yet here he was, hugging the stuffing out of Zack and receiving a hug in return.

Chance sighed, defeated. He'd turned out to be as big a sucker as the fish.

Chance propped himself up on the examination table at the health clinic in Willowvale. Empty bottles of pain pills and muscle relaxers were stuffed in his shirt pocket. As soon as the physician refilled his prescriptions he was leaving Rocking T. The whole situation had gotten to him, and besides, he had long since paid the entry fees for the rodeo in Fort Worth.

He had to get out of here, Chance kept telling himself. It wasn't because he was restless, anxious to return to the rodeo circuit. It was because of Alexa and Zack. He'd let them get too close, let them matter too damn much.

Leaving was going to kill him, he knew.

Staying would kill him, too.

Seeing Alexa without being able to touch her, without being able to toss a teasing comment to make her smile was torment, pure and simple. Hiding his feelings from

Howard made him feel devious and ungrateful. But damn it, Chance was between the proverbial rock and hard spot.

That fishing expedition with Zack the previous night had been another form of torture for Chance. The kid had gotten entirely too attached, starting to dream up ways to ensure Chance remained at Rocking T. To a child, things seemed so simple and uncomplicated, easy to fix. To adults, things like conflicting emotions and outside influences muddied the water.

Accepting the responsibility of another man's family, especially the Tipton family, was overwhelming to Chance. He had so few family experiences to draw upon. What if he followed the insane impulse to stay a while longer, then turned out to be as big a jerk as Dan Tipton? What if the call to follow the only life-style he knew and understood got so intense that he took his frustration out on Alexa and Zack?

No, Chance told himself for the umpteenth time, he had unintentionally disrupted life at Rocking T too much already. He had stirred up emotions he'd kept dead and buried since childhood. His heart and head kept battling over what was the right thing to do. Heaven knew, Chance's attempt to do his good deed for the year had caused more complications than he'd ever imagined.

When the door swung open, Chance manufactured a cheerful smile for Kurt Stevenson, M.D. "Howdy, Harvard." Chance thought the teasing nickname fit the Easterner perfectly. "How's the world treating you?"

Kurt returned the smile. "Can't complain." He glanced at the information sheet on the clipboard that Chance had filled out during his stint in the reception room. "How many times have you injured this strained knee of yours?"

"This year?" Chance asked nonchalantly. "Just once."

Kurt raised a sandy-colored brow. "This is an aggravated injury, I presume. You failed to fill in that particular blank on the questionnaire."

Chance grinned. "My hand was getting tired of writing. You know how us cowboys are, Doc. All we know is how to hang on to the back of a bronc and bull."

"Right." Kurt smirked wryly. "My educated guess is that the code of rodeo cowboys states than anyone who fusses and whines about his injuries is labeled a sissy. Therefore, answering medical questionnaires is taboo."

Chance chuckled. "You catch on quick, Harvard. That's where the phrase 'cowboy up' applies. Riding and competing while injured is a way of life on the suicide circuit. The only time you back down is when you can't physically hold your seat on a saddle."

Kurt nodded pensively. "Tough way to make a living."

Not so tough, thought Chance. The physical pain—he'd found out recently—was easier to bear than the emotional anguish of waging war between good sense and reckless whim. Being horse-kicked only hurt for a day or two. But remembering the look on Zack's face—when Chance turned down the arrangements for him and Alexa to marry and become a family—hung on like a terminal illness. Chance wasn't sure he'd ever recover from the kaleidoscope of emotions that kid put him through during their fishing expedition.

"Well, let's have a look at the knee," Kurt said as he approached the examination table.

When the physician raised Chance's gimpy leg to a sharp angle, then extended it, Chance bit back a grimace. While Kurt poked, prodded and manipulated the leg into several killer positions, Chance ordered himself not to let out a betraying howl of agony.

"Have you had an X-ray?" Kurt questioned in a businesslike tone.

Chance winced again as Kurt rotated his scarred leg. "Look, Harvard, I realize you're a conscientious physician, and I appreciate the fact that you're just doing your job here. But I don't need a clean bill of health with your notarized signature to return to the rodeo circuit. All I need is refills for my prescription in case I strain the knee at Fort Worth.''

Kurt stared him squarely in the eye. ''You realize you need surgery to repair all the ligament and tendon damage around the patella, don't you? There's a reason why this knee comes out of its socket when pressure is placed on it. There is very little cartilage to hold the patella and tibia in place. In your case, this brace is more than just protective gear. It is quite literally holding your leg together.''

''Then I guess I got a real bargain, didn't I? This brace is worth twice as much as I paid for it,'' Chance replied flippantly.

Kurt snorted in disapproval. ''A little more healing time spent at Rocking T is what this doctor orders.''

''No can do, Harvard. I've got places to go and things to do.''

Kurt cocked a brow as he extended his hand, silently requesting the chance to look at the prescription bottles. ''Oh really? It seemed to me that you and Alexa were getting along quite well last weekend. What's the rush to leave? No man in his right mind would be anxious to leave a woman like Alexa behind.''

''Who said anything about being in my right mind?'' Chance popped off.

Kurt shook his head. ''Too bad I can't write out prescriptions to cure fools. I'd have you ingesting double doses of medication.''

Chance scowled. He was losing his good disposition and Harvard was prying into matters that were none of his concern. ''I didn't come here for psychological counseling. Just write me a prescription and I'm out of here.''

''My recommendation is surgery. My second recommendation is an entire month of R and R.''

If Chance stayed at Rocking T for another month he would need psychological consultation. His emotions, his forbidden dreams, were already in a state of traumatic turmoil. No, he wasn't staying here. It was time to hit the road.

While Chance fastened himself into his blue jeans, Kurt leaned casually against the counter, staring pensively at the cowboy. "Since you don't seem receptive to advice, maybe you could give it."

Chance's thick brow quirked. The preppy doctor wanted *his* opinion on something? "Sure, I can spout cowboy philosophy from dusk till dawn. What kind of advice are you looking for?"

Kurt gazed very solemnly at him. "How do you get a country girl like Deb Parsons to take you seriously?"

The question startled Chance. Why wouldn't any woman be interested in a distinguished, refined, good-looking physician who had more degrees than a thermometer?

"She doesn't?" Chance chirped.

Kurt shook his head. "She seems to enjoy herself when we're together, but she is seeing other men. I don't want to sound like some Neanderthal, but I'd prefer to be the only man in her life right now."

Chance wasn't sure he was the man to supply Harvard—who'd apparently gotten hooked on the fun-loving Deb Parsons—with advice. Hell, Chance couldn't even hold on to the one relationship that had ever meant anything to him. He was a fine one to give suggestions to Harvard.

"All I can suggest is sweeping the lady off her feet and keep turning her head," Chance said finally. "Show her there is something deeper than the reserved doctor under those scrubs."

Kurt blinked. "You think I'm too stuffy?"

Chance eased off the examination table and held out his hand, requesting the prescriptions. "I didn't say that, you did. Of course, I'm too rough-and-tumble and unsophisticated for most people's taste, so what the hell do I know?"

Absently, Kurt scribbled the prescriptions. "Maybe

you're right. Maybe the reason Debra doesn't take me seriously is because she thinks I'm too serious minded.'' He tried out a reckless grin. ''Better?''

''Much,'' Chance complimented.

''So, how much do I owe you for the consultation?''

Chance smiled in amusement. He kinda liked Harvard, though they were obviously cut from different bolts of cloth. ''Not a thing, but I would like for you to repay me by keeping an eye out for Alexa and her kid.''

''Consider it done, Country,'' Kurt teased. ''And go easy on that knee or I'll haul you back here to surgically implant pins in that leg.''

''There's a cheery thought,'' Chance said as he limped out the door.

During the drive to the ranch, Chance mentally prepared himself for his final departure. He'd give Zack intensive lessons in basketball. And after a few more pointers for baseball, he would encourage Alexa to use the notes she'd taken to remind Zack of his newly acquired skills. Alexa would see that Zack didn't forget what he'd learned.

Alexa...

A maelstrom of emotions strummed through Chance as he steered the jalopy truck off the paved highway and followed the gravel road to the ranch. Sometimes he wished he'd never met her, wished he could have gone merrily on his way without getting sentimentally attached. He just hoped she hadn't gotten overly attached to him. He didn't want to hurt her. Heaven knew she had endured enough hurt in her lifetime....

Chance blinked, startled. What the hell was happening here? *He* was hurting, too. *He* had endured his share of anguish during his rotten childhood. But he was more concerned about how Alexa felt, how she would deal with his absence.

Oh man, he couldn't afford to love Alexa and her adorable kid. How could he focus on rodeo competition if he was carrying emotional baggage like that in the saddle with him?

But there it was, flat out, right smack-dab in the open. Chance had gone and fallen in love with both of them. Although he was pretty sure he had convinced Alexa that he was nothing like her husband, Chance and Dan shared the same profession—one Alexa strongly disapproved of.

She had good reason, Chance allowed. She'd never had a shoulder to cry on, the emotional support occasionally needed. Even if Howard Tipton didn't loom between him and Alexa like an impassable mountain range, Alexa's distaste for Chance's profession would always be a sore spot between them.

As for Chance, accepting the responsibility of being loved and relied upon, after years of living footloose, raised all sorts of alarming questions. What if he didn't have staying power? His parents hadn't. They broke up like a meteor hitting the earth's atmosphere. All Chance had to his credit was how *not* to handle a relationship, how *not* to raise a child.

No, it was more sensible to remain on the path he'd followed for years. Dealing with contrary horses and cattle in an arena didn't involve emotional impacts, only physical ones. Failing in a rodeo event simply meant the loss of a paycheck, eating dirt and bruising pride. But failing at a relationship that might involve life-altering repercussions? He was the product of those repercussions and he wouldn't wish his life on his worst enemy.

Gather your gear and ride off, cowboy, Chance told himself.

Alexa didn't need a man in her life. Hell, she had managed just fine until Chance showed up. He didn't need a woman, and he had survived well enough. He would simply board the plane for Texas, knowing it was for the best, knowing he had no other choice—not without stirring up a whole new set of problems.

Chapter Ten

Alexa sat on the porch, watching intently as Chance gave Zack the final sports lesson. Her heart was breaking, knowing this cowboy was walking out of their lives first thing in the morning. Howard had already lined up another hired hand who had sustained cracked ribs when the bull he was riding threw him on the turf and stepped on him. In fact, Howard was waiting at the airport to pick up the next cowboy bound for Rocking T's rehab center.

Alexa studied Chance with the intensity of a woman who longed to commit every gesture, every easy smile, to memory. She would recall the sound of his voice, his laughter, the husky whisper that sent tingles flooding through her.

She could get through this, she told herself. She had to. She wouldn't ask Chance to make return visits. That would be too painful. Better to make a clean break. Better for Zack, too.

Glancing up, Alexa watched Howard and the injured cowboy pull into the driveway. The young man, Pecos

Smith, who looked to be about the same age as her sister, eased down from the truck. He looked like a man in considerable pain. His colorless face held a pinched expression. His lips were compressed in a line as tight as stretched fence wire. How Pecos was supposed to handle ranch chores in his condition Alexa couldn't imagine. But Howard would undoubtedly assign minimal duties while Pecos was under the weather.

For all Howard's faults, his policy of lending a helping hand to down-on-their-luck cowboys was admirable. Men who had nowhere to go, who needed room and board, found sanctuary here. Howard was a decent man; he simply had the compulsive need to keep his son's memory alive.

As for his habit of taking Alexa for granted, she could deal with that, had dealt with being overlooked for years. Howard was good to his grandson, and that counted for a lot in Alexa's book.

After quick introductions, Chance showed Pecos to the bunkhouse. Zack dogged Chance's heels. The boy was going to miss Chance terribly. Hopefully, Pecos wouldn't ignore Zack completely, Alexa mused.

"It's a good thing Chance is leaving," Howard mumbled as he watched the cowboys amble away. "It bothers me the way Zack has been carrying on. All I've heard lately is 'Chance did this. Chance did that. Chance said this and that.'" Howard snorted in annoyance. "If I hear how perfect Chance Butler is one more time, I'll be ready to pull out what's left of my hair."

Alexa said nothing. Howard would throw a ring-tailed fit if he knew she thought Chance Butler was perfect in every way but one. He was still a rodeo cowboy.

"Pecos didn't get to eat on the plane," Howard said as he spun toward the house. "Fix him something to eat, will you? I'm due at my poker game this evening."

"Sure, no problem." Alexa followed Howard into the kitchen to reheat leftovers.

No problem, she could handle everything. She'd done it dozens of times. This was just another day in the life of Riley.

Except for one minor detail, thought Alexa. The man who had given her life new meaning was about to ride away forever.

No problem?

Yeah, right.

Chance wore a rut in the floorboards with his restless pacing. He couldn't turn on the TV in the bunkhouse, because Pecos was sleeping. Chance supposed he could stroll up to the house for a game of checkers with Zack, but he didn't think he could stand being in the same room with Alexa without touching her.

Chance checked his watch. Nine-thirty. Zack would already be tucked in bed by now. The kid had a school bus to catch bright and early in the morning. By now, Alexa would have the kitchen tidied up. She was probably working on the advertising flyers for the B-and-B. Chance should save his goodbye until morning....

A shadow moved past the window. Chance glanced toward the storm door to see a trim silhouette standing on the porch. Every consoling platitude he'd preached to himself during the day flew out the window the instant he saw Alexa standing on the other side of the glass door, staring at him.

Chance cast the sleeping Pecos a quick glance, then eased open the door. "Something wrong, Al?"

He would try to keep the mood light, he told himself. He would thank her for her hospitality, make all the right noises about how he'd enjoyed his stay at Rocking T. Then he would say farewell and crawl into his bunk and count several flocks of sheep, in hopes of falling asleep sometime before dawn.

Alexa stepped off the porch so she wouldn't disturb the

sleeping cowboy. Chance found himself limping along behind her, his hands tucked deep in his hip pockets so he didn't give way to the temptation of reaching out to touch her—and lose all ability to think logically.

"I just wanted you to know how much I appreciate all your help with my construction project, all the tips you gave Zack," Alexa murmured without glancing in his direction.

"Glad to do it, Al. Working with Zack appeased the deprived kid in me."

Alexa shifted uneasily from one booted foot to the other. So did Chance.

"Well, I won't keep you. I'm sure you have packing to do."

When she turned and walked away Chance's stomach dropped to his aching knee. He shouldn't follow her back to the house—but his boots were already doing the walking. She seemed to know why he was following her, didn't object.

Without a word, Chance took her hand and led her through the kitchen, up the staircase. When they reached the second floor Alexa turned to the left, walking silently toward the end of the hall.

Chance had never set foot in her room. He expected it to be a monument to Dan. But to his surprise only one eight-by-ten glossy sat on the dresser. The room was simply furnished, testifying to Alexa's down-to-earth life-style, the lack of luxuries her husband and father-in-law sent her way.

His thoughts trailed off when Alexa walked into his arms and kissed him in a way that ignited instantaneous fires in his blood. Chance kissed her back—with the desperation of a man who understood that he was about to lose something very special and dear to him.

"I'm sorry," she whispered against his lips. "I know I shouldn't have come to the bunkhouse, but I wanted to see you one last time. I want you." She tugged on his T-shirt, her hands gliding beneath the fabric to make stimulating contact with the washboard muscles of his belly. "If I know nothing else, I know that I haven't stopped wanting you."

Chance moaned the instant her searching fingertips brushed over his flesh. One touch and he was hot and aching, shaking with need. One kiss and he was starving to death for the taste of her.

Gentle patience fell by the wayside as his arms contracted around Alexa. Just once more, he needed to experience her, absorb her, needed to express and communicate the emotions he'd carefully held in check.

Chance wasn't even sure how and when they got to the king-size bed. A trail of clothes lay on the floor—evidence of where they had been and where they were going. Chance tumbled Alexa down on the patchwork bedspread, his hands moving restlessly, aching to rediscover every satiny inch of her, to pleasure her, to share this last stolen moment he knew would end in mindless ecstasy.

To Chance's surprise, and tormented delight, Alexa stilled his hands while she brushed a path of warm, moist kisses over his collarbone, his chest. She seemed to have her heart set on arousing him.

Chance smiled to himself. Alexa was halfway there and she didn't even know it. And, he thought, it was so like Alexa to place someone else's needs above her own, to please rather than expect to be pleased....

Chance swallowed a roomful of air when she divested him of his jeans and caressed him brazenly. The touch of her hands and lips on his most sensitive flesh had him hissing through his teeth in an attempt to keep from screaming in unholy torment. His body throbbed with desire, and he fairly shook with the need she summoned so easily from him.

"No more," he wheezed. "I swear you're killing me.... Have mercy."

She raised her head to grin seductively while she held

him hot and aching in her hand. ''Mercy will have to wait her turn with you, cowboy. I'm not turning you loose just yet.''

Chance tried to chuckle, but in the next heartbeat she was moving her heated mouth over his aroused flesh and he couldn't breathe. Jaw clenched, eyes squeezed shut, he battled the wild sensations that riveted him. His body thrummed with such intense need that he feared he was about to explode with it.

Things were moving entirely too fast. He was out of control. He wanted to make love to her slowly, thoroughly, as if they had all the time in the world to pleasure each other. But instinct kicked into high gear when Alexa continued to caress him so intimately, arouse him beyond bearing.

Groaning, Chance hooked his arm around her waist and pulled her beneath him. He wanted to sink into her, become the blazing flame of passion that was him, was her. Hands shaking, he drew her knees around his hips, lifting her to him.

Though he felt like a horny teenager with a bad case of the hots, he couldn't seem to slow down. He glided over her, taking possession of her body—and became possessed by her.

Although she had asked for nothing but this moment, he felt as if he had handed his heart and soul over to her. He would never be able to make love to Alexa with just his body, he knew. She called something deeper and more powerful from him, some indefinable part of him that he hadn't realized existed until she came into his life.

Chance moved in age-old rhythm, fighting his roiling needs, vowing to take Alexa with him when he tumbled into the free fall of ecstasy. When she gasped, her nails biting into the corded tendons of his back, the world careened around him. Chance could feel her feminine body bathing him with the most intimate kind of caress, burning him in the hottest, sweetest kind of fire.

Passion slammed into him with such devastating force that all he could do was hold on to her. Shudder after helpless shudder rocked him, stole his breath, numbed his mind with intense pleasure. The impact of their lovemaking was so fierce and consuming that Chance was honestly surprised he hadn't passed out.

And then he heard the words whisper from her lips. Words that were both heaven and hell.

"I love you, Chance. Love you..."

He forced himself to lift his spinning head and peer into her shadowed face—and fell into the depths of her misty-green eyes. It was all there, the open sincerity, the grim acceptance that he was leaving and that she was prepared to bear the loss as she bore all else.

"Alexa, I—"

She touched her index finger to his lips to shush him. "It's all right. You don't have to say anything," she assured him softly. "I just want you to know that wherever you are, I'll be praying for your safety, your success, your happiness. Zack and I will both be there in spirit to cheer you on."

The sensations and emotions triggered by her words would have brought Chance to his knees, had he been standing. He wanted to return the satisfaction of knowing that she was wanted and needed, without making the situation more difficult. But Alexa was better off not knowing how much he cared, how much it troubled him to walk away from the best thing that had ever happened to him. She wasn't expecting whispered words of love from him.

If she believed he wouldn't be back, had already accepted it, then she was already way ahead of him in the count. Chance hadn't quite adjusted to the idea of his leaving, but obviously Alexa had. She had been down this road before, had learned to dodge every pothole in her path.

But just because Chance was reluctant to voice the emotion she aroused in him, didn't mean he couldn't express his affection in the silent language of passion. And to that dedicated purpose he touched Alexa with all the gentleness that was within him to give, with a tenderness that spun a web of erotic pleasure around her. He worshiped her with intimate caresses and kisses, shared every heated response. He felt her come undone in his arms and heard her words of love whispering over him as he made love to her with all that he was.

And for that sweet, stolen moment in time, every forbidden dream, every whimsical impossibility, was theirs for the taking.

Howard Tipton puffed on his cigar, then sipped his Jack Daniel's whiskey. Squinting through the smoke that hovered around him, he studied his poker hand. The joker winked back at him from between two red aces.

"You gonna raise or call, Tipton," Shorty McClain prompted impatiently. "It's getting late and I ain't getting any younger."

Howard tossed a five-spot into the center of the table in Shorty's musty basement, then he grinned smugly.

"Whoa, boys." Clem Sanders chuckled as he bit down on his stogie. "Ol' Howard must have himself one hell of a hand, judging by his expression. When this tightwad starts flashing around five-spots we're all in trouble." Clem slouched in his chair and shook his bald head. "This pot is getting too rich for my blood. I'm folding my tent and getting out before I get burned."

Shorty shot a glance at Howard's smile, then reevaluated his hand. "Oh hell," he said finally. "I'm out, too."

Pete Fowler tossed in his cards. "Okay, Tipton, show us what you've got. We know you're bursting with the need to flaunt that power hand."

A wide grin crinkled Howard's wrinkled features as he

spread each card on the table so his friends could see his hand. "Full house, aces and kings. Read 'em and weep."

As Howard raked in his winnings the other men scowled in frustration.

"Lucky old goat," Shorty grunted. "That's the second time this month you've cleaned me out of pocket change. How am I gonna take my sweet little granddaughter out for ice cream when I'm broke?"

Still grinning, Howard stuffed the money in the front pouch in his overalls, then polished off his drink. "Next week you can sign over your social security check," he teased.

"Me and the wife couldn't pay the bills if I did that." Ben Claremore took a long drag on his cigar, then eyed Howard quizzically. "Saw your daughter-in-law last weekend. How long has she been dating that stiff-legged cowboy that's staying at Rocking T?"

Howard's hand clenched around his glass. "You mean Chance Butler?"

"Don't know his name. I saw him and Alexa at the restaurant last Saturday night." He grinned around his smoking stogie. "That is some kind of good-looking woman when she's all dolled up."

Howard wasn't sure what he said next, couldn't remember anything except the raw fury pounding through him. Alexa had been fooling around with Chance while Howard was out of town?

Feelings of outrage and betrayal roiled through him as he stalked toward his pickup. He had to get home, had to ensure his carefully protected world wasn't falling down around his ankles.

"Damn her," Howard snarled as he mashed on the accelerator. "After all I've done for her!"

Taking the back roads home, Howard drove like a bat out of hell. He couldn't risk being pulled over by a cop, not when he'd had too much to drink and was seeing furious red.

"Damn Butler," Howard snarled as he kicked up a cloud of dust behind him.

Alexa accompanied Chance downstairs—and found her worst nightmare standing at the bottom of the steps. She could see the old man shaking, his fists clenched at his sides, his chest heaving with fury. Oh God! What was she going to say to defuse this situation?

When Chance moved protectively in front of her, Alexa tried to duck under his arm, but he held her at bay. "I'll handle this."

"Damn right you will," Howard seethed. "I offered you my hospitality, my generosity, a paycheck, and this is how you repay me. I told you Alexa was off-limits. You heard me loud and clear. Get your gear and get the hell off this ranch right this minute!"

"I'm sorry, Howard. I know you're feeling—"

"You don't know a damned thing about how I feel," Howard cut in. "*Perfect* Chance." Howard erupted in a disdainful snort. "Well, Zack wouldn't think you're so damn *perfect* in every way if he knew you were sneaking behind his back to sleep with his mother, betraying his trust and his father's memory!"

"Howard—" Alexa tried to cut in.

"I will deal with you later, Jezebel." Howard glared at her.

"This isn't her fault," Chance insisted as he boldly approached the outraged old man. "It's mine. All the anger you're feeling should be directed toward me."

Alexa felt tears burning her eyes and scalding her cheeks. Never had anyone stood up for her the way Chance was doing. Even when they both knew for a fact that she was the one who had gone to him, Chance accepted all the blame. *He* had the courage to take on Howard in the height of his towering fury.

"How long has this been going on, Butler?" Howard sneered hatefully. "I bet you couldn't wait for me and my grandson to hightail it to Tulsa so you could play house under my roof."

Howard's chest swelled like a hot-air balloon, and his eyes shot sparks that penetrated like pieces of shrapnel. "Well, I hope you twist off your damn knee at Fort Worth. And don't think you can come hobbling back here, because you aren't welcome, will never be welcome again! I'll get a restraining order if I have to. This is *my* home, *my* family, and you aren't going to sweet-talk your way in here to take over what I've spent years building!"

"No one is trying to take your ranch away from you," Chance said calmly. "No one is taking anything that belongs to you, Howard."

The old man's gnarled hand shot toward Alexa. "*She* does. My *grandson* does." He spit hatefully.

"Howard, you've got to calm down," Alexa insisted as she inched down the steps, alarmed by the wild look in his eyes, the erratic rise and fall of his chest. His face was such a bright shade of crimson that she feared he was about to work himself into a stroke.

When Alexa reached for Howard, he jerked away as if she were a poisonous snake about to strike him. "You really pulled the wool over my eyes with all your false concern for sending Zack off to the rodeo," he sputtered furiously. "But you were just itching for me to take Zack away for the weekend, weren't you? Then you got dressed up fit to kill and walked the streets so you could humiliate me from one end of town to the other!"

"Howard, lower your voice," Alexa murmured, casting an apprehensive glance upstairs where Zack slept. "You'll wake up the boy."

"You're a fine one to show concern now," Howard said

in disgust. "It's obvious that the only time you take Zack into consideration is when he doesn't interfere with this fling you have going with the not-so-perfect Chance Butler!"

"That's enough, Howard," Chance gritted out. "Alexa has done nothing to deserve your crude insults."

"Like hell she hasn't. She's turning out to be as much a flirt as her sister, who runs around with different men to match her moods. Well, I won't have the townfolks whispering that Alexa is a man's sure thing!"

"You leave Deb out of this," Alexa said heatedly. "This has nothing to do with her."

Howard flung Alexa a murderous glance, then hitched his thumb at Chance. "Get the hell out of here. If you're here in the morning, I'm calling the cops to haul you off. As far as I'm concerned, you both deserve a good shooting!"

Cursing mightily, Howard stormed toward his bedroom, then slammed the door.

Alexa sank limply onto the step, her face in her hands. "I'm so sorry," she said brokenly. "I was afraid he might find out, but I hoped it would be after you left. I never—"

Chance drew her to her feet and into the comforting circle of his arms. "I don't care what Howard thinks of me. It's you I'm worried about. I can't leave here, wondering and worrying what he might do. I want you to come with me."

Alexa gave her head a wild shake, her eyes glistening with tears. "I can't leave. This isn't your battle to fight, and it will be easier for me to return to Howard's good graces when you're gone. I'll find a way to smooth over the situation, even if I have to give a sworn statement in blood that I'll never go near another man."

And that was when Chance realized for certain that Alexa's whispered confession of love wasn't simply a mindless phrase uttered in the heat of passion. She cared enough to cut herself off from life again, to give Howard what he wanted—a permanent maid and waitress who catered to his every whim. There would be no other man in Alexa's life, no personal pleasure, only continual sacrifice. She would try to live up to Howard's expectations and allow the old man to fling Dan Tipton's memory in her face.

"I can't let you stay here," Chance told her. "We'll take Zack and—"

She stepped away from him. Her chin lifted to that determined angle he was quick to recognize. "Don't get all noble on me, Butler. I admit that I love you, but do you really think I need a man? I didn't have one around while I was married. You think I won't get over this? Better think again. I thought I loved Dan, too. I survived every disappointment and rejection, accepted the fact that I wasn't a priority in his life. I'm not a priority in your life, either. I *chose* to live for the moment. But the moment is gone and you will be, too."

Chance stood there, watching tears dribble down her cheeks, watching her wrap fierce pride and determination around her like an invisible shield. He knew she was nobly offering him an easy way out. It was so like her, damn it. She stayed to fight, to cope, to tolerate. He was expected to skulk away because that was what she had learned to expect from men like him.

The easy way out. That was the road Chance had followed all his life. No commitments except to himself, no emotional ties to bind, no burdensome responsibility. And now that he was standing here on the threshold of accepted responsibility—wondering if he would be reliable and adequate, wondering if he could become all the things his own father *hadn't* been—Alexa was slamming the door in his face. She was prepared to do it, in order to save him from the frustration and displeasure of dealing with the outraged Howard Tipton.

Damn noble of her, but infuriating, thought Chance. No

matter how much Alexa claimed to care for him, she still expected him to disappoint her, expected him to live down to her low opinion of cowboys. Her faith and trust in him were obviously limited.

"I've already said goodbye," she whispered through her tears. "Take my truck to town. The keys are in it. Leave it at the airport and I'll ask my sister to drive me in to pick it up tomorrow."

"Alexa—"

"Please leave," she interrupted. "If you care anything about me at all, get out of here. That's what you planned to do. That's what I want you to do. Now, damn it, do it!"

If he cared? Chance was awash with so many emotions that he didn't know what the hell to say or do. And when he stared into her wan face, watching her bleed tears, he felt a sinking sensation in the pit of his belly and then found himself doing as she requested.

Chance turned and limped out the door. He didn't look back, didn't need to. He would carry the image of Alexa standing there until his dying day—possibly longer.

Chance hobbled to the bunkhouse to collect his belongings. The ache in the pit of his stomach made it hard to breathe. He braced his hand against the wall and tried like hell to pull himself together. He wished he knew Howard well enough to know how vindictive the old man would be, wished Alexa had enough faith in him to let him stay and shoulder the blame for her.

A grim smile flattened Chance's lips as he reached for his duffel bag. Alexa claimed to love him, but her words were all the assurance he needed that she had no faith in his staying power. Or rather, he mused, she was afraid to place faith in him, just in case he disappointed her.

Given her background, he supposed he couldn't really blame her. But it still hurt like hell to know that she didn't consider him responsible enough to withstand the difficult situation.

What a mess, Chance thought as he stuffed his toiletries into the bag. He'd known the situation had complication written all over it when he found himself attracted to Alexa, found himself drawn to that lonely kid. Sure enough, things had blown up in his face.

Chance glanced toward the sleeping cowboy. Striding forward, he shook Pecos awake—no small task because the injured cowboy was out like a light. "Hey, Pecos, I need to ask a favor."

"If it involves physical exertion, we're in trouble," Pecos wheezed, holding his arm protectively against his throbbing ribs. "Every breath I take is pure torture."

Chance eased down on the edge of the bed, then grabbed the pen and paper off the nightstand. "I'm leaving the phone number of my motel in Fort Worth. I'll be calling you tomorrow night, and the night after, to check on things here."

Pecos managed a crooked grin, though his lips were pasty-white. "Hell, Chance, didn't know you cared so much about me."

"Knock it off, pretty boy. This is serious. Howard and I got crosswise tonight. I don't want him to do anything crazy."

"Why? Because of the knockout in faded blue jeans?" Pecos guessed. "The cowboy crew that was here a couple of weeks ago was talking about how you were sweet on Alexa. Turns out they're right, huh?"

Chance scowled. Sometimes cowboys could gossip worse than old hens. He'd probably take a razzing when he returned to the circuit, but it was nothing compared to the ridicule Alexa was likely to face with Howard.

"Yeah, well, things got a little complicated around here, and I want you to keep tabs on Alexa for me."

Pecos smiled knowingly. "The old man laid down the law to me on the way from the airport. He didn't approve of you messing with his daughter-in-law, did he?"

"You could say that," Chance grumbled.

Pecos shifted carefully on the bed. "You can count on me, Chance. I'll keep my eyes peeled for possible trouble. If Howard says anything that could be considered remotely threatening I'll even call the fairgrounds at Fort Worth if I need to get in touch with you immediately."

"Thanks. I owe you one."

"No, you don't," Pecos insisted. "Two years ago you gave me traveling money from your winnings in Mesquite, Texas so I could compete in the next rodeo on the circuit. I haven't paid you back yet."

"You just did," Chance said as he levered onto his feet. "Spend a little time with the kid, too. Remind Zack to keep his elbow up when he pitches and shoots hoops. Oh, and he's the Atlanta Braves' biggest fan. If you don't know the starting lineup, familiarize yourself. And tell Alexa—"

Chance broke off abruptly, averting his gaze from Pecos's unblinking stare. "Just watch out for her, Pecos. She is determined to finish that bed-and-breakfast by herself, and she's a daredevil on the ladder. Don't let her get hurt."

"Anything else?"

"Yeah, get well quick," he said as he scooped up his duffel bag. "I'll tell the men on the circuit that you send your love."

Pecos chuckled, then groaned miserably and hugged his arms against his tender ribs.

Chance walked out the door.

It was the hardest thing he'd ever done.

Chapter Eleven

For the past few days Alexa felt as if she were walking around the ranch barefoot—on broken glass. Howard rarely spoke to her, wouldn't look at her. She knew she had shattered his ideals and expectations, but she wasn't sorry, didn't regret those precious moments spent with Chance. He'd brought pleasure back into her life, even if it had been short-termed and ended in turmoil.

She had been touched by Chance's defensive gestures of accepting the blame and offering to take her away with him. She loved him even more for that, and it had nearly killed her to send him away with those harsh words of assurance that she could live without a man in her life.

Yet, the determining factor was that Chance had planned to leave *before* the fiasco with Howard. She had known the rules when she began the affair with Chance. He was a professional cowboy who traveled constantly. They had no commitment to each other.

They lived their stolen moments without looking too far

into the future. Now their affair was over and Chance was
gone.

Life went on, Alexa reminded herself realistically.

Alexa switched on the blinker and hung a left turn in the
truck. She had driven into town to show her ideas for advertising to the graphic-design specialist at the print shop.
Before she could open her bed-and-breakfast for business,
she needed publicity flyers, needed to spread the word that
she was accepting reservations to her countrified retreat.

Although her financial budget was already bursting at the
seams, Alexa had placed several ads in area newspapers
and called radio and TV stations to offer interviews and
tours.

The sooner she filled the rooms of the B-and-B, the
sooner she could convince Howard that she was going to
make a major contribution to ranch profits.

One day he might actually thank her for it.

If he ever got over being furious with her.

Alexa shook herself loose from her dismal thoughts and
climbed down from the truck. She had scores of errands to
attend to this afternoon. Deb was bringing out the knickknacks and artwork to decorate the B-and-B after she
closed up her craft shop for the evening. Truckloads of
furniture were scheduled to arrive in three days. Alexa
planned to have the place ready.

Having delivered her proposals for posters, Alexa
zoomed off. Twice, she caught herself wondering how
Chance had fared during the first two go-rounds at Fort
Worth. She hoped he didn't sustain further injury. The man
had been banged up enough to last a normal man a lifetime.

But then, Chance Butler wasn't a normal man, she reminded herself. If he was, he couldn't have taken Alexa's
heart with him when he left Rocking T.

"That kind of thinking will land you in a state of depression," she lectured herself.

For her own sake, for Zack's sake, Alexa had to maintain

a cheerful, positive attitude. Zack was suffering enough because of Chance's absence in his life. Fortunately, Pecos Smith had given the boy a little attention now and then. The young cowboy had even asked after her, Alexa remembered.

Her errands completed, Alexa swung by school to give Zack a ride home. Hoping to lift his glum mood, she treated him to an ice-cream cone and a trip to the park, and promised to play catch as soon as they arrived at the ranch.

Lacking his usual enthusiasm, Zack moped outside with his glove in one hand, ball and bat in the other. Trying to distract him, Alexa questioned Zack about school while they warmed up their pitching arms. But nothing helped. The boy couldn't get into the swing of things, even when Alexa repeated all the pointers Chance had given.

"I'm not in the mood to play ball," Zack mumbled. "It's not the same without Chance."

Nothing was ever going to be the same again—without Chance—but Alexa didn't have the heart to tell Zack so. "Chance would be disappointed if he knew you weren't working on your fundamentals," she tried to reason with him.

"It wasn't just playing ball, Mom. It was being with him, as if I had a dad."

Wide, doleful eyes lifted to her, and Alexa felt her heart drop to the pit of her stomach. "Oh, honey, I know it hurts right now, but we have to give ourselves time. We have to keep doing all the things we did before."

Zack dropped his mitt in the grass, then gave it an angry kick. "I don't want to play anymore with you. I just want Chance back," he wailed, then turned tail and dashed into the house.

"I hope you're happy." Howard scowled at Alexa as he stepped around the side of the house. "Not only did you put my life in turmoil, but you let your son get attached to that worthless cowboy."

It was the first time Howard had spoken directly to her since the incident. She wished he hadn't broken the silence. Alexa was feeling bad enough without Howard showing up to rub Zack's misery in her face.

The sound of an approaching vehicle drew Alexa's attention. Leaving Howard to mutter that another Jezebel had arrived, Alexa strode off to greet her sister.

Deb cast an expectant glance at Howard's departing back. "How is the silent war going?"

"He finally spoke," she reported.

"And had nothing nice to say, I'm sure," Deb predicted.

Alexa shrugged. "Howard is still in his pouting phase, but I've been on such good behavior that he's had little to complain about," she said as she scooped up a box of wooden crafts from the car seat. "He's smart enough to know that if he boots me off the ranch his laundry will pile up and he'll starve to death. I think the only reason he's letting me stay is because he realizes he'd have to pay someone to do the things that I've been doing around here for free."

"Damn," Deb grumbled. "I really screwed up your life when I insisted you date Butler."

"No, you didn't," Alexa contradicted. "I was the one who accepted the date, then came running to you for a makeover. I could have called it off. I knew there was the chance Howard might find out about it and take it badly. I hold myself personally accountable for everything that happened."

"Well, if you ask me, that weasel Butler should have stuck around," Deb said bitterly. "The man disappointed me."

Alexa rounded on her sister. "I will not have you blaming him for this. I sent him away, insisted that he leave, even after he offered to stay."

Deb blinked, stunned. "You didn't mention that before. Damn, sis, how many kinds of fool are you?"

"Is this a multiple-choice question?" Alexa flung back. Deb was not to be put off. "Why did you send him away?"

"Because he was already on his way out the door when the confrontation with Howard came up." Alexa shouldered her way into the newly completed dining area. "I didn't expect Chance to stay, just because Howard got his nose out of joint."

"Did you give Chance a helpful shove out the door?" Deb quizzed her. "Didn't you think you deserved to be happy?"

Alexa glared at her sister, then realized Deb saw a little deeper, a little clearer than Alexa preferred.

Deb slammed the box of crafts down on the kitchen counter, planted her fists on her hips and squared off against her sister. "Lady, you are badly in need of an attitude adjustment. You deserve all the happiness, consideration and respect you can get.

"Dan really did a job on you, didn't he? When he cheated with every rodeo groupie that tucked her phone number in the front pocket of his tight-fitting jeans, you presumed that you weren't doing something right at home and that was what caused him to stray."

"Pipe down," Alexa whispered, glaring expectantly at the door. "Zack might come barreling in here any minute. I don't want him to hear this."

"Fine, I'll whisper." She lowered her voice several decibels. "But you have to listen to me, Alexa. You are not second-rate, even if Dan left you with that impression. And maybe Butler really did want to hang around to work through the difficulties. Maybe he needed to know that you really wanted him here."

Alexa stared at the air over Deb's head. "I told him I loved him, so it wasn't as if he didn't know how I felt."

"And what did he say?" Deb fired back at her.

Alexa shifted awkwardly from one foot to the other beneath Deb's piercing scrutiny. "I didn't let him say anything."

"Why? Because you were afraid he wouldn't be able to return the words?" Deb threw up her hands in exasperation. "Atta girl, sis. Keep the situation under your control. Don't give the man a chance to speak his piece, just in case he wouldn't say what you wanted to hear.

"Honestly, Alexa, I never realized you were such a coward. You might have thrown away a chance at happiness, just because you were afraid Butler might not feel the way you do. What if he does?"

Alexa wheeled away, carrying a box of small wooden shelves and the appropriate knickknacks to set on them.

"Those thingamabobs don't go over there," Deb called out. "That wall is too long for short shelves. I have a particular painting in mind for that spot."

Alexa whipped around. "Fine, you decorate the place. That isn't my field of expertise anyway. I'm not even sure I have one. Obviously relationships are impossible for me to handle properly. I'll go upstairs and hang the ceiling fan in the executive suite. That, I can do."

"Are you sure?" Deb taunted her unmercifully. "You couldn't handle your first and only affair properly. You sent out mixed signals to the man, you know. You got your heart broke, though you're putting up an admirable front for my benefit. But I can see right through you, Alexa, don't think I can't."

"Thanks for the support, sis. Makes me feel so much better that I want to jump for joy," Alexa muttered sourly, then stalked up the steps.

"Don't electrocute yourself," Deb called after her. "I have a date with the doctor tonight. I don't want him hanging around the emergency room resuscitating you."

"Don't worry, I wouldn't dream of spoiling your date," Alexa threw over her shoulder, along with a scowl.

Alexa grabbed the ladder that Chance had named Grace,

then stalked down the hall. Deb's words were still burning her ears as she retrieved the boxed ceiling fan.

Had her fear of disappointment and rejection truly set off her defense mechanism? Alexa asked herself. Had she refused to let Chance speak because she wanted to protect herself from possible hurt? Had she refused to let Chance stay because she was afraid he would grow tired of her, just as Dan had? Or had she refused because she assumed Chance was willing—because of a sense of guilt—to hang around until she resolved the situation with Howard?

More muddy water under the bridge, Alexa told herself as she toted Grace into the executive suite. She wouldn't have to feel slighted by the man she loved if he wasn't around to hurt her, now would she? She didn't have to keep up pretenses for Howard's benefit, either. She was safe in her world and her emotions didn't have to suffer another round of abuse.

She would make her mark on the world as a savvy businesswoman, maybe even win the award for Mother of the Year. And if she was very lucky, maybe Howard would eventually forgive her for betraying the memory of his son.

Resolved to making the most of her situation, Alexa unpacked the ceiling fan and checked the colored strands of electrical wiring, just as Chester instructed her to do. Her mind buzzing with a dozen different thoughts, she set to work on the fan, trying desperately to ignore the ache that missing Chance left burning in her soul.

Chance Butler didn't drink, but he was definitely drunk. He was down in Fort Worth, on the run from himself, on the run from his emotions. He'd ordered cocktails the minute he boarded the plane in Tulsa and refused to let his glass go dry until he landed in Texas. Hell, Chance didn't even remember riding in the first and second go-round at the rodeo. He could barely recall his first telephone conversation with Pecos Smith. All Chance remembered was that Howard hadn't gone on a shooting spree at Rocking T. According to Pecos, Alexa and Zack were alive and well.

Propped on his bed at the motel, Chance poured himself another drink of hooch. His head felt as if it were full of cobwebs, his mouth full of cotton, but he didn't care. Sooner or later the whiskey would numb the ache in his chest. It had to. Sitting here alone with his soul, missing Alexa and Zack until hell wouldn't have it, was driving him nuts.

Chance felt like a damn coward, an irresponsible jerk. He should have stayed in Oklahoma, despite Alexa's refusal to let him run interference for her. As for Howard, he could take a flying leap. The old goat was dictating Alexa's life. And she let him, damn it! Chance should have stayed, should have stepped in to mediate the situation. He sure as hell wasn't accomplishing anything in Texas, except getting himself rip-roaring drunk for the first time in his life.

You should have told Alexa how you felt, even if she refused to listen, came the silent voice that had been nagging him for two endless days. Just because the words stuck in his throat, just because he'd never bared his heart to another living soul before, just because he felt as awkward, uncomfortable and exposed as if he'd dropped his jeans in the middle of a rodeo arena was no excuse.

Chance laid back his head and cursed in dismay. Damn, he'd screwed up Alexa's life, and now he was screwing up his own. He'd made an absolute fool of himself with the rodeo cowboy crowd that evening. He had staggered down the lanes to chew out the chute boss for refusing to call his name and number in the calf-roping event. When the chute boss ignored him, Chance had grabbed the man by his shirt and wheeled him around, demanding to know when he'd have his turn in the event.

To Chance's humiliation, the chute boss, with an audience of cowboys surrounding him, informed Chance that he had already competed in the event early that afternoon and that he had come in first in the go-round—but was obviously too drunk to remember it.

Turned out Chance was leading the other contestants by a wide margin and stood to win a hefty prize purse. Fort Worth Rodeo was being better to Chance than he was being to himself. As for his knee, it hurt like hell, but Chance refused to mix whiskey and pain pills. He figured that would make matters worse than they already were!

When the phone rang, Chance groped for the receiver—and accidentally dropped it on the floor. Slurring curses, he sprawled over the edge of his rumpled bed to retrieve the slippery damn thing.

"'Lo," he mumbled.

"Chance? Is that you?"

He knew that voice, but he couldn't place it while he was up to his ears in booze.

"Chance?"

"Yeah?" he slurred out.

"I got your number from Pecos Smith," the shaky voice informed him. "I'm sorry to bother you, but I thought you might like to know that Alexa has had an accident."

Chance shot straight off the bed, staggered, then hit his knees—though he didn't have two good ones to fall on. "Who is this?"

"It's Deb. My sister was hanging a ceiling fan in one of the upstairs rooms at the B-and-B. She was on the ladder—"

Oh God. *Oh God!* She'd taken another fall from Grace and broken her neck. Damn it, why couldn't that woman hire experienced help to complete her project? Hadn't he told Pecos not to let Alexa near any ladders? Where the hell was that cowboy when disaster struck?

Where the hell were *you*, Butler?

"Is she okay?" Chance wheezed over the thunderous pounding of his heart.

"Not exactly," Deb said grimly.

"Well, spit it out," Chance demanded, fear and concern eating at his belly like battery acid. "How is she, *exactly?* She's still alive, isn't she?"

"She's alive," Deb confirmed bleakly. "But she's in serious condition. She suffered an electrical shock that knocked her off the ladder."

"Damn it, don't tell me she forgot to throw the breaker before she hooked up the ceiling fan!" Chance roared in frustration.

"Fine, I won't tell you that," Deb snapped back at him. "This isn't easy for me, you know. This is my big sister we're talking about and I'm worried sick."

Chance swore under his breath. "Is she going to recover?"

"Kurt...Dr. Stevenson...says it will take time. She'll have to remain hospitalized until the wound heals and the swelling goes down. He can't put a cast on her broken arm until it does."

Wound? What wound? The one caused from electrical burns? Horrible visions tangled with the cobwebs cluttering Chance's mind. He'd heard of electrical currents passing through bodies and blowing out through the skin like discharging bullets. The thought of Alexa suffering left him shaken. And poor Zack, the kid worshiped his mother.

"How is Zack holding up?" Chance wanted to know.

"He's staying in town with me. He's pretty broken up, because..."

When her voice trailed off, Chance swallowed hard, his fist clenched around the phone in a death grip. "Go on."

"It gets worse, Chance."

"Damn."

"Howard suffered a heart attack when he saw the shape Alexa was in when the ambulance hauled her away. I know this isn't your problem, that you're committed to perform this weekend—"

"I'm there," Chance said without a moment's hesitation.

"If you can manage to leave the old truck at the airport in Willowvale, I'll be on the first available flight."

"Thank you, Chance," Deb murmured gratefully. "I don't know anything about running the ranch, and Pecos can only do so much while he's nursing cracked ribs."

"I'm on my way," Chance promised, then hung up the phone.

The call left him trembling, had him beating himself black and blue for leaving Rocking T. Despite the excessive amount of whiskey he'd consumed, Chance shook his head to clear his thoughts, then made the necessary calls to book a flight and withdraw from rodeo competition.

Chance stumbled out the door and wobbled across the street to the convenience store for coffee. He downed a quart of it, showered for a half hour, then paced his room.

He should have been there for Alexa, even if she ordered him to leave. Damn it, damn it, damn it! He'd been so busy trying to obey her wish, trying *not* to step on her independent toes and trying to prove that he was nothing like Dan, that he'd screwed up in reverse! He should have taken control of the situation—whether Alexa wanted him to or not, which she obviously didn't.

Chance knew Alexa had learned to take care of herself and didn't appreciate domineering men. And so Chance had tried to accommodate her. But now she was going to have to deal with the dominant aspects of his personality. Like it or not, Rocking T was going to be under his command until Howard and Alexa were back on their feet.

By the time Chance caught a northbound plane, he still didn't know exactly how he was going to handle Howard, who wouldn't be the least receptive to his return. The old man despised him. But nothing was going to stand in Chance's way when it came to providing moral support for Alexa and Zack. And this was the last time Chance was going to bow out graciously when he was needed!

The full impact of Chance's hellish hangover hit him somewhere over Oklahoma City. It was a doozy, but it didn't slow him down. He refused to let it. He figured he was getting what he deserved for trying to drown his frustrations in a bottle. That had been his father's way, but it wasn't Chance's way—at least it hadn't been until the turmoil of leaving Rocking T left him looking for consolation in the bottom of a whiskey bottle.

Chance intended to grab the bull by the horns. If even one member of the Tipton family objected, that was too damned bad! None of this would have happened if Chance had remained on the ranch, despite Alexa's insistence that he leave. He was never going to forgive himself for not being there when she needed him!

"Hold it right there, mister. You may look like a walking greenhouse, but you aren't getting past this nurses' station. Hospital visiting hours are over."

Chance poked his head around the monstrous flower arrangement he had ordered in Dallas and had waiting for him to pick up at Willowvale Airport. A sturdy, gruff-looking nurse stood as a human barricade, bearing down on him with the evil eye.

Chance mustered his most disarming smile for the nurse—who he was sure must have worked as a prison warden or drill sergeant in another life. She stood with hands on broad hips, feet askance, blocking the hallway.

"I flew back into town the minute I heard about Alexa Tipton's accident," he explained.

"Alexa?" The nurse's dark eyes widened and she glanced right, then left. "Are you that nice cowboy Chester told me about?"

"Are you Mildred?" Chance questioned the question.

A smile spread across the woman's face, altering her stern appearance. "That's me. Chester Whitmier is my husband."

"I've come a long way on a bad leg," Chance said as he gestured his head toward his brace. "I dropped what I was doing in Fort Worth as soon as Alexa's sister called me. I can't rest or relax until I see Alexa."

His hopeful expression must have done the trick, for Mildred contemplated bending her strict rules.

"All right, cowboy," she murmured, motioning for him to follow her down the hall. "But if you spread word around town that I'm a pushover, I'll come after you with a scalpel and hypodermic needle."

"Mum's the word, ma'am," Chance promised.

On the way down the hall, Mildred shook her Brillo pad head and sighed. "That poor girl. Talk about bad timing for an accident. Alexa has been racing all over town, making arrangements for publicity and promotion for the bed-and-breakfast. Then this happened. I told Chester to get his butt out to the ranch and put the finishing touches on that construction project for her. And he better not charge her a red cent for doing it, or he'll hear plenty from me on the subject. I hope to smile that you returned to manage the ranch while Howard is laid up…uh-oh…"

Chance glanced around the oversize flower arrangement and then blinked in astonishment. Kurt Stevenson, M.D., had taken on a westernized image since Chance last saw him. The preppy doctor was decked out in Mercedes boots, Riata dress jeans and a colorful Western shirt.

"Chance Butler? Is that you behind that wall of flowers?" Kurt questioned.

"Yep." Chance levered the vase against his hip and outstretched his hand. "I approve of the change in appearance, Harvard," he said as he shook Kurt's hand.

"I gave Mr. Butler permission to drop off the flowers," Mildred was quick to explain. "You can take it from here, Dr. Stevenson. I need to get back to the desk."

Chance winked and smiled at the hefty nurse.

"Thanks, Mildred, you're a sweetheart."

Mildred harrumphed as she wheeled around and marched off. "You won't think *sweetheart* if you try bending my rules on a regular basis, cowboy."

Chance's grin melted as he fixed his concerned gaze on the physician. "How's Alexa doing?"

"All things considered—"

Chance cringed apprehensively. He didn't like the sound of that opening statement.

"—she's doing all right. We think Alexa was standing on top of the ladder trying to reach the sixteen-foot ceiling," Kurt continued as he ambled down the hall.

Chance grimaced at the vision of Alexa teetering atop the stepladder, which carried a warning label stating, in plain English, that the top rung was *not* to be used as a step. No doubt, Alexa had taken quite a spill from that height.

"The electrical jolt that went through Alexa burned her hands and exited through her elbow, leaving an open wound."

Chance squeezed his eyes shut, speculating on how much pain she'd suffered.

"If Debra hadn't heard the commotion and dashed upstairs to give Alexa mouth-to-mouth resuscitation she might not be here now."

Chance's heart missed several beats. His breath clogged in his chest. Damn, things were worse than he thought.

"When Alexa fell, she hit her chin on the top of the ladder, splitting the skin. The arm she landed on is broken in two places, but I can't cast it until the wound heals properly. She also received a concussion, and I have her on an IV and antibiotic."

"Is that it?" Chance asked grimly.

"Except for the twisted ankle, a nasty bruise on her hip and the guilt-trip express train she's been riding on since she learned of Howard's heart attack, that's it. She was very lucky."

Chance smirked. "Don't try to convince her of that. I doubt she'll buy it."

Kurt halted in front of the closed door. "Alexa looks every bit as bad as she feels. I hope seeing you will lift her spirits. Heaven knows she needs that."

Chance mentally prepared himself for the encounter. If ever he needed to look—and sound—cheerful this was the time. "Thanks for taking care of her, Harvard."

Kurt nodded and smiled. "Find a way to cheer her up, Country. I'll take care of her physical recuperation."

"Still seeing Deb?" Chance asked.

Kurt nodded. His smile widened considerably. "Although it came at Alexa's expense, Debra and I have been seeing a great deal of each other. She likes my country look. Says I'm not so intimidating since I gave up my preppy wardrobe."

Chance stared at the closed door. "I'm spending the night here. Can you clear it with Mildred?"

"Mildred has a special place in her by-the-rules heart for Alexa. Our head nurse has run her legs off checking on her favorite patient. There won't be a problem with you staying overnight."

When the physician strode off to complete his rounds, Chance drew himself up to full stature, then inhaled a deep breath. No matter how bad Alexa looked he vowed not to show the slightest reaction to her battered appearance. Whatever Alexa needed, however she needed it, Chance promised himself she would have it.

He just hoped Alexa didn't get even more bent out of shape than she already was when he walked back into her life—and took over....

Chapter Twelve

When Chance stepped into the hospital room to see Alexa hooked up to the IV, looking fragile and vulnerable, his stomach clenched. She looked every bit as bad as Chance had imagined—worse maybe. Her left arm was bandaged, she had burns on her hands, a black eye, and her long auburn hair fanned out in a mass of tangles.

Never in his life had Chance wished for the ability to take someone's agony and bear it as his own. He was prepared to do that for Alexa, right here, right now, from then on.

A less noble part of him wanted to rail at her for climbing up that damn ladder, for not hiring a certified electrician to hang those blasted ceiling fans. But he figured that lecturing Alexa wouldn't do any good since she was sleeping—or heavily sedated, Chance didn't know which.

Chance set the huge flower arrangement on the nightstand, then hovered beside the bed for several minutes. Then he bent to brush his lips over her unresponsive mouth.

Damn, he could imagine Zack's reaction to seeing his mother lying here battered and mangled. The poor kid had already lost his father—and came close to losing his mother and grandfather. Chance hadn't asked about Howard's condition, but he suspected the old man was suffering—which only intensified Zack's stress.

Uncomfortable though the vinyl chair looked to be, Chance sank down to keep the vigil. The hangover that had followed him all the way from Texas was beginning to subside, replaced by his gnawing concern for Alexa. It was going to be weeks before she could function normally, he predicted. He wondered how well an active, independent woman like Alexa would cope with her immobility—and Chance's announcement that he had returned to run her business for her.

That should set well, Chance mused, smiling for the first time in a week. But Alexa wasn't getting rid of him so easily this time. The B-and-B was important to her, and he was here to see that the establishment opened on schedule, to ensure that the horseback-riding trail through the panoramic Oklahoma Hills was laid out and the mounts were trained to take a leisurely walk over hill and dale.

Chance vowed to stay as long as he was needed, even if Howard objected. The old man needed him, too, whether Howard would swallow his obstinate pride and admit it or not.

On that grim thought, Chance laid back his head, stretched out his gimpy leg, reached over to take Alexa's limp hand in his, then fell asleep.

It was the first time he'd relaxed since he walked away from Rocking T four days earlier.

It seemed more like a year....

Alexa moaned as she tried to squirm to a different position in her hospital bed. She had been drifting in and out so much since the accident that it took several minutes to orient herself. Then she suffered through several anxious moments when she remembered she couldn't afford to be laid up in the hospital. This accident was costing her time and money. If the B-and-B wasn't open for business soon, she wouldn't be able to pay the interest on the loan. She would be bankrupt before she had the chance to make a success of her business.

And Howard would never let her hear the end of that, she mused. As if he didn't have enough to hold over her already.

She vaguely remembered Zack coming to visit, and she had tried to put up a cheerful front when she saw the fear and concern in his eyes. Trouble was, she had been so groggy and uncomfortable that she wasn't sure she had reassured her son.

The poor child's world had fallen apart a second time. Thank goodness Deb was around to ride herd over Zack....

Alexa frowned when she realized something strong and warm encased her bandaged hand. Squinting, she stared at the gigantic flower arrangement beside her bed, then focused her fuzzy gaze on the masculine arm that was swallowed up by roses, baby's breath and carnations.

A jolt of surprise riveted her when Chance's hazy image appeared from a sea of flowers.

"Hi, gorgeous, 'bout time you woke up."

Alexa's mouth dropped open. "Chance? What are you doing here?"

"You need me so I'm here," he said matter-of-factly.

"But what about Fort Worth? What day is this? Did you compete—"

He flung up his free hand to halt her rapid-fire questions. "I was leading the calf roping and holding down third in bulldogging when Deb called to inform me that you took another fall from Grace. Not smart, Al," he muttered darkly.

Alexa blinked. "You came back because of me?"

Never during her years of marriage had Dan dropped what he was doing in a family crisis. He hadn't even returned the night she called to tell him she was on her way to deliver Zack. Alexa had to drive herself to the hospital, because Howard was at his poker party. Dan showed up a week later to see his son.

Chance rose stiffly from the chair and leaned over to drop a kiss to her lips. "What's one rodeo when you have a B-and-B to open?"

"I don't expect you to—"

"I know." He smiled tenderly at her. "And you'll probably be cursing me before I leave Rocking T, but here's the deal, Al. I'm putting myself in charge. I'm handling all the arrangements while you recuperate. Zack and I will be staying at the ranch. That's his home and he'll feel more comfortable there. I'm not the world's greatest cook, I'll admit, but Zack and I can rough it."

Alexa's jaw was still scraping her chest when he finished speaking. She wasn't accustomed to having someone fill in for her, assume her responsibilities or tell her what to do. She wasn't sure she was comfortable with the feeling.

Chance braced his arms on either side of her shoulders and leaned down to stare her squarely in the eye. "If you have a problem with me running your affairs then you'll just have to get over it, because that's exactly what's going to happen. My way may not be your way, but things *will* get done on time."

"But what about the circuit?"

He grinned wryly. "The electric circuit? I'll switch off the breaker before I finish hanging the fans."

"No, the rodeo circuit," she said, her lips pursing in response to Chance's infectious grin.

He shrugged lackadaisically. "No big deal, Al. The good thing about the circuit is that you can pay your entry fees and be back in action in a couple of weeks."

"I really can't let you do this," she insisted.

"No? How do you plan to stop me?"

"I don't know, but I'll feel worse than I already do if I let you sacrifice your contention for national finals."

"Well, you don't have a choice in the matter. Since you aren't physically able to kick me out of town, you're stuck with me."

Alexa blinked away the mist of tears that clouded her already blurred vision. "I don't know how to repay you for this."

"All you have to do is get well. That's all the payment I want."

"But Howard—"

Her breath hitched, and the tears she tried to hold in check came dribbling down her cheeks. "I've already upset him twice and your reappearance might—"

"Let me handle Howard," Chance interrupted as he leaned over to retrieve a tissue to blot her cheek. "Let me do my thing while you concentrate on getting back on your feet."

"Chance! You're back!"

Zack's excited voice barely beat him across the room. He charged directly toward Chance, and Chance scooped the kid off the floor to ruffle his hair.

"Hey, rookie, good to see you."

Chance returned the zealous hug bestowed on him. Before he knew it, Zack buried his head on Chance's shoulder and clung to him as if he were a life preserver.

"Mom doesn't look too good, does she?" Zack mumbled against Chance's neck.

"People get knocked down and bumped around sometimes," Chance whispered. "But Dr. Stevenson told me he was taking extra special care of your mom." He glanced over Zack's ruffled head and smiled a greeting at Deb, who sagged in relief at the sight of him.

"If it's okay with you, kid, we'll be staying at the ranch.

We'll make sure things run smoothly until your mom comes home.''

Zack lifted his head, then nodded vigorously. ''I'll help with the chores.''

''I was hoping I could count on you.'' Chance set Zack on the edge of the bed. ''Give your mom a kiss before you head off to school. I'll be waiting for you when you get off the bus tonight.''

Zack leaned down and carefully kissed Alexa. She felt another wave of tears flood her eyes. She knew Chance's return was a mixed blessing. It was going to be even more difficult for Zack when Chance left Rocking T once again.

And it would be difficult for her, too. Even now, she found herself wishing Chance could be a permanent resident. But she quickly reminded herself that Chance had returned out of a sense of duty, obligation and concern. She had to be careful not to read more into the situation than was actually there.

''Come on, Zack, I don't want you to be late for school,'' Deb insisted. ''We gotta go.''

''Don't worry, Mom, Chance and I will take care of things,'' Zack promised as he eased off the bed.

When Deb and Zack exited, Alexa stared at the haggard cowboy, who was badly in need of a shave and a good night's sleep—in a bed, not an uncomfortable chair. But just seeing Chance diminished her aches and pains. Not only was he a good and decent man, but his smile had the power to heal.

Alexa admitted that he had made a marked difference in her life. Yet she knew she could never be satisfied with the kind of long-distance relationship she'd had with Dan. She had to keep in mind that the love she felt for Chance wouldn't evolve into a lasting relationship. She had to withhold a part of her heart or she would be devastated when he left again.

When Chance dipped his head to feather a kiss across

her lips Alexa reminded herself that Chance had come because of his strong sense of honor and duty. And he probably experienced the same feelings of guilt that hounded her after Howard collapsed. She couldn't let herself misinterpret Chance's motives for being here, no matter how much she would like to think he had sacrificed his time and earnings on the circuit because he cared so deeply for her.

"I hate to kiss and run, doll face, but I've got things to do," Chance murmured. "Zack and I will be back to see you tonight."

With a cheery smile he limped away, leaving Alexa to choke down the bland meal delivered two minutes later.

"Oh, God," she muttered as she chewed on the dry toast. "How am I going to cook at the B-and-B while wearing a cast and limping around on crutches?"

Wouldn't that be loads of fun!

Well, she would simply have to find a way, she told herself determinedly. She would manage the feat—somehow.

Chance stepped from the hospital room to see the physician making his morning rounds. "Yo, Harvard, I need to ask a favor."

Kurt pivoted and raised a blond brow. "What's the problem?"

Chance halted directly in front of Kurt. "The problem is Howard Tipton. How stable is his condition? Can he tolerate a visit from his least favorite person?"

"Well," Kurt said slowly, "he's out of intensive care, but I still have him hooked up to monitors. He doesn't need undue stress. According to Debra he was upset when he learned you and Alexa were seeing each other."

"That's an understatement." Chance smirked.

"The shock of seeing Alexa unconscious after being electrocuted sent him over the edge. At his age, I don't want to test that old-wives' tale about the third time being the charm.''

"I need to speak with him," Chance said earnestly. "I wonder if you could man the monitors while I'm in his room. I won't stay long."

Kurt frowned warily. "I'm not sure that's a good idea."

"Neither is fretting about who is in charge of the ranch while he's hospitalized," Chance parried. "No doubt, Howard is concerned."

Kurt nodded hesitantly. "Okay, you can see him briefly. Just be tactful with him. If he gets riled up I'll be in that room in a flash."

Chance strode down the hall, mentally rehearsing what he intended to say to Howard. Chance didn't want to send the old man into cardiac arrest, but he didn't want Howard thinking Chance was going behind his back, either.

The instant Chance entered the room, Howard's eyes widened and he clenched his gnarled hands around the newspaper he was reading. "What the hell are you doing here? It says right here in the paper that you're leading the calf roping event in the Fort Worth Rodeo."

"I came back to help out," Chance told him simply, directly. "Pecos is in no condition to handle all the ranch chores for you."

"I'll find someone I can *trust*," Howard muttered, glaring at Chance.

Chance halted at the foot of the bed, despite Howard's unwelcoming glower. "I know you have little use for me, but I'm offering my assistance, free of charge. I care about Alexa and Zack, though I know you disapprove—"

"You got that right," Howard said, and scowled.

Chance clamped his hands on the railing at the end of the bed and stared the old man straight in the eye. "I'm not trying to take your son's place. I'm not trying to take your place, either, Howard. Deep down, I think you're afraid that might happen. But I believe in lending a helping hand when it's needed. You provided me with a place to stay and paid me wages while I was too injured to compete. One good turn deserves another, don't you agree?''

Howard regarded him for a long, silent moment. ''And then you'll leave when I'm back on my feet?''

Chance nodded. ''When you can handle the chores without overexerting yourself, I'll turn the reins over to you and get the hell out of your sight.''

''I'll bet you will.'' He sniffed caustically. ''You're probably hoping I'll keel over so you can waltz in and take over the ranch. Well, I won't let that happen. I'll get well to spite you!''

''You do that, old man.'' Chance grinned at him. ''Now that we have that settled, when do you want to sell your feeder steers? The livestock market price is high in anticipation of good wheat pasture this winter. You could turn a profit if you sell within the next two weeks.''

To Chance's relief, Howard set aside his personal grudge to talk business. But in the end, Howard's wary suspicion got the better of him.

''I better not find out you sold fifty head of cattle and pocketed the profit on a half dozen calves for yourself. And I better not find anything missing from my house or barns after you're gone, Butler. I'll have the cops track you down, don't think I won't.''

There were only two things Chance considered taking from Howard's ranch—Alexa and Zack. In his opinion those were the only two valuables. But he wasn't going to upset the old man further by blurting that out.

''Now get some rest,'' Chance said, his tone matching Howard's in gruffness. ''I've got work to do at Rocking T and it won't get done while I'm standing here jawing.''

He turned to leave, hesitated, then glanced back at Howard. ''While you're here recuperating it would be a good time to consider all the things your daughter-in-law has done for you over the years. I don't think you realize how fortunate you are to have a woman like that under your roof.''

For a moment Chance thought Howard was going to respond. But the old man clamped his mouth shut and glanced away. Although Chance doubted his last comments would be taken to heart, he was greatly relieved that Howard hadn't worked himself into a lather when Chance made an appearance. If the old man's condition were in jeopardy, the doctor would have been here in the bat of an eyelash. Apparently, Howard's blood pressure and pulse hadn't shot through the roof.

On his way out of the hospital Chance kept wondering if Howard appreciated this gesture of assistance, though he was too proud and stubborn to express gratitude to a man he clearly despised. Although Chance wasn't sure what made the old man tick, he suspected the fear of losing his daughter-in-law and grandson weighed heavily on his mind.

Howard Tipton had wrapped his life around what was left of his family. He used the memory of his son as the cement that bound him to Alexa and Zack. Any man who showed interest in Alexa was considered a dangerous threat.

In some ways Chance could understand Howard's fears, his need to protect his position in the family. Yet the old man wasn't being fair to Alexa and Zack. He was preventing them from getting on with their lives by holding on too tightly to the past.

Convincing Howard to change his attitude wouldn't be easy, Chance speculated. But if he could convince Howard to treat Alexa with the consideration and courtesy she deserved it would give Chance peace of mind. And if Chance could walk away with a smidgen of Howard's respect it would be more than he expected.

In the meantime, there was work to be done. Chance sure as hell hoped Pecos could pitch in and help. If not, Chance would be working long days for the next few weeks.

The prospect of hard work didn't bother Chance. It was this feeling of satisfaction that came from helping a family in need that really got to him. This, he realized, was what family was about. He'd never experienced the sensation before, and had been reluctant to become emotionally involved in unfamiliar situations. Though he still risked becoming so attached that leaving Rocking T again might be as painful as taking a beating, Chance decided the worthwhile deed of holding this family together was worth the risks.

Somewhere along the way, what Alexa and Zack—and even that cantankerous old man—needed had become top priority in his life.

Being the man Alexa could rely on was important to Chance. He wanted her to see her dreams come true... because seeing her happy made him happy.

And seeing her injured nearly destroyed him.

"Oh, hell," Chance muttered as he drove off in the clunker truck Deb had left for him at the airport. He was going to be hurt badly when Howard gave him the nod to leave Rocking T. And Chance would probably know the full meaning of loneliness when he walked away a second time. Now that he had accepted the responsibility of caring for this family he would feel lost, as sure as hell blazed.

Things would be the same as they were when he was a kid, he mused. Forever the outsider. Well, he ought to be used to that, he reminded himself. No matter how much things changed it seemed they were ultimately the same.

Story of his life, Chance thought as he headed for the ranch.

Since Chance didn't consider himself much of a cook—and had never had much opportunity to practice culinary skills—he made certain the kitchen was well stocked with cookies and fruit for Zack's after-school snacks.

Fortunately, Zack wasn't a picky eater. He gobbled up

the microwavable dinners Chance set in front of him. And thankfully, Zack never whined when Chance requested they cut baseball practice short so they could finish evening chores.

The kid proved himself to be a trouper, and Chance's fondness for the boy grew by such bounds and leaps during the week that followed that he couldn't imagine what his life was going to be like without that reddish-blond-haired rookie in it. Chance and Zack became inseparable from the moment Zack hopped off the bus and came dashing down the driveway.

Chance had learned the names of every third-grader in Zack's class. He checked over the boy's school papers and helped with difficult homework assignments. Chance had somehow become the substitute parent whose care and concern placed Zack at the top of his list of priorities. Chance had discovered that he had missed some of life's most rewarding and enjoyable experiences by not having a family. The responsibilities that had once concerned him, made him question his inabilities and inadequacies, fell by the wayside in the span of a week.

Hell, not even an evening passed that Chance didn't find himself propped on Zack's bed, reading from the latest issue of *Sports Illustrated* and discussing the Atlanta Braves' ERAs and batting averages. It had become a ritual that Chance anticipated and thoroughly enjoyed.

As for Chance's concern for Alexa's condition, he ran himself ragged to ensure he and Zack made nightly visits to the hospital. Alexa was developing a serious case of cabin fever, and Chance and Zack delivered a series of lectures on the need for her to stay off her feet so her mangled body could heal properly.

The woman was so accustomed to constant activity that lying in bed drove her up the walls. She squirmed, fidgeted and muttered about how the interest on her loan was mounting up and she needed to open for business immediately.

Despite all Chance's reassurances that the B-and-B would open on schedule, Alexa wanted to be at the ranch to oversee the progress that had been made. She simply couldn't imagine how things could get done when she wasn't there to do them herself.

Chance was amused—in a frustrated sort of way—by Alexa's inability to depend on someone other than herself. He supposed she'd become so self-reliant over the years that she had never delegated authority or placed the reins of responsibility in anyone's hands. She was uncomfortable with the whole process of lounging in bed while Chance ruled the roost.

And if Alexa had said it once she'd said fifty times that she felt terrible about heaping all of Rocking T's chores on Chance. She didn't want him sacrificing the winnings he could have earned while traveling the rodeo circuit. She was certain she had ruined his chances of competing at national finals in Las Vegas. She apologized up one side and down the other about tying him down in one place.

No matter how many times Chance insisted that he was exactly where he wanted to be, he couldn't convince Alexa that it was the truth. She couldn't comprehend that he cared enough to want to see her dream of opening the B-and-B come true.

That was what it had come down to, Chance realized as he escorted Zack upstairs to bed. What Chance wanted, personally, professionally, was no longer a consideration. He was determined to see Alexa happy. He wished he could wave his arms like a mystical wizard and put her world aright, ensure her business venture was highly successful.

"How come Mom seems so grouchy lately?" Zack asked as he retrieved his sports magazines for the evening reading session.

Chance stretched out on the double bed to give his leg a much-needed rest. "I don't think inactivity agrees with her."

"Guess not. She never stayed in the same place very long until the doctor told her she couldn't get out of bed."

Zack presented Chance with the magazine, then snuggled up against him. "Are you sure you don't want me to fix it with Mom so you could marry her? You make an awful good dad."

Chance felt his throat close and his heart melt down the ladder of his ribs. "Do I, rookie?" he squeaked.

Zack nodded with great conviction. "You're the best kind of dad. Even better than the dads my friends have. I've been telling them how you make snacks, cook supper, wash my clothes and play ball with me every night. They said their dads don't do all that stuff for them. They think you're a real cool dude."

A cool dude? Chance Butler was considered a real cool dude in the third-grade crowd? Who would have thought that a man with his childhood background could impress kids? He must have been doing more things right this week than he thought.

Chance hadn't had a clue how to care for an eight-year-old, until necessity demanded that he lend a helping hand. Chance had thought back to his younger days, then tried to be all the things—do all the things—he'd ached for when he was a kid.

There had been times when he'd wished for a sturdy shoulder to lean on, someone to prepare meals and ensure he had clean clothes to wear. He had longed for someone to be there waiting to greet him when he came home from school, instead of walking into an empty house that was sorely in need of a thorough cleaning.

The awesome responsibility of a family, a child, hadn't been so intimidating once Chance got his feet wet. Maybe the fact that he wanted to supply all the things his own parents had neglected made Chance a model parent—at least in this eight-year-old's eyes.

Not a model parent, Chance quickly amended. Just a

substitute parent. Howard would have a hissy fit if he realized Chance and Zack had grown so close this past week. Alexa would stew about it, too, he predicted. Zack was her number-one priority, and she didn't want to see the boy hurt in any way.

She spoke—and thought—in terms of Chance's temporary presence on Rocking T. She expected nothing permanent from a rodeo cowboy, because she had spent nine years married to the worst stereotype in the profession.

"Chance, aren't you gonna read to me tonight?" Zack propped himself up on his elbow and peered quizzically at him. "You look kinda sad. Is something wrong?"

Chance smiled as he ruffled the kid's mop of hair. "How could I possibly be sad with you here, rookie? I was just trying to think of a way to cheer up your mom while she's stuck in the hospital. Got any ideas?"

Zack pondered the question for a moment. "Cookies," he said. "We should bake her some cookies. She likes chocolate chips as much as I do."

Chance winced. He'd never made cookies in his life, and he doubted Zack had soloed, either. But what the hell. Living at Rocking T had been filled with all sorts of firsts for Chance. "Sounds like a winner to me, kid. Soon as you get home tomorrow we'll fire up the stove and start baking."

Satisfied, Zack snuggled beneath the quilt. Chance set aside his meandering thoughts and read the article about the NBA's highly publicized prospects for the upcoming basketball season.

Chance couldn't help but wonder who was going to bake cookies for, or read to Zack, when Howard returned to the ranch, declaring that he was physically able to resume control. Both Howard and Alexa expected Chance to resume his quest for another world title in professional rodeo.

God, his life was going to seem unbelievably empty, Chance thought as he eased away from the sleeping boy.

Now that he knew exactly what he had been missing, how much he *enjoyed* the responsibility of caring for a child, how much he delighted in being the recipient of Zack's enthusiastic smiles, anything less was going to be a lousy substitute for personal satisfaction.

Damn it, why had he allowed himself get all tangled up in someone else's life? In a few weeks he was going to be hurting worse than the kind of pain a wild bronc or unruly steer could deliver in an arena. He'd gone and broken his own rule about not getting emotionally attached in an impossible situation.

"Face it, cowboy," Chance muttered as he sprawled on Alexa's bed. "You're walking in quicksand."

On that dismal thought, Chance faded off to sleep, dreaming forbidden dreams, drifting in memories of a green-eyed woman and her adorable son...and knowing that caring so much would eventually leave him alone and miserable.

Chapter Thirteen

"Well, how are we doing this morning?" Deb asked as she breezed into Alexa's hospital room.

Alexa glowered thunderclouds on Deb's sunny smile. "We aren't doing worth a damn, but thanks for asking. I wish you would use your influence on the good doctor and convince him to spring me. I'm going stir-crazy in this sterilized condo."

Deb shook her head ruefully. "Too bad you and Howard aren't sharing the same space. Cranky as you two are, you should be snarling at each other."

Alexa threw up her good arm in a gesture of exasperation. Her other arm was now encased in plaster. It itched. It throbbed. The stitches under her chin felt as tight as shoelaces. Putting weight on her swollen ankle still made her nauseated. And if she weren't allowed a change of scenery pretty darn quick she'd be a basket case!

"You try parking your carcass in bed, staring at bare

walls and having nurses poke and prod at you, and we'll see how well you adapt,'' Alexa said, then scowled.

Deb sighed dramatically. ''And here I brought you doughnuts for a special pick-me-up treat. I suppose you don't appreciate the gesture any more than you appreciate my daily visits here.''

Alexa plunked her head against her foam pillow. She hated foam pillows. They caused her to wake up with a crick in her neck. She needed down-filled pillows, damn it!

''I'm sorry, sis,'' she apologized. ''It's just that I have so much to do in preparation for the grand opening. I feel awful about heaping my burdens on Chance. He's missing another rodeo this weekend, ruining his chance to compete in national finals.

''You've seen him in action. You know damn well that he's exceptionally good at what he does—the best, in fact. My careless accident is costing him big time! My conscience is hounding me to death. And Zack is probably badgering Chance with so many questions that he can't wait to hightail it off Rocking T.''

''You think so? Last time I saw the inseparable twosome they seemed satisfied with their situation. And pardon me for pointing this out to you, sis, but you can't measure a man like Chance Butler with the same yardstick you used for your husband. They look to be entirely different creatures. Chance seems to enjoy Zack's company far more than Dan ever did.''

''I'm glad Chance does, but this isn't going to make things easy on Zack,'' Alexa murmured fretfully. ''My kid is getting too attached. He'll be depressed and disappointed when Chance leaves again.''

Deb was silent for a moment. ''Why does Chance have to leave at all? Knowing how you and Zack feel about him, I thought perhaps—''

''Don't go getting all romantic on me,'' Alexa cut in. ''I care too much about Chance to ask him to sacrifice his personal ambitions. I told you, he's damn good at what he does. Although he's modest about his accomplishments, he *is* the rodeo superstar Dan *dreamed of* being. And besides my refusal to tie Chance down, considering he even wanted to be, there is Howard to contend with. My father-in-law operates from a position of power here. He never lets me forget that.''

Alexa gave her head a decisive shake. ''No, I will not even allow myself to entertain such whimsical possibilities. When I made the decision to borrow money against my half of the ranch to build the bed-and-breakfast I locked myself in for the duration. I can't leave Rocking T and Chance can't stay.''

Deb leaned forward in her chair, resting her elbows on her knees. ''Falling in love is for the birds, isn't it, sis? It hits when you least expect it and tangles up your life.''

Alexa did a double take. ''You and Harvard...I mean Kurt?''

Reluctantly, Deb nodded. ''I never wanted to let a man close enough that I could get hurt, in case things didn't work out. After losing our parents, after watching the way Dan ignored your affection for him, I vowed to avoid the pain of caring too much. I watched you wrap up your feelings and stash them away, then go through the paces of handling your responsibilities. Even when you fell for Chance Butler, you refused to let yourself put any hopes or expectations in the situation.

''In my own way, I guess I packed my emotions in storage.'' Deb chuckled humorously as she slouched in the chair. ''Keep it light, I told myself. Don't take men, or yourself, seriously. But I swear, watching Kurt with his patients, especially with you, got to me. The compassion he offered me while I was so distressed about your condition got to me. I've seen too much good in him. Too much competence and tenderness. The fact that he changed his preppy image to fit into our rural community so he could put me and his patients at ease was touching, too.

"How the heck did this happen? I was going merrily on my way, and then wham! Suddenly I'm getting this warm, fuzzy feeling every time I see the man."

Alexa knew that sensation all too well. Although she knew she was cranky and irritable because of her extended hospital stay, she got this funny little tingle each evening when Chance arrived for a visit. His attentiveness, his concern for her tugged at her heartstrings. The way he kept a constant, protective watch on Zack stirred her deeply.

Half the time, Dan had been so wrapped up in his own world that he didn't know his son was underfoot, expected Alexa to be the only caregiver. But Chance treated Zack as if he was important, as if the boy's presence was welcomed and wanted. Chance had strengthened his sense of security and self-confidence by noticeable degrees.

Lord, Alexa and Zack were going to need time to recover from Chance's absence. He had made such a strong impression, such a drastic difference in their lives.

"Well, sis, I don't have time to sit here pouring my heart out to you. I need to open my shop. I have several consignment orders coming in this morning and book work to do." Deb strode over to give Alexa a sisterly hug. "Try not to be so cranky. Kurt says you're progressing well, physically speaking. A few more days and you can go home...*if* you sign a sworn statement that you'll stay off ladders and never go near electrical circuits, that is."

"Believe me," Alexa muttered, staring at her plaster-coated arm, "I won't be able to stuff an appliance plug into an electrical outlet for years without remembering what a shocking experience it can be. Chester already stopped by to inform me that he and Chance installed the ceiling fans and that I have been fired as apprentice electrician."

"Good. Electricity is definitely not your true calling in

life.'' Deb waved goodbye on her way out the door. ''See you after work, sis.''

Alexa lounged on her bed, twiddling her thumbs. Despite doctor's orders, she knew she needed to pay Howard a visit. Whether he would be happy to see her wasn't the issue. They were family, in spite of their conflicts, and families stuck together.

Although Kurt reported that Howard was recovering nicely, Alexa needed to see for herself, to assure the old man that she was concerned about his condition.

Alexa levered herself onto the edge of the bed, devoured the chocolate-covered doughnuts Deb had sneaked in via her oversize purse, then grabbed her crutches. She had to apologize to Howard for causing the stress and shock that incited his heart attack. He might not accept her apology, but she *needed* to give it.

''Good gawd, woman, you look like hell!'' Howard croaked when Alexa hobbled into his room. His astonished gaze swept over her, lingering on her burned hands, her plaster cast, then dropped to her bandaged ankle. ''It's a wonder you survived. When I first got a look at you that day I didn't think you'd make it. I thought…I'd lost you.…''

Alexa stopped in her tracks when the old man's voice cracked. He was afraid he'd lost her? Did he really mean that? Did he actually see her as more than chief cook, bottle washer and hired hand at Rocking T?

''I'm so sorry I alarmed you with my stupid stunt,'' she apologized. ''Regaining consciousness to discover that I'd caused you to collapse was as bad as suffering from electrical shock.''

Howard squirmed uncomfortably on the bed, then fiddled with the cords that monitored his heartbeat. He looked pale, drawn, uneasy.

"I'm not upsetting you by paying this visit, am I?" Alexa asked.

"No, no. Sit down and take a load off your leg. You shouldn't be moving around, not by the looks of you."

Howard was worried about her? Stunned, Alexa sank into the chair. Was this the same man who had accused her of betraying his son's memory, who had refused to speak to her after he saw her with Chance?

"I've been…um…meaning to thank you for putting up with me all these years," Howard mumbled awkwardly. "I know I'm not an easy man to live with. I'm used to doing things my way, on my own terms, and all that."

Alexa's mouth dropped open far enough for a quail to roost. Her eyes popped.

"Don't look at me like that." Howard scowled, then shifted uneasily on the bed. He refused to meet her astounded gaze. "When Chance Butler barged in here to inform me that he had appointed himself king of Rocking T for the duration of my hospital stay, he said I should spend some time thinking about all the things you've done for me."

"He said that?" she chirped.

Howard nodded his balding head, but he didn't glance in Alexa's direction. "The man's got gumption, I'll give him that. Just limped in here, took over and had the nerve to lecture me."

Alexa winced, wondering if Howard had suffered a setback after Chance's unexpected visit. She wouldn't be surprised. Chance Butler wasn't one of Howard's favorite people nowadays.

The old man leaned over to retrieve an envelope from the top drawer of the nightstand. "Butler dropped by yesterday to deliver the check from the stockyards. He sold some steers for me. I double-checked with the stockyards to see if he sold any cattle under his name."

"And?" Alexa prompted, holding her breath.

"And he hauled fifty head of cattle to Willowvale's stockyards in my trailer and had fifty head sold in my name."

Alexa waited for Howard to finally meet her gaze. "He's an honest man, Howard. He has been nothing but kind, considerate and helpful since he showed up at Rocking T."

Howard nodded as he stared at the check in his hand. "So it seems. But Dan pulled that scam on me a couple of times when he was running low on cash for his rodeo tours. He didn't bother to ask me if I minded giving him a cut of the profit. He just took it."

To her recollection, this was the first time Howard had mentioned one of Dan's failing graces since his death. There had been nothing but glowing praise since the traffic accident. Finally, Howard had accepted the fact that Dan was human, that he had flaws that caused previous hard feelings.

"Dan did...um...a lot of things I didn't approve of—"

Howard's voice dried up, and Alexa realized how difficult it was for Howard to admit that. His one and only son was nowhere near close to perfect. Chance Butler showed Howard more consideration and respect than Dan had. Dan's continuous complaint that Howard could have been more financially generous than he was had never set well with Alexa. She got the impression Dan thought his father owed him financial support, even though Dan wasn't home often enough to help with chores and resolve crises.

"Dan wasn't the kind of husband you deserved, either," Howard murmured.

Alexa gaped at Howard, aware of the mist in his eyes. Did he know Dan had been unfaithful to her? She had never flung the fact in the old man's face, not even when she was exasperated with him.

"There were a few times that I thought my loyalty to Dan was disregarded," she said carefully.

Howard dipped his head slightly. "It's hard for an old

man like me to admit that he's been wrong. I threw Dan's memory in your face constantly. I appeared to take you for granted, because I—''

His voice cracked as he clutched at his chest. When his face lost all color and his shoulders shook, Alexa clambered from her chair, ignoring the sharp pain that shot up her leg.

''Howard, are you all right? Do you want me to call a nurse?''

His chest rose and fell. His breath came in ragged spurts. ''I can't talk about this anymore. Get somebody in here. I'm not feeling well.''

Despite her own injuries, Alexa hopped to the door on one leg to summon assistance. Mildred Whitmier and her assistant barreled down the hall the instant they heard Alexa's frantic call.

''How'd you get down here, young lady?'' Mildred muttered as she whizzed past Alexa. ''Dr. Stevenson hasn't given you permission to be up and around until he's certain you aren't suffering side effects from your concussion. You can't take another fall in your condition.''

''Howard can't breathe,'' Alexa put in quickly. ''Make sure he's all right.''

The nurses swarmed toward Howard, who gasped and sputtered for breath. Alexa clamped herself against the door as Mildred stuffed an oxygen mask over the old man's whitewashed face.

''Don't even think about giving up, Howard,'' Alexa ordered through the stream of tears. ''We need each other. You know that, don't you? Zack needs you, too.''

Despite his sputters and gasps, Alexa saw Howard's gaze swing to her. He stared at her, as if there was more he wanted to say—and couldn't.

Alexa fretted all the way back to her room. She seemed to have the disconcerting knack of upsetting Howard—no matter how good her intentions. Clearly, her visit caused a setback. But no matter what their conflicts through the years, she had never wished ill to him. Would never wish ill to him.

Even though he stood firmly between any relationship she might have had with Chance, she would never sacrifice Howard for her personal happiness. Never! She couldn't have lived with herself if she contemplated such a morbid possibility.

That old man had become a substitute father after her own father was killed in the plane crash. Howard had always been there to protect her, even though he got carried away with his possessiveness at times.

If Howard died...Alexa squeezed her eyes shut and maneuvered into bed. He damned well better not check out! If he got to thinking that was the easiest way to keep from acknowledging the affection she felt for Chance, the affection Zack felt for Chance...

The frantic thought put Alexa right back on her feet. She had to reassure Howard that nothing would change—that she refused to let it change. That was what Howard wanted and needed—to know that he was important to her.

If Alexa had to choose, she knew she had to choose Howard. He had to know that, so he wouldn't hang it all up and let this heart condition get the better of him.

By the time Alexa wobbled down the hall, using the wall for support, Mildred and her aide had Howard resting comfortably. The mask was still in place, the oxygen machine hissing and spitting to break the silence.

"Howard, can you hear me?" Alexa braced herself in the doorway.

Howard open his eyes and stared at her.

"I think you already realize that I'm in love with Chance Butler. I didn't want it to happen, didn't expect it to happen, but it did. But there's something else you should know, Howard," she went on hurriedly. "If I have to choose between you and him, I'll choose you. We need each other. When we get out of here, things will be as they have always been. That is something you can count on. Do you understand what I'm saying, Howard? What I want doesn't matter. I'm not leaving you—ever.''

Alexa didn't realize tears were streaming down her cheeks until after she'd said her piece. The words caused her belly to twist in knots. She was forsaking Chance, casting aside her love for Chance, in order to reassure Howard. Speaking the words caused a riptide of conflicting emotions to whirl through her. She was betraying the one man who had placed her needs above his own when she desperately needed assistance. And yet she knew she would feel the same way if it were Chance lying there in life-threatening condition. She would have betrayed Howard to save Chance, too. But it was Chance who was the stronger of the two men, Chance who had the will to live.

''You have to get better, Howard,'' she sobbed, feeling as if she were being pulled in two directions at once, torn apart by contrasting affections. ''Do you hear me, Howard?''

He closed his eyes. No sound penetrated the silence, except the oxygen tank's methodical cadence—and Alexa's wailing soul crying out in anguish.

Alexa turned away, swiping at the tears. In order to save the old man's life, to provide him with the will to live, she had sacrificed her own chance at fulfillment and happiness. But she owed Howard for the years of support. Dan might have turned his back on his own father, but Alexa couldn't. And she was dying on the inside, knowing the man she could have loved forever could never be a part of her life.

The kitchen was a disaster. It looked as if a flour bomb had exploded on the counter. Cookie ingredients were everywhere—the sink, the floor, the handle on the stove, in Chance and Zack's hair and on the front of their shirts. The first batch of cookies was in the trash, burned beyond recognition.

Chance and Zack's efforts were better the second time around—at least, the cookies weren't burned to a crisp. They were tough as leather, however. Chance was sure Zack had gotten carried away when measuring the flour. Either that or the boy had used a short cup of Crisco. But nonetheless, Zack was beaming in culinary triumph. He had a container of chocolate chip cookies to deliver to his mother.

"Ready to go, Chance?" Zack questioned as he scooped up the plastic container, then headed for the door.

"Whoa, half-pint," Chance called after him. "You can't go to the hospital dressed like that. You look like the Pillsbury Dough Boy."

Zack gave himself a quick perusal, then dusted flour off his shirt and jeans. "There. Clean as a whistle."

Chance begged to disagree. "You go barging into the hospital with white specks on your arms and face and the nurses might think you've contracted some rare disease. Can't have you holed up in the hospital, now can we? Who would help me with all these chores? Certainly not Pecos. He's still waddling around like a lame duck."

Zack surveyed his bespeckled arms. "You think I look diseased?"

Chance grinned. "Unclean, at the very least. You know how particular those nurses are about sanitary conditions for their patients. I think I prefer to shower at home than take a chance of being mopped with disinfectant." He unbuttoned his soiled shirt on the way down the hall. "Don't know about you, rookie, but I'm going to shower before we deliver the cookies."

To Chance's relief, Zack beat him upstairs to shower and change. Chuckling, Chance ambled into Alexa's private bathroom. A man had to stay on his toes if he wanted to reason with a kid.

Forty-five minutes later, Zack was scurrying down the hospital hall, his Air Jordan tennis shoes squeaking with each hurried step. The kid was so proud of his culinary accomplishment that he was about to pop. Chance watched in amusement as Zack burst into his mother's room. The kid wore a smile that stretched from the eastern border of Oklahoma to the tip of the panhandle.

"We made cookies to make you feel better, Mom," Zack announced.

Chance stopped in his tracks when he noted the lackluster in Alexa's eyes, the bleak expression that bracketed her mouth. His pulse stalled out. He knew something was dreadfully wrong.

It was amazing how he had come to read Alexa's moods as if he had radar. He detected her inner turmoil, felt it vibrate through him as if it were his own.

Although Alexa mustered a smile for Zack's benefit, Chance noticed that it didn't begin to reach her eyes. "You baked cookies for me?" she asked, her voice wobbly.

Chance's concern intensified, but he hung back, hoping Zack's arrival would lift Alexa's flagging spirits.

"Me and Chance…Chance and I," he corrected himself hastily, "baked them just for you. But don't worry, Mom, we'll clean up the mess in the kitchen before I go to bed tonight."

Her dull-eyed gaze swung to Chance, then flitted away. He couldn't imagine why she couldn't meet his eyes. It was as if she had committed some terrible sin against him and couldn't bear her own guilt, or the prospect of his reaction. My God, what had happened!

Chance battled the overwhelming urge to scoop Alexa in his arms and assure her that whatever disturbed her could be handled satisfactorily. He would solve whatever problem she faced. He would make everything right—somehow.

While Zack reported on his schoolday—hour by hour—then rattled on about how he had been picked first when the third-graders chose teams in gym class, Chance held up the wall, remaining in the background. Zack was still babbling like a brook when the announcement that visiting hours were over interrupted him.

Giving his mom a smacking kiss on the cheek, Zack bounded off the bed. "I gotta go see Grandpa," he insisted.

"Zack, wait," Alexa called after him. "Grandpa didn't have a good day. The nurses don't want him disturbed. Better wait until tomorrow to visit him."

Chance fixed his attention on Alexa's bleak expression. Was Howard's condition troubling her? Had the old man suffered a serious setback? Was guilt and concern eating her alive?

He knew she held herself personally responsible for frightening and upsetting Howard. Chance felt responsible, too. He had worried for days that his confrontation with the old man would worsen his fragile condition.

According to Harvard, the old man had been recuperating nicely. What happened today that disrupted his recovery?

Chance didn't have a clue, and it was days later before Kurt Stevenson informed him that Howard's condition had finally stabilized. As for Alexa, she never recovered from being unnaturally quiet and withdrawn.

It wasn't until the day Alexa was released from the hospital that Chance noticed the slightest enthusiasm in her voice or sparkle in her eyes.

Chance picked up Alexa from the hospital, but there was nothing but small talk between them. He couldn't bring himself to press her, not on her first day of freedom in two weeks. She was satisfied just to absorb fresh air and admire the outside world.

The only reaction he received from her was a startled gasp when she spied the recently completed patio attached to the cedar barn.

"Oh, Chance," she murmured. "I can't believe how much difference the lattice portico makes in the appearance of the barn! And the cedar benches! When did you find time to do all this?"

Chance helped Alexa from the truck, then lent a supporting arm as she made a beeline toward the B-and-B. "Chester and I got the idea from one of those country-living magazines of yours." Chance held open the barn door and gestured toward the new addition to the dining area. "Deb came up with the idea of using cedar lattice as dividers, giving the tables a look of privacy. She insisted that people came to places like this looking for a getaway that offered a cozy atmosphere. Chester and I agreed with her. With this arrangement, you can tuck yourself into a corner and feel as if you have your own piece of the world."

Alexa scanned the marvelous changes that provided the dining area with the kind of atmosphere she wanted to project. Tears filled her eyes, realizing that she was seeing her dream come true, painfully aware of the sacrifices she had to make to keep it. As much as she longed to fulfill this dream of hers, her enthusiasm was overridden by the fierce ache in her heart. She would give it all up in the bat of an eyelash if she and Chance could have a future together.

Yet, circumstances made it impossible.

Alexa recognized the extent to which she had come to rely and depend on Chance. She had grown to love him even more when she observed the way he interacted with Zack, how happy and well adjusted Zack had become, despite this ordeal. Chance had made all the difference. He had made personal sacrifices for her benefit.

And she had betrayed him in order to provide Howard with the hope needed to fight for his life. Worse, Alexa hadn't been able to find the words to tell Chance that she had promised Howard that his world would remain as it had been.

"Hey, darlin', don't cry. The barn doesn't look that bad, does it?"

Alexa couldn't blink away the tears that dribbled down her cheeks, couldn't find her voice to speak. She wrapped her arms around Chance's neck—and accidentally knocked him upside the head with her clumsy cast.

"Hey, watch it. That arm is dangerous," he said, trying to tease her into good humor. "If you—"

Impulsively, urgently, Alexa pulled his head to hers and kissed him with all the pent-up emotion boiling inside her. She kissed him for all the empty days and broken dreams that lay ahead of her. She held on to him with the desperation of a woman who knew she would never enjoy her heart's fondest desire. And Chance returned all the emotion she poured out to him, holding her with a gentleness that incited more tears.

"I love you," Alexa choked out. "No matter what, I want you to know that, believe that. I love you for all the things you've done, for the way you make me feel inside. There aren't enough words to express how I feel about you, Chance."

Very tenderly, he framed her face in his hands and stared deeply into her eyes. "Do you love me enough to give up this dream of yours, to come away with me, no matter where I asked you to go?"

"Chance, I—"

His thumb skimmed her quivering lips. "How much, Alexa? Enough to make the sacrifices for me that I've made for you?"

His question was like a knife twisting in her heart. She wanted to scream in misery and frustration. "Yes," she whispered brokenly. "I—"

"I love you, too, Alexa," he murmured, then brushed his lips over hers. "I've missed so much in life, things I wasn't even aware of until I came here, until I came to know you and Zack. I was leery of any responsibility that might prove I was like my own father. But spending this week with Zack taught me that I'm nothing like my father. Caring for you and Zack makes me happy, fulfills a need that has been growing stronger each day. I—"

"Chance," she wailed in torment. "Please... Oh God, I didn't know..."

Her voice trailed off into a tortured sob. Why couldn't he have told her days ago? And yet, would it have altered her crucial decision if he had? She still would have had to choose and someone had to lose, she realized. There could be no compromise, no satisfactory resolution.

"Don't love me," she whimpered in anguish. "I don't deserve you. I can't have you!"

"Don't deserve me?" Chance frowned at the near-hysterical expression in her eyes. "I swore it was the other way around. We can make things work. We'll find a way—"

"No," Alexa cut in. Tears burned down her cheeks, her breath seesawed in and out. She couldn't stop the flow of tormented emotion she had held in check for a week. "There's no way. When Howard had a relapse I was in his room. I was afraid he was going to give up. I told him how I felt about you, and I told him that in spite of my own hopes and dreams I would be there with him always—"

Her voice broke and she pushed away from the circle of his arms, feeling ashamed, frustrated, cruel. "Don't you understand, Chance? When Howard's life was on the line I had to choose him and he had to know it. I did the very thing I secretly despised Dan for doing!"

Alexa heard her voice rise to a wild pitch, but was helpless to control it. These feelings of betrayal and hopelessness swallowed her alive. The hurt expression that claimed Chance's rugged features left her soul to bleed.

"I placed Howard as the higher priority, because he needed to know he was needed. He's an old man and he has no one else to turn to. I sacrificed *us,* Chance. I made the agonizing mistake of letting myself chase a selfish dream, just for the chance to be with you, to live with you for a moment out of time. Giving you up is the price I have to pay to provide an old man with the will to live. You don't deserve this, and it's killing me to know that I'm going to lose you...."

Chance stood there, immobilized, while Alexa burst into sobs and wheeled away. She hobbled toward the house, accompanied by the sound of her own whimpers. He wanted to stalk after her, to rail at her for forsaking the best thing that had ever happened to him. Chance felt betrayed, cheated, slighted. He had given up his way of life to see that Alexa had her dream of opening the B-and-B. He had let himself get impossibly attached to her and that adorable kid. And pow! His dreams of a family went up in a puff of smoke.

He'd known it would hurt like hell if things didn't work out according to his hopeful expectations. But the pain that bore down on the throbbing cavity in his chest made it difficult to draw breath, difficult to find reason to draw breath.

Now what are you going to do, Butler? Stay here, bleeding on the inside, waiting until Howard is back on his feet so he can personally order you off the property? Are you going to refuse to speak to Alexa, because of the choice she made to instill the will to live in the old man?

The will to live... The words kept rumbling through his mind like thunder. Alexa had sacrificed any chance of true happiness, because Howard Tipton—for better or worse—had always been there. Alexa's loyalty was unfaltering, but she tossed the prospect of love aside because...

Chance swore colorfully. He had Dan Tipton's infidelity to thank for Alexa's lack of faith in the power of love and stability. She had discovered, the hard way, that love didn't always last, that it wasn't necessarily a two-way street.

Loyalty, now there was the sure bet, as far as Alexa was concerned. She knew what to expect from the old man, had learned to deal with him through the years. What she was afraid to count on was that Chance wouldn't succumb to the lure of the rowdy nightlife that went hand in hand with the rodeo circuit. She expected Chance to come and go like the seasons of the sun. She expected him to lose interest in her eventually. She didn't have confidence in her ability to satisfy a man—for as long as they both lived.

Damn it, he knew those reasons influenced her decision to remain loyal to Howard. So how the hell could he prove that he had staying power when he wouldn't be allowed to stay?

Scowling, swearing, Chance spun around and stormed toward the bunkhouse. Pecos Smith pulled up short when Chance shouldered past him.

"Did you bring Alexa home from the hospital?" Pecos asked as Chance whizzed inside.

"Yes," Chance snapped gruffly.

"How is she?"

"Fine."

Pecos blinked at Chance's harsh tone, but Chance was too frustrated to apologize. He needed some space to think things through. He needed to pack his gear and get the hell out of here.

"I'm putting you in charge of Rocking T. According to the physician, Howard won't get his walking papers for another week. You will be here that long."

"I will?" Pecos asked.

"Damn right you will."

"But it's okay for you to bail out, is that right?"

Chance glared steak knives at the younger cowboy. "Yeah, that's right, pal. You stay and I go."

"You're going to leave before the grand opening next weekend?" Pecos questioned as Chance rummaged around for belongings he might have overlooked. "What the hell's the matter with you?"

Chance rounded on Pecos, wishing he could hit something, throw something, but he refused to take his anger out on an innocent victim. "I'll tell you what's the matter. I fell in love with an impossible dream, with an impossible woman in an impossible situation. Do yourself a favor, Pecos, don't make the same disastrous mistake. Love will rip out your heart.''

In a flash, Chance was out the door. He didn't bother to collect the belongings he'd left at the house. What he left behind could be replaced....

Now there was a laugh. How did a man replace his own heart and soul? It wasn't as if they were sitting on a shelf at the local convenience store where a man could swagger in and pick up replacements when he was fresh out.

Gunning the clunker truck, Chance sprayed gravel on his way down the driveway. His hands were clenched so tightly around the steering wheel that his knuckles turned white. His belly flipped over, then knotted up. He spewed a few obscenities to ease his frustration as he drove away.

He had opened his heart, taken the risk of falling in love, and he had nothing to show for the experience but bittersweet memories.

Damn it to hell and back! Hadn't he known better than to get involved? Hadn't he predicted something like this would happen?

Well, here he was, staring misery in the face. And misery, he figured, was about to become his ever-constant companion.

Chapter Fourteen

Chance got as far as Willowvale before he realized he couldn't walk away. His aching heart had already changed his mind for him. Both his heart and head were in agreement that if he walked, he would prove what Alexa believed to be true: During a series of crises, she could never depend on a man to be there with her, for her.

Damn it, he and Alexa loved each other! Didn't that count for anything? Was there any truth to that cliché about love conquering all?

Applying the brake, Chance waited for the stoplight on Main Street to turn green. His mind raced like a Thoroughbred. He had given Howard Tipton his word that the ranch would be in proper working order when the old man returned home. Chance had obligations to fulfill, even if he had to drive to and from Rocking T.

Maybe he couldn't bear to live at the ranch, tossing and turning each night, wishing he could hold Alexa in his arms, but he could hole up in a local motel, the way he did while he traveled the rodeo circuit. He would see to the farm chores, then make himself scarce in the evenings. If nothing else, he would prove to Alexa, and to Howard, that he was a man of honor, a man who took responsibility seriously.

Chance had tolerated all the hurt and disappointments life tossed his way when he was a child. He could endure this feeling of betrayal, this sense of loss.

When the impatient driver behind him honked twice, Chance glanced up at the green light and cruised through the intersection. Within a few minutes he located Sleepe Hollow Motel. The quarters were cramped, luxury-sparse, but the room was reasonably clean. Chance had sure as hell bedded down in worse places while he followed the suicide circuit.

While he was sprawled on the double bed, holding the remote control to the TV in one hand, a can of cola in the other, he asked himself how he was going to explain his absence in Zack's life. He and the rookie had become so close the past month that Chance couldn't bear the thought of removing himself from Zack's life without so much as a goodbye.

Chance's parents had pulled that stunt on him, and he knew how it felt to be abandoned and left thinking that it was his fault that his parents lacked affection for him.

Zack was not going to suffer that kind of mental anguish. No child deserved to harbor those feelings of inadequacy!

Chance checked his watch. If he skedaddled over to the elementary school, he could speak to Zack before the boy piled onto the bus. In a flash, Chance was out the door and in the jalopy truck. He had no idea what in the hell he was going to say, but Zack had a right to know Chance wouldn't be waiting at home.

"Chance!" Zack called excitedly. He rushed forward, clutching his math book in one arm and waving wildly with the other.

Chance smiled faintly when several third-graders wheeled around to peer up at him. It seemed all of Zack's friends were eager to look their fill at the real cool dude Zack had described.

Tipping his hat politely, Chance nodded greetings to the half-pint crowd that closed in around him.

"You're the rodeo star, aren't you?" a towheaded youngster asked. "Do you really practice baseball with Zack every night?"

Chance inwardly grimaced. Those practice sessions were about to come to a screeching halt. "Unless it rains," he hedged. "We definitely don't practice when lightning strikes. Much too dangerous."

"Did you really put up an adjustable basketball goal for Zack?" another youngster wanted to know.

Chance nodded. "Gotta have a place to practice if you're going to get good at something."

"And you actually took Zack fishing, and you didn't even yell at him when he accidentally caused you to fall in the water?"

Chance was amazed that these third-graders knew so much about his activities. That was proof enough that Zack took pride and satisfaction in the time Chance spent with him.

"No, I didn't yell at him. I was too busy laughing," Chance said. "Now, if y'all will excuse me, I'd like to speak privately with Zack before he catches the bus."

Proudly, Zack matched Chance's step as they strode to a vacant corner of the building. "Man, the guys won't be able to say I made up all that stuff about you. Thanks, Chance."

"No problem, rookie." Despite the pain in his knee,

Chance squatted down to Zack's level. "We don't have much time here, rookie. I just wanted you to know that I won't be around the ranch much when you get home from school."

The stricken look on Zack's face was like a spike driven into Chance's chest.

"Why not?" Zack wheezed.

Why not? There were a dozen complicated reasons why, none of which Zack would understand.

"The fact is that I'm not really a part of your family, Zack. Sometimes grown-ups have to go away, but that doesn't mean that they don't care. I care about you, and I wish things could have turned out differently. I'll be around town a while longer, until your grandpa is feeling better. But now that your mom is home from the hospital—"

"But I want you there!" Zack burst out, his bottom lip quivering as he battled tears.

"It's going to be okay, rookie," Chance assured him quickly. "We'll work it out so we can spend time together. Maybe we can go to the park together. Your mom says it's one of your favorite places."

"But it won't be the same." Zack wiped the tears from his eyes and hugged his math book tightly to his chest.

Chance glanced over his shoulder. The steady stream of students clambering onto the bus had thinned out. He was running out of time.

"You'd better load up, rookie. Your mom is home waiting for you. I'll make arrangements to see you soon. Now behave yourself. I'll be thinking about you."

When Zack didn't budge, Chance gave him a gentle nudge. "Take care of your mom. Don't let her overdo on her first day home."

Zack didn't reply. He just walked away with a wounded look on his face that had Chance swearing under his breath.

Damn it all, Chance thought as he limped back to the

clunker truck. Kids always got caught in the middle of turmoil that wasn't of their own making. Chance would have to schedule visits with Zack to assure the boy that he was cared about. Chance had to let Zack down gradually. A clean break was inadvisable—for the kid *and* for him.

God! This was killing Chance by inches. He wanted Zack and Alexa in his life, wanted to be an important part of theirs. But he was forever the outcast, the outsider.

Some things never seemed to change.

Scowling, Chance drove to the motel and channel-surfed the TV. Ironic, he thought hours later. Flipping from one television channel to the next seemed symbolic of his life. He'd never been able to stay in one place long enough to make sense of anything. He sure as hell couldn't make sense of this relationship with Alexa. Loving her, being unable to have her, was tearing him apart!

Alexa bathed and washed away the steady stream of tears that dripped down her cheeks. For the past two days she had been so tormented and miserable that nothing seemed to matter. She felt as if she had one nerve left—and it was badly frayed. There were times, like now—especially now—that she wished she could adopt her late husband's habit of walking away when situations got tough. But that had never been her style.

Chance would never know how she wished she could shrug off the cloak of responsibility and follow him wherever he wanted to go. But she couldn't live on pipe dreams. She had promises to keep, prior commitments. Ah, if only his declaration of love had come sooner. If only…

Alexa muffled a sniff as she scooped up the fresh-baked cookies and set them aside to cool. She had to get her act together before Zack returned from school. He had arrived the previous afternoon looking sullen and fighting tears. Alexa had tried to explain to him that Chance wouldn't be around now that she was back home. To her surprise, Zack informed her that Chance had stopped by school to tell him in person.

Alexa was deeply touched by Chance's thoughtful gesture. And frankly, she was amazed that he had shown up bright and early this morning to tend the chores and check the cattle. Although he made no attempt to see her, he was honoring his promise to Howard.

That made Alexa feel all the worse. Her love, admiration and respect for Chance had grown by gigantic proportions. She knew how much she was losing, knew she would never experience the kind of happiness he brought into her life.

Alexa blotted away the infuriating tears that had her eyes dripping like a leaky faucet. She didn't want Zack to see her like this again tonight. Last night had been enough. She had tried to be good company, to play catch—though the plaster cast and crutches limited her. But Zack lacked enthusiasm, refused to let her take Chance's place during ball practice sessions.

Tonight, Alexa vowed, she was going to pull herself together and put up a cheerful front....

Thunder boomed overhead, and Alexa nearly jumped out of her plaster cast. Great, she thought. Just what she needed—a rainstorm to put a damper on her already bleak mood.

Before she pulled the second sheet of cookies from the oven huge raindrops hammered against the windowpane. Even though the pastures could use the rain to provide forage for the cattle, Alexa would have preferred the cloudburst to hold off until the school bus arrived.

But then, she asked herself, when did life go exactly as she preferred?

Switching off the oven, Alexa wrapped a plastic bag around her cast, then headed for the door. She wouldn't let Zack make the quarter-mile walk from the bus stop, not with lightning popping and thunder rolling. The kid would be drenched before he reached home.

Hobbling on her tender ankle, Alexa headed for her pickup. Five minutes later, she was still waiting for the bus. Knowing road conditions were deteriorating from the downpour, she gave the bus another fifteen minutes.

And thirty minutes later, the bus still hadn't pulled into sight.

Alexa's anxiety intensified. She wondered if the bus had been involved in an accident. The thought of children being tossed around inside the bus had her praying nonstop.

Alexa drove toward town, following the bus route. She arrived at school in time to flag down the young teacher who served as bus driver.

"Zack didn't come home today," Alexa hollered over the sound of pounding rain.

The teacher ducked into his car before he became drenched completely. "Zack wasn't on the bus," he informed her. "The other students said he had made arrangements to stay in town."

Alexa frowned as the teacher waved and drove away. Had Chance made arrangements to spend time with Zack? No one had bothered to inform her. That didn't sound like Chance. Although she knew he was hurt and disillusioned, she couldn't imagine that kind of spiteful behavior from him. If nothing else, she had learned that Chance Butler was consistent, reliable.

Her mind buzzing, Alexa sped toward her sister's craft shop. The store was within walking distance of the school, and Zack had made the jaunt several times while Alexa was in the hospital.

Protectively covering her cast, Alexa hobbled through the downpour to reach the craft shop. Deb blinked in surprise when Alexa came in with a draft of wind.

"Alexa? What the devil are you doing out in this toad-strangler?'' Deb demanded. ''You're supposed to be home recuperating.''

''Have you seen Zack?'' Alexa asked without preamble. ''He didn't ride home on the bus. I spoke to the driver a few minutes ago and he said Zack made arrangements to stay in town. Is he here?''

''No, I haven't seen him.'' Deb frowned. ''Maybe he came through the back exit to my office. When he was staying with me, he made a habit of doing his homework at my desk until I closed up shop. I'll go check.''

While Deb hurried off, Alexa wrung her hands nervously. It wasn't like Zack to wander away without checking with her. His disappearance had her conjuring up all sorts of worse-case scenarios. If she hadn't tracked her son down within the hour, she was definitely calling the police. In this storm Zack would be difficult to track, and she needed all the assistance she could get....

Howard! Alexa remembered that Zack had asked her to take him into town the previous night to visit his grandfather. Alexa had put him off. Maybe Zack had taken it upon himself to pay Howard a call.

''He's not in my office, sis,'' Deb called from the rear of the store.

''I'll try the hospital,'' Alexa announced.

''Hold on a sec and I'll go with you.''

Deb trotted down the aisle that was lined with colorful crafts and refinished antiques to grab her bank deposit pouch and purse. In less than a minute she was leading the way through the rain to her car.

''I can't imagine Zack pulling a stunt like this,'' Deb said as she flipped on the windshield wipers.

Alexa stared straight ahead, her fists knotted in the hem of her T-shirt. ''His life is in turmoil again.''

''Meaning what?'' Deb interrogated.

"Meaning Chance is no longer staying at the ranch. I think Zack holds me responsible for Chance's absence."

"He's gone?" Wide-eyed, Deb glanced at Alexa, then focused her attention on the rain-slick street. "When did this happen?"

"Yesterday afternoon. We...um...I told Chance that nothing could ever come of our relationship because I couldn't abandon Howard, especially not after his heart attack."

Deb groaned aloud. "Great, just great. Remind me to take lessons from you if I get a hankering to screw up my life. You need Chance at the ranch. How are you going to manage the chores and final arrangements for opening the B-and-B? And why didn't Chance have the guts to tell Zack he was leaving?"

"He did," Alexa said in his defense. "Chance still comes out to handle the chores. The man isn't at fault."

Deb frowned pensively. "Well then, maybe Zack went looking for Chance. The kid is fiercely attached to him, after all."

Alexa's shoulder's sagged. "I have no idea where Chance is staying. I'm not sure Zack knows, either."

"Duh," Deb said, and snorted. "How many places can the man be, for heaven's sake? This town has two dumpy motels to its credit. We can check both places."

"Let's try the hospital first," Alexa insisted.

She didn't want to face Chance unless absolutely necessary. Seeing him at a distance, while he tended the chores at Rocking T, was difficult. Face-to-face would be pure torture. Besides, Chance probably despised her—and she honestly couldn't blame him if he did—for the decision she'd made.

Before Deb came to a complete stop in the hospital parking lot, Alexa opened her door. Oblivious to the steady downpour, she limped inside. Mildred Whitmier's gaze narrowed as she gave Alexa the once-over.

"Young lady, I specifically heard Doc Stevenson tell you to stay off that injured ankle. What are you doing here?"

"I'm looking for my son," she explained hurriedly. "He didn't ride the bus home, and I thought maybe he took it upon himself to visit his grandpa."

Mildred glanced over her broad shoulder. "I haven't seen the boy, but the entire nursing staff has been run ragged. This storm sent several traffic-accident victims to the emergency room. We've been informed that another wreck occurred—"

No sooner were the words out of her mouth than the intercom buzzed, requesting that all available staff report to the emergency room. When the nurses scurried off, Alexa aimed herself toward Howard's room. Deb darted off in the opposite direction to grab a phone book to check the motels, in hopes of locating Chance.

Alexa crossed her fingers, hoping Zack was tucked safely in Howard's room. To her dismay, Howard was alone. He was picking over the plate of food that sat in front of him.

His waxen face registered surprise when Alexa approached him. "Why are you all wet?"

Alexa supplied a silly answer to the silly question. "It's raining outside."

"Well, you shouldn't be here," Howard lectured her crossly. "You should be home resting."

"I had a few errands to run in town, so I thought I'd drop in to say hello," Alexa lied through her teeth.

No way in hell was she going to jeopardize Howard's condition by mentioning Zack's disappearance. If she was lucky, she would locate her son and Howard would never know about the incident.

"I'm feeling better," Howard informed her, then wrinkled his nose as he stared distastefully at the tray of food.

"But to borrow a word from Zack's vocabulary—this meat loaf *sucks*."

"Doesn't matter," Alexa insisted. "You are going to eat it and like it. You need to regain yourself strength so you can come home."

He muttered under his breath—something about slop unfit for hogs. Alexa was in too much of a rush to ask him to repeat the comment.

"Finish your meal, Howard," she said as she pivoted on her good leg. "I'll see you tomorrow."

"Where's Zack? I'd like to see the boy."

So would Alexa. Soon as she did, she was going to read that kid every paragraph of the riot act. He'd better not pull this stunt again!

"Zack has plans this afternoon," Alexa answered. She dearly wished she knew what those plans were!

"Alexa, I—"

"I'll bring Zack in for an extended visit tomorrow," she cut in quickly. "I have several stops to make before supper. Take care, Howard."

Deb stood at the nurses' station, watching her sister's limping approach. "No Zack," she presumed.

Alexa shook her head dismally. "I didn't want to alarm Howard. I've caused him enough distress. When we find Zack—" not *if*, but *when* "—Howard will never know about this. I want that understood, Deb. Howard can't endure repeated shock and stress right now."

Deb nodded agreeably as they strode out into the rain. "I checked both motels. Chance is staying at Sleepe Hollow. I think that should be our next stop."

"I don't think I can face him. Oh, Deb, I swear I'm going crazy!" she burst out as she plunked on the car seat. "Chance claims he loves me. He wanted me to gather up Zack and walk away with him. I swear that request was some sort of test to see if I meant what I said about loving him. I failed the test. I failed *him.* I've been grossly unfair to him, and he has been nothing but supportive and reliable...."

When Alexa dissolved into tears, Deb reached over to pat her quaking shoulder. "Let's solve one crisis at a time here, shall we?"

Alexa managed a watery smile. How many times during Deb's turbulent teenage years had Alexa said those very words to her sister? At least two dozen that she could recall off the top of her head.

"I'll do the talking," Deb volunteered. "When we locate Chance, you can stay in the car."

"No." Alexa inhaled deeply, scrambling for hard-won composure. "I screwed up everyone's life. I'll accept responsibility for it and deal with it."

"Well, fine," Deb muttered as she wheeled into the motel. "Go ahead and play the martyr, as usual. But I'll be your moral support. Heaven knows, you've been mine for years." Deb opened her door to climb out. "Just hang tight while I check with the front desk. When I tried to call Chance from the hospital he wasn't in. I want to make sure he didn't check out."

One minute after Deb entered the office, the jalopy truck rumbled in and pulled up to room seven. Alexa hopped from the car, holding her breath, hoping to see Zack scoot from the passenger door.

But Chance didn't have a passenger. He carried a sack from a local fast-food restaurant.

When Chance caught sight of her, she noted the look of resentment before he could mask the emotion. Clearly, he wasn't prepared to face her any more than she wanted to face him. Well, their personal problems had to wait, Alexa told herself determinedly. Zack's whereabouts took precedence.

"Something wrong?" Chance asked, staring at the air over her wet head.

"Zack didn't take the school bus home," Alexa informed him. "I was hoping he was with you."

"God, the kid isn't running around loose during this storm, is he?" Chance gasped.

"If he is, it's my fault," Alexa muttered. "Everything is entirely my fault—Howard's condition, Zack's disappearance, your disappointment. Cause and effect, turn of events and all that. I started this mess!"

"Alexa, calm down."

The moment he grabbed hold of her good arm, she flew at him like a lost ship searching for a port in a storm. She had no right to cry on his shoulder, no right to ask for his help. She had treated him abominably, forsaken him, and still he offered comfort and compassion. She didn't deserve him, damn it!

"I'm sorry, Chance," she blubbered. "Since I can't help loving you, I keep turning to you. I've had nowhere to turn but to myself for years. But after what I did to you, to us—"

"Sh-sh!" he interrupted, cuddling her close. "None of that matters. Zack is important. We'll track him down and make certain he doesn't pull this kind of shenanigan again."

"He's missing you badly." She lifted her head from his shoulder and stared into those intense silver-blue eyes that haunted her waking hours and consumed her dreams. "I tried to make him understand, tried to prevent him from getting too attached to you, but my accident complicated the situation. Every time I turn around I have myself to blame for everything that goes wrong, and *you* to thank for everything that goes right. I swear I'm some kind of jinx—"

Chance gave her a firm shake. "Stop it. Quit being so

damned hard on yourself. No more apologies. No more one-way guilt trips. I'll turn this town upside down to find that kid.''

Fighting another embarrassing round of tears, Alexa nodded. "Thank you for being here when I need you.''

"I was ready to make the commitment to always be there when I'm needed, but I discovered loving wasn't always enough—" Chance scowled as he ushered her toward the passenger side of the jalopy. "I shouldn't have said that. It was a cheap shot.''

"I deserved it," Alexa murmured.

"Chance! Thank God!" Deb called, then came dashing through the rain. "I presume you haven't seen or heard from Zack, either.''

Chance limped around to the driver's side of the truck. "Afraid not. I'm taking Alexa with me to search the streets. Call the police and report Zack's disappearance. Maybe a cop will spot him while on patrol. Do you know if Harvard is off duty?''

"Yes," Deb replied. "He had the afternoon off. We were supposed to see a movie tonight.''

"Good. Give the cops Harvard's phone number. We'll check in every quarter of an hour. In the meantime, you cruise the west side of town and we'll take the east side. Harvard's house will be our base of operation.''

Deb managed a smile and gave him a snappy salute. "Yes sir, General Butler, sir.''

When Deb sprinted to her car, Alexa focused absolute attention on the man who turned out to be *not* just another cowboy who showed up at Rocking T. Chance Butler's organizational skills were impressive. When things got tough, he became assertive and decisive. Although it felt unnatural to let someone else take charge, Alexa felt herself relax slightly. If she hadn't realized it before, she knew now that Chance had become her strength, her support, her dearest friend.

She hadn't thought it possible to love him more than she already did, but she did. Yep, she realized, when he left town for good, she was definitely going to be miserable for the rest of her life. She only hoped to God that she had Zack with her to ease the ache of losing the most precious love of her life, a love that wasn't meant to be.

Zack huddled under the sprawling cedar near the slipper-slide in the park. He had walked from one side of town to the other, trying to locate Chance, but he was nowhere to be found. Even though Zack loved his mom with all his heart, he loved Chance, too, and wanted him back.

He'd thought it all out. Every sentence of his speech to Chance. Zack was going to list all the reasons why Chance should marry Mom. Chance would be the coolest dad in town, and every kid at school thought Chance was something special.

Grown-ups got everything tangled up, and Zack wanted to straighten things out. He might have, too, but he couldn't find Chance.

And then it started raining...and it got dark....

Zack hated to admit it, but he'd gotten scared when that greasy-haired creep who looked as big as a gorilla started following him. Zack had hightailed it down the nearest alley, and he didn't even cry when the goon started yelling foul curses at him. Zack wasn't a crybaby. He was just a little shook up right now, that was all.

Thunder boomed overhead, and Zack ducked instinctively. Pea-size hail thudded into the overhanging cedar limbs. Zack shrank deeper into the protection of the tree.

Soon as the rain let up, he had to come up with a plan. He couldn't stay here all night, not with that greasy baboon roaming around out there.

Zack had swung by Aunt Debs' shop when he got real hungry, but she had closed up for the night. He considered hiking to her house to call home, but he figured his mom would be pretty mad about the whole thing. Better let her calm down, Zack reasoned. If he could have found Aunt Debs or Chance, things might have been okay.

As rain dripped off the tree limbs, Zack tucked himself into a tight ball and battled his tears. He wasn't gonna cry. Chance wouldn't have cried. Mostly he laughed and smiled and did what needed to be done without complaining. Zack wanted to be like that when he grew up.

When the rain finally slacked off, Zack made his decision. He'd finally figured out what to do. There was one place he could go that was a sure thing. He was annoyed with himself for not thinking of it earlier. That sure was dumb of him. His grandpa was in the hospital, and he wasn't coming home for a week. Zack could visit Grandpa and call Aunt Debs.

Zack wasn't ready to face Mom yet. He'd worry about that later, he decided.

Peering from the thick tree branches, Zack tried to get his bearings in the darkness. He'd follow the alleys through town until he reached the hospital. He wished he had enough pocket change to buy a snack from the hospital vending machines. He sure was hungry, and tired. His legs were aching something fierce from all that running and walking.

Chilled to the bone, legs wobbling, Zack scrambled through the park toward the alley. Dogs raised a ruckus, and Zack got scared all over again, because he couldn't see where he was going in the darkness and rain. He had only streetlights to guide him, but he told himself he could find Grandpa. Grandpa Tipton would make sure Mom didn't yell at him too much.

And next time Zack decided to track down Chance, he

needed to come up with a better plan. This one had turned out to be a complete flop.

"We'll try the park," Chance announced after a futile thirty-minute search-and-rescue attempt.

Alexa shook her head and squirmed worriedly. "How can an eight-year-old boy drop out of sight so fast? And how old does Zack think he is anyway? He knows better than to go traipsing off alone. We've had that talk several times."

"Calm down," Chance soothed. "We'll find him. Working yourself into hysterics won't help. Zack is usually a levelheaded kid."

"He'll be levelheaded after I pound some sense into him for scaring ten good years off my life," Alexa erupted.

"Kids are more durable than you think," Chance told her as he cruised toward the park. "When I was eight I was taking care of an alcoholic father. Granted, it should have been the other way around, but I survived the ordeal."

Alexa reached out to touch his arm. "I'm sorry," she whispered. "I wish you'd grown up differently. I wish my own mistakes hadn't sent Zack out alone tonight."

"And I wish you'd stop blaming yourself. We'll find him, Alexa."

Chance hoped to hell he located the kid before disaster struck. Fact was, he was every bit as worried as Alexa. Chance would lay down his life if it would ensure Zack returned home safely. Until that kid was found, Chance vowed to search low and high. Someone had to have seen that kid, Chance reassured himself.

The police department was doing their thing, he mused. Every boy in Zack's class was being contacted, and word spread fast in small towns like Willowvale. The community was like an extended family that pulled together during a crisis. Chance liked that. He wished he could be around to enjoy that aspect of the community.

Sooner or later, Zack would be home where he belonged. Chance sincerely hoped it was sooner. He couldn't bear to see Alexa fall apart. She was still recovering from her mishap. He wanted to offer her all the moral support she needed, but hell! Fretting about Zack had Chance tied up in knots!

Chapter Fifteen

"Mildred?"

Mildred Whitmier wheeled around to see nothing but an abandoned hall beyond the nurses' station.

"Yes?" she said to the hall at large.

"It's me. I'm down here."

Mildred leaned over the tall counter to see a wet head and green eyes peering up at her. "Zack? Where have you been? Everybody in town is looking for you."

"I came to see my grandpa," Zack announced. "I forgot which room he was in. They all look alike."

Mildred whizzed around the desk and grabbed the soggy youngster by the hand. "I'll deliver you personally to your grandpa. I want you to promise to stay put until your mom comes to pick you up. She's worried sick."

Zack groaned miserably. "You aren't going to put her back in the hospital, are you?"

"No, sugar, she's not that kind of sick," Mildred clarified as she tramped down the hall. "But you have to make sure your mom gets plenty of rest after she chased around town all night trying to find you."

"She's gonna be pretty mad, I guess," Zack mumbled uneasily.

"Can't say I blame her," Mildred harrumphed. She halted at Howard's door. "Go snuggle up with your grandpa and I'll make some phone calls. Have you had supper yet?"

Zack shook his head.

"I'll send one of the nurses down with a few snacks to tide you over." Mildred shoved Zack into the room. "Go on now, sugar. Keep your grandpa company."

When the nurse galumphed away, Zack approached the bed. Grandpa was sleeping, and Zack didn't know if he should disturb Howard.

His wet shoes squeaking, Zack tiptoed across the floor. He climbed onto the chair, then onto the bed.

When Howard's eyes fluttered open, Zack smiled. He sure was glad to see his grandpa.

"Zack? What are you doing here?" Howard questioned. "What happened to your clothes?"

"They got wet," Zack replied. "I'm kinda cold. Could I crawl under your cover?"

Howard scooted sideways to accommodate his grandson. The twosome snuggled up, nice and cozy, waiting for the nurse to bring snacks.

"Mildred told me to remind you to stay put," the nurse said as she whizzed into the room. "We're trying to track down your mother."

Howard raised an eyebrow, then stared at Zack who squirmed uncomfortably. "Your mom doesn't know where you are? How did that happen?"

Zack ripped open the sack of potato chips the nurse provided. "I decided to go see Chance after school," he explained. "But I couldn't find him anywhere in town."

Howard's face paled. He told himself to remain calm. This was no time to hyperventilate. "Why did you need to find Chance? Was there a problem at the ranch?"

"It's like this." Zack paused to cram a handful of chips in his mouth. He chewed hurriedly, then chased the food with the can of cola the nurse had given him. "Chance isn't staying at the ranch. Mom is awfully unhappy. I could tell because her eyes were all red and puffy when I came home from school yesterday. She was happy when Chance was around, and she smiled and laughed a lot. Chance was good at making her do that. He was good at making me happy, too, because we played ball and stuff after school. We even baked cookies for Mom when she was injured. I was going to bring some to you, but that was the day you weren't feeling so good and the nurse wouldn't let me come see you."

Howard clenched his hand in the sheet and waited for Zack to gobble up the remainder of his chips. Howard hadn't realized how much the turmoil between him and Alexa and Chance had affected Zack. It hurt to learn that Zack had run to Chance to make everything right again.

"What did you need to see Chance about?" Howard asked.

"He seemed kind of sad, because he couldn't stay at the ranch, so I thought I could talk him into marrying Mom. Then we could all be a family."

Howard gasped for breath, but he swore he was not going to collapse in front of his grandson. The boy didn't need another scare. "But you have a dad, Zack. Just because he can't be here in person doesn't mean he isn't with you."

The look in Zack's eyes nearly broke Howard's heart—and it wasn't in good shape at the moment. "I love Chance, Grandpa. When Mom was in the hospital Chance took real good care of me, and I tried to take care of him, too. And Chance said we had to take care of things for you, because he didn't want you to overex...ex—''

"Overexert," Howard supplied.

"Yeah, that was the word. Chance said it means to do too much when you're not feeling good."

Zack paused to sip his cola, then continued. "I thought if Chance liked Mom that I could tell her so, then I could let Chance know if Mom liked him, too."

Howard smiled despite his own tormented emotion. "Is that how the kids at school go about lining up boyfriends and girlfriends?"

Zack nodded his head, while unwrapping his candy bar. "Yep. That's exactly how it works. You tell your friend if you like a girl, then he asks the girl if she wants to be your girlfriend. If she says yes, then it's set. Chelsea McClain is my girlfriend. We worked that all out last week at recess. It doesn't take long if you don't have to run all over town passing the word back and forth."

"Shorty McClain's granddaughter is your girlfriend?" Howard questioned. "She's a cute one, all that long blond hair and blue eyes."

Zack nodded, then bit into the candy. "I want to get things worked out for Mom and Chance, but I can't find him. I sure hope he didn't leave town. I want him to come back and stay forever. Don't you, Grandpa?"

The question went unanswered. Howard flicked on the TV and stared at the screen while Zack polished off his candy bar and cola.

Halfway through the ten o'clock news, Howard glanced down to see his grandson nestled beside him, fast asleep. Tenderly, Howard tucked the quilt under the boy's chin.

Howard's tears fell unnoticed, and Zack missed the sports report. The Atlanta Braves clinched a double header against the New York Mets. Chipper Jones had knocked one out of the park.

And the words of an eight-year-old boy spun around the old man's head, leaving him to do some serious soul-searching.

Chance applied the brake when he recognized Deb's car—with its emergency lights blinking. He rolled down the window when Deb halted beside him.

"Any news?" he asked.

"Kurt just received word that Zack showed up at the hospital to see his grandfather," Deb reported.

"Is he okay?" Alexa questioned anxiously.

Deb bobbed her blond head. "Soaked to the bone and hungry, but unharmed."

"Thank God!" Alexa slumped on the seat. "Thank you, Deb. We'll swing by your shop to get my pickup."

Chance made a U-turn to follow Deb. He figured he was about to be cut out of the loop, as soon as Alexa manned the wheel of her own vehicle. But Chance needed to see—with his own eyes—that Zack was safe and sound. He felt responsible for Zack's ordeal.

"I'm going to the hospital to see Zack before you haul him home," Chance declared, then stared intently at Alexa, daring her to object.

She smiled at him. "I thought you would."

"You don't mind?"

She shook her head. Long strands of corkscrew curls danced around her face. "When a boy goes to such extremes to find you, and I'm pretty sure you were his destination, he's entitled to. say whatever it was he wanted to say to you. He was gravely disappointed when you left. Surely you know that."

Chance let out the breath he hadn't realized he'd been

holding. "Thanks, Alexa. And surely you realize how much I care about that kid."

"Yesterday, when you asked me if I would give up everything to—"

"That was a selfish demand," Chance cut in quickly. "I know the ranch is your home. You have your feet firmly planted in Rocking T soil. I guess I just wanted to know if you loved me enough to make a fresh new start, if it turned out that was the only way we could be together."

Alexa graced him with a watery smile. "What I want, and what I feel necessary to repay a long-standing debt to Howard are in direct conflict. I know I can't have it all, Chance, but it doesn't mean I hurt any less."

He sighed audibly as he reached for her hand, giving it a gentle squeeze. "I knew I was asking for the moon, but I guess I'll settle for a few stars. I made a commitment to Howard to manage things during his absence. I want to see you and Zack as often as I can. I want the right to return occasionally. Can you at least give me that, Alexa?"

Alexa felt like bursting into tears again. Until recently she'd had no idea she had so much water in her. Heavens, she could have filled a dried-up farm pond! She loved Chance so deeply, so completely, for a thousand justifiable reasons. She was prepared to settle for bits and pieces of his time, to treasure every stolen moment.

It wasn't so long ago that she swore off professional rodeo dynamos and their here-today-gone-tomorrow lifestyle. But Chance proved to her, time and again, that he wasn't just another cowboy. He had seen Alexa through every crisis, seen her at her best and worst and every mood in between. He pitched in to help when she needed an extra hand. He taught her the gentlest kind of passion and the hottest, sweetest brand of desire. He treated Zack like his own son, compensated for the emptiness in Zack's life.

Chance Butler had come to mean all things to Alexa and Zack, and she longed to dream the forbidden dream.

Alexa needed Chance, wanted him more than she'd wanted anything in life—including the bed-and-breakfast that she had poured her time and labor into.

"Alexa?" Chance prompted as he pulled into the parking lot of the arts and crafts shop. "You didn't answer me. Can I see you and Zack when I'm going to and from rodeos—"

She was in his arms before Chance could punctuate his question. He didn't even care that she whacked him on the shoulder with her plaster cast. She held on to him as if she didn't want to let him go. Chance knew, there and then, that no matter where he was, no matter what geographical distance separated him from Alexa, she would always be home to him. He would carry their love for each other with him wherever he went.

"Any time, any place, cowboy," she whispered as she clung desperately to Chance. "I'll find a way to come to you, to savor the minutes you can spare. I want my goodbye back. Yesterday nearly killed me. I love you and nothing is going to change that."

Chance crushed her to him, ever mindful not to apply pressure to places still tender from her fall from Grace. "Don't ever stop loving me, honey. If I can't have you and Zack with me all the time, I need to know you're there, that I can pick up the phone and hear your voice. You're the home I never really had. You're my heart, I swear it—"

"If the two of you can tear yourselves away from each other for a few minutes, there's a kid at the hospital. Remember him? Big green eyes, reddish-blond hair. Fires questions like torpedoes?" Deb taunted as she mashed her nose against the steamed-up window and made comical faces.

Reluctantly, Chance released Alexa so she could scoot

across the seat. He could have sat there all night, holding her, filling up his heart so he could leave on a full tank.

That was what his life had come down to, he realized. He had to make pit stops at Rocking T when his heart and soul ran on fumes. He'd have to refuel, then be on his way. He wanted more than a roadhouse, yet circumstances at Rocking T forced him to run on half-empty dreams.

"Here's how I have this planned out," Deb said as Alexa hobbled to her truck. "I'll bring Zack to my place for the night. I still have a few of his clothes in the laundry. I'll feed him breakfast and take him to school while the two of you—" She smiled wryly at Alexa, then glanced at Chance. "Well, you're consenting adults. I don't have to tell you what you can do."

"I think Zack better come home," Alexa insisted, though she appreciated her sister's offer to grant them privacy.

"Are you kidding?" Deb sniffed. "Zack will leap at the chance to avoid you. I predict he expects you to yell at him for scaring you witless. He'd probably like to wait until you cool down before he faces the music."

Chance's heart lurched when Alexa glanced at him, as if she were including him in the decision-making that affected Zack. The faith and trust she placed in him was overwhelming.

"Thanks for the offer, Deb, but I think the rookie needs to be tucked in his own bed after the night he's had. The ranch is his *querencia*."

"His what?" Deb and Alexa asked in unison.

"*Querencia,* his safe, secure haven," Chance translated the Spanish word. "Zack also needs to know that running away from a difficult situation, one in which he might receive a reprimand, is unacceptable. He has to learn that you hang around to work out problems."

Alexa met Chance's gaze, seeing the sparkle of reassurance, of commitment. "He's right, Deb," she chimed in. "Zack needs to go home with us."

Home with us…Alexa's words whispered through Chance's mind during his drive to the hospital. She wanted him with her as much as possible, until Howard came home. And then…

Chance decided to cross that bridge when he got there. He had promised Howard that he'd leave when the old man came home, but Chance hadn't promised not to leave his heart and soul behind. Alexa was *his querencia.*

Alexa mentally prepared herself for her encounter with Howard as she walked down the dimly lit hall of the hospital. She knew Howard would be upset with her for neglecting to tell him about Zack's disappearance. But she had tried to spare him the stress of worrying about his grandson. She also wished she could spare Howard from confronting Chance, who was right beside her, every step of the way.

But she could no longer deny her need to have Chance in her life. She couldn't completely sacrifice her love for Chance. She cared too much, and she would insist that Howard compromise. If he was going to get upset about it, this was the place to do it, she reminded herself.

Alexa instinctively reached for Chance's hand as they approached the door. Odd, wasn't it? She had relied on herself for years, and suddenly she was reaching out to Chance for moral support. He hadn't failed her yet, and she had come to understand that he never would.

This wasn't the one-way street she'd been traveling during her marriage to Dan. Chance Butler had successfully launched into orbit her cynical theories on men.

Pausing to inhale a fortifying breath, Alexa stepped into the room. Her gaze landed on the touching scene before her. Zack was propped against his grandfather. The boy's ruffled head was tucked under Howard's right arm. Candy and potato chip wrappers lay on Howard's lap. The old man cocked a graying brow when Alexa and Chance approached his bed.

"Tried to spare me from worry, did you?" Howard asked quietly.

Alexa nodded. "I've distressed you enough, Howard. I didn't want you to be upset until I knew if there was something to be upset about."

Howard stared at Alexa, then at Chance. His gaze swung to the boy nestled at his side. "I don't think Zack will need an in-depth lecture about leaving school without consulting you first. I think he gave himself a pretty good scare and a dousing of wet logic tonight."

"Howard, maybe this isn't the time, but—" Alexa compressed her lips when Howard held up a hand to forestall her.

"Howard, there is something—" Chance's attempt to take up where Alexa left off was met with a loud sh-sh-sh!

"I'm going to do the talking here and you're going to do the listening," Howard insisted. "Zack told me where he was headed after school. He also told me the purpose of the visit he tried to make to Chance."

Alexa tensed, then shot Chance a discreet glance. Together, they waited for Howard to continue.

"Tonight I was granted insight through the eyes of an eight-year-old child. It turned out to be quite a revelation," Howard murmured as he curled his arm around his sleeping grandson. "Zack had thought the matter through. As he saw it, Alexa wasn't happy after Chance left. Neither was Zack. He was on a mission to see if Chance would like to marry Alexa, so we could be a family."

Alexa's heart fluttered like a caged sparrow. She could just imagine the shock Howard suffered when Zack explained his crusade to his grandfather.

Although the old man's narrowed gaze was boring into Chance, he broke into a grin—he couldn't help it. That eight-year-old matchmaker had tried to simplify a situation far too complex for him to understand. The kid, like his mother, had the kind of determination that wouldn't quit.

"Once Zack got the okay from Chance, the boy planned to hightail it home to square things with his mom," Howard went on. "According to Zack, that's how this sort of thing is done in the third grade. That's how Chelsea McClain came to be Zack's girlfriend. A mutual acquaintance worked out the details for them."

Chance's grin broadened. "I like the kid's style. It's simple, straightforward and to the point."

"Figured you would," Howard said, and smirked.

"While we are on the subject—" Alexa tried to put in.

Again, Howard cut her off with a dismissive flick of his wrist. "I'm not finished, Alexa. I have something to say. After I say it, you can take Zack home and put him to bed where he belongs. I—"

Howard's voice dried up and he squeezed his eyes shut momentarily, as if battling for control. Alexa went to his side immediately.

"Howard, it's okay," she reassured him.

"No, it's not okay," he wheezed. "I was...*a-frai-d.*" The words came out in broken syllables, as if bubbling up from a deep well. He focused his misty gaze on Alexa as he reached for her hand. "I was...afraid...of losing the only family I have." The words came more quickly now, flowing from the hidden depths. "I was afraid I'd lose my place in this family if a man came along to turn your head. You wouldn't need me anymore. You'd leave me and take Zack with you. The boy is all I have left of my wife and my son, and you, Alexa. I thought if we stayed together, kept outsiders at a distance, that we could live out our lives and that would be enough for you. I kept my son's memory alive so Zack wouldn't forget, so you wouldn't forget.''

He paused for breath. Tears clouded his eyes and slipped down his wrinkled cheeks. ''I didn't want to face the truth about my son and his lack of responsibility to his family. But I know he was never fair to you, Alexa. I ended up being just as unfair by being so possessive and demanding of you. I tried to keep you from seeking your own happiness. The torment of knowing what I was doing to you, knowing I was selfishly keeping you from Chance, brought on my heart attack. But it was easier to blame you and Chance than myself.''

His gaze locked with Chance's. Howard was silent for a long moment while he struggled for composure. ''It's not easy for a hidebound old fool like me to admit he's scared, to admit he's getting old and can't handle the duties that Rocking T demands. It's even more difficult to admit my son's failings. Since you came here, you accepted every responsibility I thrust at you and spent your spare time helping Alexa with her project. You treated her with consideration and respect and you gave Zack the kind of attention I can't provide.''

''I love that little squirt,'' Chance said softly, sincerely.

''I realize that,'' Howard murmured. ''But fear and envy make a man say and do unforgivable things.''

''I tried to give Zack all the time and attention I never received from my own father,'' Chance confided, then paused for breath before plunging ahead. ''I love Alexa, Howard. I'm asking for the privilege of visiting Rocking T every chance I get. I don't expect your blessing, but I would like your permission.''

''You think you can waltz in here between rodeos and shack up with my daughter-in-law?'' Howard snorted disdainfully. ''No way, Butler. I won't allow that.''

Howard gently nudged Zack awake. The boy stirred

sluggishly, then squinted in the light. "Mom! Chance!" He
bolted straight up, then slumped against his grandpa. "Uh-
oh, I'm in big trouble."

"It's all right, boy," Howard consoled Zack. "I already
told them that you had learned your lesson about striking
out on your own. You promise never to do that again, don't
you?"

Still huddled against his grandfather—just in case the fur
flew—Zack nodded his head vigorously.

"Now then, Zack, since you went to a lot of trouble to
locate Chance so you could ask him a question, you might
as well ask him," Howard insisted.

"With Mom here?" Zack peered at his grandfather.
"That's not how it's done."

Howard grinned affectionately. "Since we aren't dealing
with third-graders we can bend the rules a bit." He elbowed
the kid. "Get to it, boy. It's late and we all need our beauty
sleep."

Zack propped himself up to stare directly at Chance, pre-
tending his mother wasn't in the room. "I was trying to
find you so I could ask you one more time if you might be
interested in marrying my mom, so you could be my dad."

Chance smiled in amusement as he watched embarrassment flood Alexa's cheeks. "I can't think of anything I'd
like better, rookie. Do you think you could convince your
mom that it would be a good idea?" He glanced at Howard,
then shifted his attention back to Zack. "And maybe you
could square it with your grandpa so he could be the dad
I never really had. Since you're in the matchmaking business, maybe you could work it out so all four of us could
be a family."

Zack nodded his tousled head. "Sure, but you have to
wait until I ask Mom. You can't get too many things going
at once. My teacher at school says it's best to complete one

assignment before starting the next one. That way you don't get mixed up."

"Wise teacher," Chance agreed. "We wouldn't want to break any more third-grade rules than we have to."

Zack turned his attention to Alexa. "Mom, Chance would like to marry you. Is that okay with you?"

Suddenly, the room shrank to the watery image of Chance standing at the foot of Howard's bed. Love, respect and hope glistened in Chance's eyes as he met Alexa's gaze. More than anything Alexa wished she could give Chance what he never had—a place he could truly call home, a family whose thoughts and affection accompanied him wherever he went.

Secretly, she wanted to ask Chance to remain at Rocking T, even if Howard squirmed a bit at having him there permanently. But Alexa couldn't ask Chance to walk away from the success of the life he'd led. He was a three-time world champion, a contender for another title. She refused to be that selfish. She would force herself to take what she could get and live every moment with Chance to its fullest.

"Yes, I'd like to marry Chance," she murmured, her heart in her eyes.

"All right!" Zack cheered. He raised his hand to give Howard the high five. "It's all set, Grandpa. We'll get them married tomorrow. Now then, Chance wants you to be his dad, if it's okay with you."

Chance held his breath. He knew he was asking a great deal of Howard. The old man had immortalized his son for more than a year. All Chance wanted was the opportunity to earn Howard's respect, to repay him for a privilege that meant the world to Chance.

"I'd be honored to adopt Chance as my son," Howard whispered.

"Oh, Howard!" Alexa eased down on the bed to hug him close. "We'll make this work, I promise."

"Damn right we'll make it work," Howard declared. He clung to Alexa, but his gaze was fixed on Chance. "I've decided to deed my half of Rocking T to Zack, and I'm going to sit back and take it easy, enjoy my retirement. When you decide to give up the circuit, we'll be waiting for you to take over the management of the ranch. I expect you'll handle it as well as you have while I've been cooped up in the hospital."

Chance stood there, his mouth hanging open. "You want me here?" he croaked like a waterlogged bullfrog.

Howard nodded. "Seems we all do, *son*."

Chance was astounded, overwhelmed. His legs wobbled, his heart pounded. Tears misted his eyes as emotion roiled inside him. After all these years, after all the trials and torments of his youth, he finally had a place to call home, someplace where he was wanted, needed, accepted. A place where he belonged.

Zack bounded off the bed and charged toward Chance, who swung him up and settled him on one hip. Chance nuzzled his forehead against Zack's, then ruffled the kid's hair. "Thanks, rookie. You did good, really good."

Zack hooked his arms around Chance's neck and beamed at his mother and grandfather. "Can I go home now? I need to get things ready for the wedding tomorrow."

"Whoa, pardner," Chance drawled. "It's not easy to make those kinds of arrangements in a day."

"No?" Zack asked.

"No," Chance confirmed.

"That's what you said the first time I asked if you wanted to marry my mom. Didn't seem so hard to me."

Chance peered into the kid's face—one that radiated innocence and happiness. "Okay, rookie, do your thing. Official or unofficial, we'll have a wedding tomorrow. Then we'll make sure all those complicated legal matters that grown-ups insist upon are taken care of later."

"I'll officiate," Howard volunteered. "Be here tomorrow after school."

"What does officiate mean?" Zack wanted to know.

"That means someone is in charge of making sure the bride and groom say the I-dos," Alexa explained. "We also have to have a marriage license. No one gets married without a license."

"I'll take care of it," Zack insisted. "Do you want it written in cursive or printed? I can do both. I got an A in penmanship."

"Then you're hired, rookie," Chance confirmed, grinning broadly.

"Chance and I will make cookies for refreshments. We've had practice," Zack spoke up.

"Come on, squirt. Considering the busy day you've planned, we better get you to bed."

When Chance carried Zack from the room—with the boy clinging to him like Spanish moss—Alexa turned her teary smile on Howard. "Thank you for everything," she whispered.

"Know what, hon, I feel better since I got that load off my chest. Being unfair to you and battling my private fears was a heavy burden to bear. Like you said, Chance Butler is a good and decent man. And a damn fine rodeo cowboy. One of the best I've ever seen."

Too choked up to speak, Alexa nodded in agreement.

"Go home," Howard ordered. "I need to rest up for tomorrow. If I would've listened to Zack a long time ago I could've made things simple for all of us. That boy has the right idea. Grown-ups make things too complicated."

"Mmm…" was all Alexa could add to the conversation.

"I'll see you tomorrow." Howard gave Alexa a nudge toward the door. "Invite that sister of yours to the ceremony. That girl turned out all right, thanks to you."

Alexa made it to the door before she felt the need to glance back at Howard. "I love you. Never doubt that."

Howard smiled. "I know, honey. You proved it when you were willing to give up your own happiness to assure me that I was wanted and needed. This is my way of assuring you how much you and Zack mean to me. And that cowboy, too," he added. "This may be an unusual kind of family, but then, I've come to realize that families are folks who support each other, help each other, care about each other. That's what it's all about."

Alexa walked away—floated on air was nearer the mark. The best she'd hoped for was a workable compromise with Howard. Instead, he had set aside his private fears and opened his heart to those nearest and dearest to him. Alexa vowed that not one member of this family would be slighted. She had enough love and happiness in her heart to spread around for at least two lifetimes!

Chance stood at Zack's bedroom door, watching the boy sleep. He had cut short their evening ritual of reading from sports magazines, because the rookie had endured a harrowing evening and had a school bus to catch early in the morning. Furthermore, Zack had a wedding to organize. Zack planned to make out the invitations during the school bus ride, then he intended to print the marriage license during recess.

"Is he asleep?" Alexa whispered as she walked up to put her arms around Chance.

"Finally. The kid's brain has been buzzing like a bumblebee stuck in a bucket of tar. He's taking care of all the wedding details, but he's decided to wait until after the ceremony to bake cookies. Couldn't fit in enough time before the nuptials, and he doesn't want me to have to bake without him. Says we're a culinary duo.

"I informed him that honeymoons, not baking cookies,

usually follow weddings.'' Chance grinned rakishly. ''He wanted to know what a honeymoon was.''

''And what did you tell him?'' Alexa asked warily.

''The truth, of course. I don't lie to kids. I told him honeymoons were that special time when brides and grooms expressed and communicated their love for each other in private, without interruptions. I told him a lot of hugging and kissing went on.''

Chance's hand folded around Alexa's as he led her toward the steps. ''I didn't bother to tell him about the fantasy I've planned for tonight, though.''

''Another water-world fantasy?'' she asked, smiling.

''No, a B-and-B fantasy,'' Chance replied as he descended the steps. ''I plan to christen the executive suite. I want to be the first to make use of that king-size bed.'' He waggled his eyebrows suggestively. ''And I don't plan to be there alone, if you catch the way I'm drifting, darlin'.''

Alexa glided her good arm around his waist. ''Sounds intriguing.''

''Glad you plan to join me, because I decided to keep things open and simple and get straight to the heart of this matter.''

''We're going to let an eight-year-old dictate policy around here?'' She laughed as they strolled outside, arm in arm.

''Works for me.'' Chance pushed open the barn door and led the way upstairs. He halted at the door, then turned to stare intently at Alexa. ''One thing you should know. I don't want to come and go from Rocking T. I've spent twelve years on the circuit, living out of a duffel bag. I want to be here with you and Zack and Howard on a permanent basis.''

Alexa gaped at him in stunned belief. ''You want to give up your chance to win another world title?''

''Been there, done that, darlin','' Chance said as he led

her toward the roomy bed. "What I haven't done is made a commitment to a woman and child whom I love dearly. I haven't had a home where I've felt as if I belong. I want to invest my savings in the B-and-B and help you make the business boom while we follow Zack's upcoming sports career."

Alexa stared at him in amazement. No one had ever made her top priority before. "I don't know what to say."

"Say yes," Chance whispered and he framed her face in his hands. "Say you'll let me be the forever kind of man you can always depend on, one who depends equally on you. Say you want Zack to have a brother or sister, and I promise that Zack will never feel neglected or left out the way I did. I won't let that happen, because I know how it hurts. Say you love me as deeply as I love you…always."

"I love you like crazy," she whispered as she looped her arms around his neck. "And you've got yourself a deal, cowboy…."

When Chance tumbled with her onto the king-size bed in the executive suite, Alexa gave herself up completely, wholeheartedly. She matched Chance caress for gentle caress, kiss for breathtaking kiss. The world spun out of control as love burned its brand on two hearts and souls that blended as one.

And later, when they walked back to the house to check on Zack, Chance knew beyond all doubt that he'd found his place, his purpose in life. His new family was top priority. That was the commitment he made when he gave his heart to Alexa.

"Pinch me," Chance murmured after he'd kissed Alexa good-night at her bedroom door. "I wanna make sure this ain't no dream. Can I really be this happy?"

Giggling, Alexa grabbed the lapel of his shirt and towed him into her room. "I've got more tantalizing things in mind besides pinching you. And don't think I'm going to let you out of my sight until you sign Zack's marriage license, either. Just try walking away from me. I'll have you roped, thrown and tied in a pigging string faster than you can blink.''

''I'm hog-tied for life?'' he asked.

''Absolutely.''

''No time off to practice bad behavior?''

''Definitely not.''

''Promise?''

Alexa drew him to her bed, drew him deeper into her heart. ''You got it, cowboy, now come here and kiss me.''

Chance chuckled as they rolled playfully across the patchwork quilt. ''Pardon me, ma'am, but I already—''

When Alexa slid her leg between his thighs and glided her body seductively against his, Chance forgot what he planned to say. He decided, right then, that he didn't really need all that much sleep to see him through the first of his two upcoming weddings. He could survive quite nicely, thank you very much, just floating around on their personal cloud in paradise.

* * * * *

Silhouette®SPECIAL EDITION®

presents **THE BRIDAL CIRCLE**, a brand-new
miniseries honoring friendship, family and love...

THE BRIDAL CIRCLE

by
Andrea Edwards

**They dreamed of marrying and leaving their
small town behind—but soon discovered there's
no place like home for true love!**

IF I ONLY HAD A...HUSBAND (May '99)
Penny Donnelly had tried desperately to forget charming
millionaire Brad Corrigan. But her heart had a memory—and a
will—of its own. And Penny's heart was set on Brad becoming
her husband....

SECRET AGENT GROOM (August '99)
When shy-but-sexy Heather Mahoney bumbles onto secret agent
Alex Waterstone's undercover mission, the only way to protect the
innocent beauty is to claim her as his lady love. Will Heather
carry out her own secret agenda and claim Alex as her groom?

PREGNANT & PRACTICALLY MARRIED
(November '99)
Pregnant Karin Spencer had suddenly lost her memory and
gained a pretend fiancé. Though their match was make-believe,
Jed McCarron was her dream man. Could this bronco-bustin'
cowboy give up his rodeo days for family ways?

Available at your favorite retail outlet.

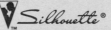
Silhouette®

And Baby Makes Three

FIRST TRIMESTER

by

SHERRYL WOODS

Three ornery Adams men are about to be roped
into fatherhood...and they don't suspect a thing!

And Baby Makes Three

APRIL 1999
The phenomenal series
from Sherryl Woods has readers
clamoring for more! And in this special collection,
we discover the stories that started it all....

Luke, Jordan and Cody are tough ranchers set in
their bachelor ways until three beautiful women
beguile them into forsaking their single lives for
instant families. Will each be a match made in
heaven...or the delivery room?

Available at your favorite retail outlet.

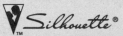